Berkley Prime Crime Books by Katherine V. Forrest

LIBERTY SQUARE
APPARITION ALLEY
SLEEPING BONES
HANCOCK PARK

Other Kate Delafield Mysteries by Katherine V. Forrest

AMATEUR CITY
MURDER AT THE NIGHTWOOD BAR
THE BEVERLY MALIBU
MURDER BY TRADITION

HANCOCK PARK

A KATE DELAFIELD MYSTERY

KATHERINE V. FORREST

BERKLEY PRIME CRIME, NEW YORK

A Berkley Prime Crime Book
Published by The Berkley Publishing Group
A division of Penguin Group (USA) Inc.
375 Hudson Street
New York, New York 10014

This book is an original publication of The Berkley Publishing Group.

First edition: May 2004

Library of Congress Cataloging-in-Publication Data

Forest, Katherine V., 1939-
    Hancock Park : a Kate Delafield mystery / Katherine V. Forrest.—1st ed.
    p. cm.
    ISBN 0-425-19598-8
    1. Delafield, Kate (Fictitious character)—Fiction. 2. Police—California—
Los Angeles—Fiction. 3. Los Angeles (Calif.)—Fiction. 4. Missing persons—
Fiction. 5. Policewomen—Fiction. 6. Lesbians—Fiction. I. Title.

PS3556.O737H36 2004
813'.54—dc22
                                                        2003063751

PRINTED IN THE UNITED STATES OF AMERICA

10   9   8   7   6   5   4   3   2   1

FOR JO

HANCOCK PARK

ONE

In a courtroom on the third floor of the Criminal Courts Building in downtown Los Angeles, Judge Jackson Terrell ordered: "Call your next witness."

"The People call Detective Kate Delafield," responded deputy district attorney Alicia Marquez from her seat at the prosecution table.

Through the gate held open by the bailiff, Kate walked into the inner court. A plump, blond clerk briskly administered the oath, and Kate stepped up to the stand to sit in its simple leather chair. After complying with the request to state and spell her name, she put her shoulder bag beside her, smoothed her jacket, laid her folder of notes on the ledge of the stand, adjusted the microphone.

Her expression carefully courteous, she made eye contact with Judge Jackson Terrell, who peered at her over the top of his rimless glasses, his thin face expressionless. An African-American, this judge ran a tightly controlled courtroom and had earned a reputation of careful, humorless competence. Kate gave the jury a swift, expressionless glance, careful not to give any impression that she was attempting to ingratiate herself. The usual mixture of gender, age, and race, they were better dressed and from a higher median income group than usual during this time of depressed employment in the upper echelons of American commerce. With the assumed right of all juries, they were unabashedly scrutinizing her and she felt the burn of their stares after she looked away.

She was nervous, but not because of Aimee, who had neither returned to the house nor called. There was no choice but to deal with that particular anxiety later. No matter how many times she testified, she never lost her awe of the courtroom, her awareness of the presiding black-robed judge and uniformed bailiffs, the solemnity and somberness of the proceedings, the spare elegance of the wooden walls and tables and benches, the seal of the state of California on the wall above the judge, who sat between the national and state flags. She took comfort only in the certain knowledge that over numerous court appearances she had learned how to present herself. How to project an air of calm certainty, of competence and credibility not only to jurors but no less importantly to judges, attorneys, clerks, and bailiffs.

On court days she took meticulous care with her appearance, selecting the simplest of black or dark blue jackets and pants, complementing them with either a plain shell or a turtleneck; never a shirt whose collar she might feel the need to adjust, no wristwatch she might inadvertently glance at and give an unintended indication of impatience or anxiety, no jewelry she would twist or tug to telegraph unease. Long since resigned to her finely textured, unmanageable hair, having lost all hope of taming it when alteration from dark to light gray changed its consistency not a whit, she simply brushed it in the morning and let it go where it may, touching it only to skim it from her face, rarely running her fingers through it as was Aimee's habit. The reward for successfully cultivating physical stillness was the far fewer clues she revealed about her emotional state to witnesses or suspects, to defense attorneys or juries.

She turned her attention to deputy district attorney Alicia Marquez, who stood behind the podium unhurriedly arranging her notes. These consisted of three legal-size yellow pads with a confetti of multicolored Post-its protruding from the ends and sides and several loose white pages interleaved in the pads. Kate was not impressed with her organizational habits. And had serious misgivings about the range of her competence.

Marquez did make a good appearance. Trim and compact, with alert dark eyes and full lips, she dressed conservatively, to-day in a dark brown jacket and skirt, a beige silk blouse, and matching wedge-heeled shoes. Kate suspected that a sizable chunk of Marquez's budget went to maintaining her attractive hairstyle, a simple ash-brown curve parted in the middle to frame the golden tones of her skin.

In a city where Hispanic influence was rapidly growing, this fifth-generation Latina had been fast-tracked. Rumor had it she'd required longer than usual to be promoted to drug-related homicides and class A felonies, and her prosecution win-loss record was undistinguished. This case was her first major break, the plum assignment of lead prosecutor on what appeared to be a medium-profile case—meaning it would make page three in the California section of the *L.A. Times*. In the opinion of the Office of the District Attorney, the case had an unexceptional defense lawyer on the other side, and the further advantage of a detective—Kate herself—whose solid investigations and preparation for court were well documented and rarely provided that major bugaboo to prosecuting attorneys, surprises.

In her meetings with Marquez, despite her best efforts to establish a connection, Kate had felt little rapport with her or personal warmth from her. She knew Marquez was a divorced parent with two teenage boys and had attained her level of success through hard work and unremitting determination. Kate admired her serious demeanor, her ambition and dedication. But she had heard via the rumor mill that Marquez thus far seemed lacking in imagination and courtroom generalship— significant deficiencies in a homicide prosecution.

Before this case had even gone to trial, Kate's apprehension about Marquez's competence had been proved justified. Three weeks ago the original defense's attorney had been replaced with Gregory Quantrill, a lawyer with a nationally growing reputation. Quantrill had asked for no continuance, obviously pleased to allow the District Attorney's Office scant maneuvering room to make changes in its own legal team. Kate had never made the mistake of thinking the courtroom was anything less than a theater, and she knew she was now a supporting player in a live production with a lead actor whose unexceptional talent and marginal stage craft could bring the production down no matter how strong her own skills might be. This case had fallen into unpredictable jeopardy.

"Detective Delafield," Marquez began in a clear voice that carried throughout the courtroom, "how long have you been a member of the Los Angeles Police Department?"

"Since nineteen seventy-two," she answered firmly.

Marquez turned a page as if searching for a note, then turned the page back, a standard courtroom tactic; she was allowing the jurors to do the math, allowing the positive message of a three-decade police career to penetrate. Kate took the opportunity to glance at the defense table, and met eyes the color of black coffee—the stare of Gregory Quantrill, so intensely focused she felt it as a physical sensation impaling her to the back of her chair. He offered the hint of a smile, confident and faintly personal, as if he had somehow read and sympathized with her pessimism over Marquez. She held Quantrill's gaze to give him no reason to think she was impressed with him or intimidated.

Marquez asked, "And what is your current assignment?"

"I'm in Homicide at Wilshire Division."

"How long have you been in Homicide?"

"Twenty years."

Again Marquez paused, and Kate shifted her attention to the defendant seated beside Quantrill. Handsomely presentable in a gray-green suit and paler green shirt and tie, he was listening attentively but not looking at her, his gaze fixed somewhere in the space between her and the jury. His quiet body language was far different from her last experience with him, his arrest, meaning that he had been thoroughly coached by the defense about courtroom demeanor.

Marquez asked, "In the ranks of homicide detectives, what is your classification?"

"I'm a detective-three, the highest classification in my rank."

She glanced over the courtroom. Now that Quantrill had entered the case, it had acquired a higher profile, but on this third day of trial, courtroom seats were sparsely filled, mostly with the victim and defendant's relatives and friends. Son and daughter Allan and Lisa Talbot were here; Rikki, the other daughter, was yet to come to court. *L.A. Times* police reporter Corey Lanier sat by herself on the aisle in the back row, head bent over a notepad. Lanier had attended opening statements, so why would she choose to hear Kate's testimony, a laying out in detail of what had been covered in Marquez's recitation to the jury of what she promised to prove?

Marquez's opening had been relatively brief; her strategy was to take advantage of the lack of pretrial publicity and to allow the cumulative power of the evidence to emerge, followed by a strong closing argument. Quantrill had been even more succinct, offering the colorful metaphor that the People's case was no more than a flimsy tissue of unproven speculation that would blow apart with one good sneeze.

The reason for Lanier's presence had to be Gregory Quantrill. Prepared as Kate was, and she was fully prepared—no thanks to Aimee's confounding behavior—she would have a thorny time on the stand under his cross-examination. A homicide case not pled out was never easy—attacking the credibility of investigating officers was what defense attorneys did for a living—but much of what they did involved predictable courtroom maneuvers in providing a competent defense, albeit one that brought in tens of thousands of dollars to private attorneys; homicide cases were exceedingly expensive to defend. Corey Lanier was here for one reason: She smelled courtroom drama and a story. The cross-examination of the lead detective would be a prime indicator of what that story might be . . .

Marquez asked, "How many cases, approximately, would you say you've investigated over the course of—"

"Your honor," Quantrill said pleasantly, rising to his six-foot-plus height, "the defense is willing to stipulate as to the detective's sterling record and experience."

Judge Terrell raised his pencil-thin eyebrows and waited for

Marquez, who cast a confused glance at Kate. Kate looked back at her incredulously. Had she forgotten the basics of law school? Was she actually considering—

"Your honor," Marquez said, shaking her head as if the appropriate response had just been delivered to her, "we will not so stipulate. This jury should hear the detective's qualifications and—"

"Proceed," Terrell said crisply. Quantrill took his seat with an amiable grin toward the jury that said, *I did my best to prevent this boring crap.*

"I've been involved in more than two hundred and fifty investigations over that period," Kate answered, doing her best to conceal her fury. Out of a staff of over one thousand deputy district attorneys serving this city, she had to get this one. A prosecutor like Linda Foster would have reacted with outrage, accusing Quantrill of attempting to sabotage the laying out of Kate's credentials—essential to establish maximum credibility for her key testimony to this jury—until the judge intervened.

Calming herself, Kate continued to answer a litany of questions about her position as a D-3 supervising detective at Wilshire Division and lead detective in homicide investigations and what that entailed, her experience as a training detective for other homicide detectives. At the edge of her mind was how awed Marquez might be by Quantrill.

That Quantrill's clients would be well heeled was a given. His first high-profile, big-money win had been Oklahoma oil mogul Damian Winfield, acquitted of murder and conspiracy to murder his wife and her lover, plus the follow-on win of a lucrative lawsuit against two tabloids for libel, plus a best-selling ghostwritten book on the case. The lengthy trial had been carried on Court TV, and the show's reporters had made him a star with their fawning praise of his smooth and deadly cross-examinations, his courtroom presence and charisma. The only reason they were not covering this trial was because their hastily made plea to do so had been denied. In a city where fall-out from the O. J. Simpson case still poisoned the atmosphere of law enforcement all these years later, televised trials were viewed with implacable hostility by much of L.A.'s judiciary.

Gregory Quantrill had come into this case fully expecting to win. Which meant, worst-case scenario, that he knew something Kate did not. Or far more likely, had detected amid the discovery documents and the defense's own detective work an avenue of reasonable doubt leading straight into the jury box. Unlike Marquez, who had to convince twelve jurors of this defendant's guilt beyond a reasonable doubt, Quantrill, if he could not persuade all twelve to acquit, had to reach only one for a hung jury, which would be viewed as a victory. By everyone except, of course, the defendant and the murder victim's family, who would be put through the same torturous process all over again.

Thus far, the prosecution's leadoff witnesses, the responding officers, had given their testimony and Quantrill, beyond politely clarifying a few details about the scene of the murder, the position and condition of the body at death, had asked not a single challenging question on cross-examination.

Marquez continued, "On May twenty-ninth of last year, in your professional capacity, were you called to an address on Oakview Road?"

"I was."

"This address is located in Hancock Park?"

"Correct."

"Would you agree that this is in general an affluent area of the city?"

Kate knew Marquez was reminding the jury of the prosperity of the defendant and that he could afford the best of lawyers. "It is affluent," she confirmed.

"At what time did you arrive at the scene?"

"At approximately eight-fifteen that morning." Her crime scene log lay on top of the stack of reports and notes in her folder if she needed to ask permission to consult it.

"You came from the station?"

"I was on my way into the station. I received notification on my cell phone and proceeded directly to the location, where I met Detective Joseph Cameron, who had driven there from the station."

"Detective Cameron was your partner?"

"He was and still is my partner."

"How long has he been your partner?"

"Three years."

"He was on the scene prior to your arrival?"

"We arrived simultaneously."

"Describe what you saw when you arrived."

"The responding officers had secured the scene—"

"Meaning they had deployed crime scene tape?"

"Yes. Among other duties."

The paramount rule of testifying was answer as briefly as possible. That course of action required closed-ended questions to elicit brief answers. But Marquez seemed to like open-ended questions whose answers she would frequently interrupt. Kate resigned herself to making her answers simple and clear to the jury, and watching their reactions, especially juror number three, a gray-haired man with a blue polo shirt stretched over his paunch; he had settled a faint, approving smile on her. She continued, "Sergeant Fred Hansen was in charge—"

"Have you worked with him before?"

"Many times. Over many years." When Marquez did not follow up, she continued, "Officer Dane Garrett was maintaining the crime scene log, a list of everyone entering the crime scene."

As the detailed questions continued, her memory of that morning sharpened into focus.

CHAPTER

TWO

She had pulled her Saturn in behind Joe Cameron, who was bent over the trunk of the slickback—a black-and-white without a lightbar—presumably retrieving evidence bags and latex gloves. Already focused on assessing the scene as she got out of her car, she absently returned his wave, then wrote the date, May 29, and time, 8:15 A.M., and temperature, approximately seventy degrees, in her notebook. The day was an anomaly: soft sunlight, filtering through the oaks and sycamores shading the street, had broken through the usual gray pall that hung over the city until midafternoon during the months of May and June.

She took in the perimeter set up by the responding officers. The entire scene looked easy enough to protect. The yellow tape designating a crime scene seemed superfluous around a home on a corner whose outer boundary provided its own barrier to the street with a high, neatly trimmed hedge and a wrought-iron gate. The hedge, she noted, was high enough and thick enough for a determined perpetrator to conceal himself. Patrol officers Felix Albedo and Rob Finch stood guard on the side-walk, but the spectators, a knot of perhaps two dozen, looked on in respectful silence from across the street. Cameron joined her just as a Channel Seven news van turned the corner, closely followed by one from Channel Nine. As usual, the press had picked up the police radio calls.

Albedo swung open the gate to a flagstone walkway. Its large flat sheets of stone, weathered and sun-bleached to a warm peach color, curved their way through a perfect green lawn to the arched entry of a traditional Spanish-style, graceful two-story home of beige stucco partially shaded by an assortment of queen palms. Spectacular bushes of white and yellow and deep orange daisies lined the front foundation. The house was not nearly as large or impressive as some in this area, stately homes of Tudor, Spanish, Mediterranean, French, Colonial, and traditional architecture, but it was aesthetically pleasing, the kind of unpretentious house she liked: quality, not quantity.

Her visits to Hancock Park on police business were rare. The affluence of the city of Los Angeles increased with every mile one traveled from east to west, but this section, bordered by La Brea Avenue, Wilton Place, Melrose Avenue, and Olympic Boulevard, was an anomaly—a wealthy enclave on whose bor-ders camped the bustling commerce and racial conflicts of Ko-reatown, the seedy western edge of Hollywood, and the ironically named Miracle Mile. In the forties and fifties the Miracle Mile had been the height of chic elegance but now, except for its Museum Row, was characterized only by an utter lack of distinction. Calls from Hancock Park for police assistance were mostly burglary and car theft, its reported deaths from accident, natural cause, or suicide. In Wilshire Division's widely varied social landscape, this northeastern quadrant was polar opposite to the southwestern corner, where poverty and crime were endemic, where the 18th Street Latino gang and its African-American counterpart, the Geer Street Crips, held sway. Hancock Park encompassed the tony Wilshire Country Club and the mansion of the Canadian Consulate General. Hancock Park dated back to the nineteen twenties, was old money, was elegant serenity, was classy.

But not totally lacking in historical controversy, she recalled. In the late forties Hancock Park became a minor footnote in the history of integration when a wealthy and famous new resident moved in, and the neighborhood welcome mat for singer Nat "King" Cole had taken the form of a burning cross on his lawn. A generation or so later, a far more ostentatious resident arrived: world champion boxer and Vietnam draft dodger Muhammad Ali. The next famous African-American resident was quiet, dignified, and held unassailable credentials. He was Tom Bradley, the first black police chief of Los Angeles, who had become its mayor-elect and was moving into Getty House, official residence in Hancock Park for the city's mayor.

Sergeant Fred Hansen stood at the arched front entryway to the house, a hand resting on his holster. She nodded to him and to Patrol Officer Dane Garrett, who was next to Hansen. "Fred, good to see you," she said as she took Garrett's posse box, signed in, and handed it to Cameron. Her greeting to Hansen was more than perfunctory. His stolid presence and competence at a homicide scene had won her respect over the years, as had the four hash marks on the sleeve of his uniform signifying twenty years of steadfast service in their beleaguered organization.

"Kate, Joe," Hansen greeted them, and as usual got straight to the business at hand, reading from his clipboard, "Victim's in the back bedroom. Female. Victoria Talbot." Looking up at them, he indicated the interior of the house with a slight incline of his head. "Messy."

Kate involuntarily sucked in her breath. When Hansen said a death scene was "messy," she knew to brace herself.

"Fifty-three years old," Hansen said. At the tone in his voice, Kate looked up from her notebook to exchange a brief glance of mutual understanding. Someone not young—like themselves—had been robbed of precious remaining years of life. "Gunshot wounds to the head and back. No weapon visible."

So this death could be neither natural nor a suicide. Her first murder in Hancock Park.

"Who called it in?" Cameron asked briskly, writing in his notebook, oblivious to nuance. In his tan suit, light blue shirt, and tie, he was his usual well-turned-out self. Over her three years with him he had become much more settled at their homicide scenes, his electric energy focused on the necessities and complexities of the vital first steps of an investigation.

"The son." Hansen looked down at his notes. "Allan Talbot. He's in the backyard. On a bench back there. Moreno is with him."

"How's he doing?" Cameron asked.

"Finding his mother like that?" Hansen's head shake was eloquent.

Kate took the latex gloves Cameron offered and tugged them on. "What else, Fred?"

"No sign of break-in but the son reports he found the back door unlocked. Thinks some jewelry's maybe missing."

"He scare the guy off?"

Hansen hesitated. "It's possible." He was obviously annoyed that he hadn't asked.

"Assault?" Cameron asked, pausing over his notebook.

"Doesn't look it, Joe. We're canvassing. SID's on the way. We already made the first call to the coroner. Everson's on standby," he added approvingly.

She nodded. She too approved; her optimum team was assembling. She exchanged a wordless glance with Cameron. They went into the house.

The entryway was a continuation of the flagstone path, but grouted and sanded and glazed to a high polish. A small, gold-trimmed French provincial table held an empty crystal flower vase under an ornately framed painting of a countryside of golden fields. Kate led the way into a spacious split-level living room with a high-arched ceiling and a well-used fireplace, its exterior hearth and façade of coral ceramic tile. The room was simply and comfortably furnished with a cream-colored leather sofa and armchairs on an oriental carpet of rich reds and blues, a conversation grouping around the fireplace. Three high bookcases, their shelves crowded with books and knickknacks, dominated one wall. The floor was a light, glossy hardwood that flowed up onto an upper-level dining room presided over by a large, oil still life of a bowl of fruit, its warm colors spilling over the room and its mission-style table and chairs. Part of a large eat-in kitchen was visible through an archway, tall white cupboards and an aquamarine banquette along one wall. Moving toward the kitchen, Kate could see a multipaned window overlooking a backyard lawn and garden of roses. She smelled, faintly, something that might be cleanser or furniture polish, or both.

She had not been remotely tempted to live in a house since

Anne's death. But she liked this one very much. Vastly more expensive than that small Glendale house they had shared, this place was faintly reminiscent of it, including—especially—that kitchen outlook into the garden. Anne had tended their garden so lovingly. As lovingly as she had tended Kate . . .

But Anne was twenty years dead in an auto accident, and now there was Aimee. And now there was also this woman who lay murdered after living what appeared to be a well-ordered existence in this well-ordered house.

"Let's check it out," she said abruptly. Cameron, crouched down to inspect at eye level a row of framed photos on the mantel, straightened up and adjusted his tie as if to enter a formal meeting.

Kate led the way, moving slowly down the hallway, checking for footprints and any vestige of blood or trace evidence on the walls or floor. Rookie patrol officer Pedro Delgado stood watching them, his back to an open door, his feet rigidly apart, hands behind his back, his jaw clenched. Rookies were still given this detail, the guarding of the dead, as a rite of passage, and she sent him a glance of sympathy.

She edged into the bedroom, Cameron beside her, both of them halting just over the threshold.

The room seemed on first glance to be as neatly organized as the rest of the house. A snow white bedspread lay perfectly smooth under an artistically arranged spray of multigold-toned pillows on a cherrywood four-poster bed. On the matching dresser four photos flanked a blue satin jewelry box, its lid open, and an assortment of cut-glass perfume bottles. A cherrywood Queen Anne–style desk, with a large array of family photos and a closed notebook computer on it, sat in an alcove formed by a bay window over the garden.

Two of the three windowpanes were dotted with bright red spots, the angled window to the left of the desk sprayed more heavily, a shower of red with gray blobs of material that Kate knew from experience was brain matter.

Just visible beyond the bed, a dark-haired woman lay supine beside an overturned desk chair, her head turned to her left. From the doorway Kate could see blood congealing around a wound in her right temple, and rivulets of blood leading from her back. The minimal bleeding from the back and the spatter pattern extending from her torso indicated she had already been down for this second shot. The left arm was under her, the right arm outthrust, its hand curled into a claw.

Cameron stood perfectly still; he had learned to wait and, more importantly, to observe. She completed her own inspection of the room, including its ceiling. Outside the window a young man sat at a picnic table, his head in his hands, Officer Donna Moreno beside him. Kate absorbed no details about him; that would come later. She did a rough sketch of the room in her notebook, focusing on placing location and position of the body correctly in context.

Cautiously, she moved closer to the body. Clad in a long-sleeved brick-colored silk shirt tucked into dark pants, and deck shoes, the dead woman was considerably overweight, with fleshy shoulders and large breasts bulging from the sides of her thick chest.

"She's a young-looking fifty-three," Cameron said softly.

"I'd say so," Kate said.

She hunkered down a few feet away and surveyed the corpse of Victoria Talbot. The eyes were shut—not often the case for homicide victims who resisted death, staring in horror at their imminent demise. Even victims in auto accidents gaped as if fixating on existence could prevent its extinction. Kate could not tell if the woman had tried to defend herself; the fingernails on her observable hand were painted with soft pink polish. The side of the head not visible to Kate, the left, had undoubtedly been shattered by the exiting bullet . . . No blood appeared to have reached the pristine bedspread.

"Star-shaped entry wound," she said to Cameron, pointing to the head wound.

"Powder tattooing," he added.

She could scarcely make out the faint freckle-like pattern above the wound; his eyes were better than hers these days. "Contact," she said. Someone had held a gun to her right temple.

He was studying the position of the body. "Put one in her head, then capped her in the back."

Kate examined the blood pattern. From where she crouched, the primary spatter from the head wound adhered to the left window facing into the garden where the young man sat. She looked again at the victim and the blood pattern around her. The woman had fallen to the left; the left side of her head held the exit wound. For the blood spatter to be on the left wall, she had been facing or had been forcibly turned toward the garden when the head shot was delivered to the right temple.

Cameron rose to his feet, made his way carefully over to the dresser, and peered into the open jewelry box. "Empty, Kate."

She couldn't tell whether the woman wore a wedding ring or possibly a watch; her left hand was under her body. But a diamond ring glittered on the middle finger of her right hand. And while they had yet to check the entire premises, there seemed to be no signs of disturbance in this very placid-appearing house, or Hansen would have said so. They could do nothing more till SID arrived. She said, "Let's go talk to the son."

———

KATE NODDED TO OFFICER DONNA MORENO, who acknowledged the nod and moved quietly away from Allan Talbot after one final, utterly sympathetic glance at him. As Kate approached, she focused on his hair, a dark brown frizz very unlike the long straight hair of his murdered mother, what her own mother would have termed a Brillo pad. A slender young man, he looked to be in his late twenties, perhaps early thirties, unshaven, whether by happenstance or by style maybe Cameron could tell if it did not become evident from the interview.

Talbot sat slumped and motionless at the redwood picnic table, not glancing up as their shadows fell over him. He appeared stupefied, as if poleaxed, a look not at all unfamiliar to Kate. After years of attending death scenes, she still felt a profound empathy for the bereaved because undoubtedly that same expression had been on her own face after she had been called into the captain's office in Wilshire Division and informed of Anne's death. But while she felt deep commonality, as a detective she took calculated advantage of the investigative benefit that shocked and unwary witnesses gave her in the aftermath of sudden death.

There were no tear tracks on Talbot's face, no redness of eye, but his grief was palpable in his waxen pallor and shrunken posture. The young man's khaki pants and polo shirt could have hung on a mannequin for all his bodily awareness of himself. Other than parents absorbing the death of a young child, she had rarely seen anyone at a homicide scene so visibly crushed under his grief; usually such suffering penetrated after the first layer of protective shock wore off.

Kate stopped in front of him, waiting until he looked up at her from where he sat at the picnic table. She was surprised by what she saw. To be sure, shock glazed his hazel eyes, but something else overlaid it, something that burned through the anguish, and when he did not look away she stared at him as long as she could, trying to define it before she felt compelled to speak.

"Mr. Talbot," she finally said, "I'm Detective Delafield. My partner is Detective Cameron." She added sincerely, "I am so sorry."

"My condolences," Cameron said, compassion in his voice; and his right arm twitched as if he were resisting the urge to reach to him.

Talbot nodded. He attempted to speak, cleared his throat, tried again. "Call me Allan," he said hoarsely.

"I know this is very hard for you, Allan," she said. "Do you think you might be able to answer a few questions?"

He nodded.

Kate removed the tape recorder from her shoulder bag, flipped it on, and quickly murmured the date and time, and that she and Cameron were speaking with Allan Talbot. "Because this is so very important, I'd like to use my tape recorder so we can be sure of our information, Allan. Is that all right with you?"

His shoulders and chest moved in a shrug-sigh. "Sure."

She placed the recorder on the table slightly behind him, where he would lose awareness of it. She opened her notebook, to use it for major points of information. "I know this is hard. Please tell us if it gets to be too hard. Can you tell us anything about what's happened here?"

He just looked at her. She would have to lead him. "When did you find her?"

"This morning."

She would really have to lead him. "Do you have any idea what time?"

"A little while ago. I guess . . . before eight?" He took two deep breaths, visibly collecting himself.

"Do you have a key?" As he nodded, she followed up: "Did you let yourself in, Allan? Was your mother expecting you?"

"I let myself in the gate. I always ring the doorbell even if she knows I'm coming . . ." His body sagged as if spent from the effort expended in speaking so many words, as if he were pressed down by a fresh new weight of grief.

Kate waited a few moments and then prompted him. "So you rang the bell."

"She didn't answer. I went around to here." He gestured to the beds of roses. "She spends—spent a lot of time out here, took her morning coffee here . . ." He coughed, as if masking a sob. Typical of the recently bereaved, he was having difficulty in adjusting his words to the past tense, to the truth that a vital presence in his life had been extinguished as suddenly as a blown lightbulb.

"The garden looks like it," Kate said gently, and looked around to give him a moment. Except for an artfully shaped rock garden overflowing with ferns and moss in the shadows of several palms and a high back fence, rosebushes crowded the yard, every color of the rose spectrum from white through yellow, pink through deep red. The beds had been recently hoed, and the aromas of rose and of well-tilled soil were a swelling, sweet richness in the nascent heat of the day. "She was quite the gardener, Allan. So then what? After you came out here?"

"Well . . . she wasn't here. So I was going to let myself in the back door, see if she picked up my message, left a note or something. But it was open. I went in."

Prints on the outside of the back door were possibly compromised. But if the shooter exited from the rear, there might be a palm print on the inside of the door. She asked, "Was the back door ajar? Or just unlocked?"

"Ajar. A little."

"What did you think about that? Was it unusual?"

He looked away from her, rubbing the stubble on his chin as he thought. "It was unusual. She'd leave it open if she was in the yard, but not when she went back inside. She was careful to—" He broke off, wincing at the absurdity of the remark; obviously no amount of care had prevented this outcome.

"After you entered the house, what did you do then?"

"I . . . don't exactly remember . . ."

Thinking that Talbot might respond more readily to questioning from a male at this point, she glanced at Cameron and he picked up his cue. "Hey, we understand, Allan. Just take your time. Anything you can think of, it will help, it could be important. Were you coming over here for some particular reason?"

She approved of the slight deflection in topic. It might ease him, and they would come back to the young man's discovery of his mother's body. As his slender frame heaved in a sigh that also held a visible shudder, Kate studied him. His thin face was almost birdlike with its fine bones, a narrow and slightly hooked nose. His lips were mobile and expressive; his diction bespoke intelligence and education. The tautness of the flesh on his body and an innate tension suggested that metabolism rather than a workout program kept the weight off him. She instinctively liked him.

"I call her every day," he said. "She didn't answer last night, I left a message, thought she might be out with Marjorie at one of those foreign films they like. But she didn't call back, didn't answer this morning . . . so I came over. Just to check."

"You must . . ." She searched for a verb that would not be in the past tense. ". . . feel very close to your mother."

"I do. She's . . . she was the best person. Ever. She's the last person on earth this should happen to, this should never . . ." He did not finish.

"You married, Allan?" Cameron inquired, putting a foot up on the picnic table's bench to make the question seem casually asked; and Kate knew he was fishing for clues as to how closely attached Talbot was to his mother.

"Divorced—two-time loser. Two kids," he said.

So Talbot had let himself be distracted from Mother at least twice. Nothing there.

"Were you on your way to work?" Cameron asked.

"No. Taking a few days' vacation."

"Where do you work?"

"LAX. Air traffic controller."

"As if you didn't have enough stress on the job," Cameron commiserated. "Now this."

Kate asked, "When you came into the house, did you notice anything? Anything to tell you right away something was wrong?"

"Yes," he said, a note in his voice Kate could not identify. Wonderment? Alarm? "Not wrong—different. The place was really cleaned up." He managed a faint, ghastly smile. "I mean, it was real early in the morning."

"She usually didn't clean that early?"

His gaze fixed on a bed of blood red roses, he was silent for some moments. "She usually didn't clean at all. Or at least hardly ever. This is Monday, Rosario comes on Wednesdays.

Rosario's the housekeeper. Anyway, I thought maybe that explained it. She'd been running the vacuum or something and didn't hear the bell. So I called out. She didn't answer, so then I looked . . ." He sucked in his breath.

"Did you notice anything disturbed in the house?" Cameron asked. Talbot shook his head. "Anything missing?"

Again a good deflection away from the body of his mother, Kate thought.

"Jewelry—her jewelry box was open." He quickly added, "Maybe other stuff, I don't know."

"We'll have you check that for us at some point, no hurry," Cameron said.

Of course there was a hurry; everything was a hurry in the first hours of a homicide investigation. But Cameron was right to say whatever would keep the young man talking.

"Did you hear anything at all as you came in?"

His hands gripping the edge of the table's redwood bench, Talbot looked at him intently, the burning in his eyes seeming to heighten. "You mean, someone was here when I rang the bell?"

"Is it possible?"

"Like, they went out through the back door before I came around here?" He shook his head. "I don't remember hearing anything. But I wasn't thinking, you know, about anything like that."

A hard question was now in order, and Kate resumed the interview. "Allan, when you found your mother . . . what did you do?"

Again he sagged in his seat. "Almost passed out," he whispered. "I mean, my knees just about gave way. The second I looked at her, I knew, I just knew. I could hardly walk, but I had to, I had to check her pulse, I had to do it anyway—"

"How?" she interjected as gently as she could; it was important to immediately know how much he had touched the body.

"At her neck." He demonstrated on himself, quickly raising and lowering a hand.

"Did you move her?"

"No. Her pulse—that's all I did."

"Who would do this, Allan?"

Again he looked away. "Robbery—maybe it's robbery?"

"It's a possibility, sure." Perhaps interrupted. Along with a potential assault. But from what she had observed, Victoria Talbot's body, beyond the horrific violation of the bullet wounds, appeared otherwise undisturbed. There was no sign of a break-in; she and Cameron had briefly looked at the doors and windows before coming out here. She decided to come back later to the topic of his mother's potential enemies.

"What about your father?"

"What about him?"

The phrase, the abruptness of tone, did not escape her. "Is he . . . Are he and your mother . . ." She waited.

"They aren't together, if that's what you mean. They haven't been . . . I guess it's maybe three years since the divorce."

"How did you feel about that?"

"She needed to. She had to get out from under . . ."

Cameron asked casually, "They get along okay afterward?"

"As far as he was concerned, they always got along okay." His mouth tightened; his gaze was focused on the rock garden. She asked, "What other family do you have?" Cameron looked at her in sharp annoyance because Talbot's answer begged follow-up, but they would have to come back to the father. Talbot seemed to be shrinking with each question asked of him, and they needed to cover as much ground as possible before they lost their key initial witness to an incoherence of grief and shock.

"Two sisters. Rikki's in Granada Hills, Lisa's in Studio City."

"Allan, are you okay to notify them? And your father?"

"No," he said. "But I need to do it. I'd have called right away but that police officer—" Scowling, he looked around for Donna Moreno. "She wouldn't let me do anything till you talked to me."

"I'm very sorry. I understand how upset you must feel about that. She was following procedure." Moreno had correctly left dissemination of information to the judgment of the case detectives, and little did Allan Talbot realize that this would be the first of many affronts to whatever dignity his family held precious. The damage in a murder case was like the concussive wave from a nuclear bomb, extending well beyond the relatively small ground zero occupied by the victim.

She said, "We'll need their addresses and phone numbers from you, Allan. And your father's. We understand your mother's fifty-three. How about your father?"

"Fifty-five."

"Your sisters?"

"Rikki's thirty. Lisa's twenty-eight."

"And yourself?"

"Thirty-three."

"Tell us about your mother, Allan. What was she like?" Hopefully, he would have something to say other than the usual clichés—something that would give them quick leads outside of family members.

"Cultivated, charming," he answered. "Loved reading, classical music. She was quiet . . ."

"Friends?" Cameron inquired.

"Lots of acquaintances, few friends. She always felt she didn't have much in common with most people."

"Any close by?"

"Marjorie Durant next door." Talbot gestured vaguely to his left. "She and my mother were pretty close."

This was a good lead. Someone who might provide a rich vein of information of all kinds. Kate wrote the name in her notebook. "How long has your mother had the house?"

"This one? About two and a half years. We lived over on Rossmore Drive before that."

"Is she sole owner?"

"Yes."

"What about other associations?" Cameron asked. He too was writing in his notebook. "Did she work? Volunteer?"

"She didn't work. Look . . . I can't . . ." He did not finish.

Talbot was visibly coming undone. Kate zeroed in. "Allan, do you know anyone who could have done this?"

"I'm sorry, I'm just real upset," Talbot said, his thin face crumpling.

Any information they got from him now would be coerced. Kate reached for her tape recorder. "Allan, thank you."

"I need to call my sisters. Oh God," Talbot said, and his shoulders heaved in a sob.

THREE

In the courtroom, Alicia Marquez said to Kate, "After you questioned the victim's son, what was your next step?"

"Detective Cameron and I returned to examine the residence and the scene of the homicide."

"From your previous testimony, hadn't you already done so?"

"Not at all. Detective Cameron and I could only do a very preliminary assessment while we waited for the criminalists."

"Did you need to obtain a search warrant?"

Kate did not reply; out of the corner of her eye she had seen a tentative hand go up from juror number six, a gray-haired man wearing a burnt orange polo shirt. The raised hand was always the agreed-upon juror request for a rest room break.

The judge saw him as well. "Ladies and gentlemen, the

court will take a ten-minute recess," he ordered, and issued the standard caution to the jury not to discuss the case until it was submitted to them.

Kate gathered up her reports, grabbed her shoulder bag, and hurried from the stand.

"It's going fine, Kate," Marquez said, directing the comment to her absently, not looking up as Kate passed by the prosecution table; Marquez was leafing through a folder of notes in the depths of her briefcase.

Kate gave a noncommittal "Mmmm" in reply. Thus far it *was* going well, well enough. But Quantrill's cross-examination loomed.

She quickly visited the rest room, and afterward sought out a seat on one of the crowded benches lining the walls of the busy corridor outside the courtroom. Some of the seated people had their heads propped back on the wall, dozing as they waited to be called into courtrooms to testify, or for their own court cases to begin or resume; others read or fidgeted or talked on their cell phones. Corey Lanier was one of the latter, and when she saw Kate, she got up and moved briskly away, establishing a generous line of demarcation between them.

Kate took Lanier's seat in grim amusement. This otherwise tenacious in-your-face *Times* reporter would be forced to keep her distance during Kate's testimony and even afterward while Kate was under admonition by the court not to discuss the case other than with colleagues in her professional capacity. Violation of this rule could and probably would banish Lanier from the courthouse, a disaster for a reporter assigned to the police beat and its allied court system.

Kate had already pulled her cell phone from her shoulder bag on her way to the rest room to check its call log for messages: none. Or at least not the one that mattered. Leaning forward on the bench, she called Aimee's office, keying her way with practiced efficiency through Pearce & Woodall's automated phone system to end up at Aimee's voice mail. She clicked off and redialed, this time reaching one of Aimee's paralegal cohorts. "It's Kate, Jenny," she said with forced brightness. "Is Aimee around somewhere?"

"Hi, Kate, how you doing? Aimee picked up a bunch of work and took it home with her."

Nothing unusual—Aimee often worked from home on complicated legal briefs. Kate thanked her and called the house number. The answering machine kicked in after the usual three rings. At the beep she asked softly, "Are you there?" No response. She called in again and this time punched in the access code for the answering machine. "You have two messages," the mechanical voice advised.

The first was a hang-up—accomplished after some hesitation. The second was the call she herself had made asking if Aimee were there. She deleted both messages.

If only my goddamn brother had kept his miserable existence hidden in the dark recesses of history. This business with Aimee was all his fault, she fumed. This brother she did not know she had until he'd barged into her life. This brother who had gone to such great lengths to locate her that he had hired a detective agency. This brother who appeared to be overjoyed when they had met at a restaurant near the airport, who appeared to be impressed with her and her military and police career. Who had called her that same evening, eager for more time with her, proposing to meet for a drink. Determined not to continue the practice of family secrets to a newly found blood relative, she had said, "I'd like to bring my partner along, have you meet her."

"Sure. Uh, you do mean . . . your police partner?"

"No. The woman who's shared my life for the past decade."

"No. Uh, no," he had stammered. "I can't have that. I had no clue—Look, forget about this. I'd just as soon—Look, I don't want my family exposed—to—"

She'd slammed down the phone so hard it had bounced off its cradle.

If only she'd done the same thing, if only she'd hung up on the asshole when he called again, she thought, seething with her memories and her anger.

She had been sitting with her feet up on the ottoman, sipping scotch and going over her case notes when Aimee had carried the portable phone over to her armchair. She'd held up her hand and shook her head emphatically, having already told Aimee she did not want to talk to anyone up to and including the chief of police—she would be on the witness stand in court tomorrow and she needed to focus on preparation to the exclusion of everything else.

But Aimee had mouthed: "Your brother."

Astounded, Kate uttered, "What the hell does he want?"

Aimee whispered, "Emergency."

Ridiculous, Kate thought, and pulled the phone from Aimee's hand. She would get rid of this call and get rid of *him,* permanently.

"What is this, Dale?" she demanded. "What the hell do you want?"

"I'm sorry to bother you—"

"You should be." She was surprised by the quaver in his voice, but unmoved. Nothing he could say, no news he could offer, mattered to her.

"Look, I'd never have called except this is an emergency. Dylan is missing."

Her police mentality immediately taking over, she asked involuntarily, "What do you mean, missing?" Whatever stood in the cross fire between herself and Dale Harrison, this niece of hers, despite the fact that they had never met, was an innocent bystander.

"She's a runaway."

She shook her head. The man was a dunce. "Dale, call the Red Bluff police."

"I've done that, but—"

"What did they tell you?"

"That she's probably with somebody she knows and will turn up."

"That's almost always the case." She should know; she had worked juvenile in the early years of her career. "How long has she been gone?"

"Six days. She left a note."

"Did you show it to the police?"

"Yeah. They say it proves she'll be back. But she won't." He exhaled the words: "Her note says we'll never accept who she really is."

The universal lament from overdisciplined teenagers, or those who thought they were. "Dale," she said impatiently, looking down at the stack of documents in her lap, "she's behaving like a teenager. She'll be back."

"Look, we think she's run off because she wants . . . she thinks she's . . . she thinks she wants to be . . . like you."

Silenced, she finally said, "I'm guessing you don't mean she wants to be a cop."

"No," said Dale Harrison.

Again she was silent. She could so easily picture the man on the other end of the phone, his thin gray hair, the face that was so eerily that of her father's. Not her young father, but the fifty-seven-year-old father she most clearly remembered because

Dale Harrison was now older than Andrew Delafield had been when he died. Dale Harrison, her full brother, five years older than she, adopted as an infant by another family owing to the circumstances of war, his existence the tightly guarded secret of her mother and her mother's sister.

All her life she had wondered whether she should have given her parents the chance to accept or reject her as a lesbian. And now this brother, this pallid *imitation* of her father, had dared to judge her . . .

She said coldly, "What do you want from me?"

"Find her. Tell her to come home."

"You're up in Red Bluff. I'm in Los Angeles. That leaves most of California between us."

"She's either there or in San Francisco. Probably there."

"How do you know?"

"We found . . . stuff. Stuff on her Mac. A computer guy helped us break her passwords. We found messages, web sites. And . . . other stuff."

Computer forensics—the New Age X ray for profiling the interior life of a computer user, the powerful new tool in assembling circumstantial evidence in criminal cases—and the newest method for parents to find out the truth about their kids, apparently. "What kind of stuff?" she asked.

Again he exhaled into the phone: "Gay stuff. She downloaded a lot of info mostly about the scene in L.A. and some new gay and lesbian center they built in San Francisco."

"How very awful for you, Dale," she sneered. She was done with this. She had to prepare for court. They knew where their daughter was. But she had to ask: "Why aren't *you* out looking?"

"Believe me, I want to. A cop up here told me I could end up in jail. A guy my age trying to get a young girl to come with him—I'd have to prove who I am from a jail cell. Even if I could do it, Nan claims we'd have to lock her up to keep her from doing it again, and so she needs to decide for herself to come back."

Nan's assessment sounded sensible to her. "If she does come back . . . how are you going to be about her?"

"She's only sixteen."

"Meaning?"

"Meaning even you have to agree she's got time to . . . to change her mind about this."

"*Change her mind*? She doesn't exactly sound confused."

"Thinking you're gay when you're only sixteen," he said sharply, "you can't tell me anybody can know for sure about this."

"Dale, I can indeed tell you that. I knew long before then. Just like you've always known your own orientation."

"Look, I've checked on this, on this . . . orientation. You don't have to be like this. You can—"

"So do I have this correct?" Kate demanded, gripping the receiver. "You want me to find your gay daughter so you can get her fixed?"

"Look, isn't it *possible* she might not be—hell, just forget I called. I told Nan this was a stupid—"

"Tell your wife something for me," Kate interrupted. "The truly stupid one in your family is you." She pushed the off button, then glared at the portable phone, wanting to hurl it at the wall, wishing she could have slammed it into a cradle as she had the last time.

She looked up into Aimee's incredulous, disapproving stare.

"*What,*" Kate demanded. She had work to do. Important work. It was Aimee's fault she'd even had to take the call from her homophobe of a brother.

"Your niece is a runaway—is that what I heard?"

"You heard right."

"And you're doing nothing about it?"

"Nothing." She didn't have time for a debate. She didn't have time for any of this shit. "You heard right. I'm doing *nothing*."

Aimee crossed her arms. She spoke slowly, enunciating each word: "This girl is your niece."

"A niece I've never laid eyes on, as you very well know."

Aimee's voice rose a level: "A niece who's a lesbian."

"And your point is?"

"You have a niece who's had to leave home because she's a lesbian!"

Kate shouted back, "And your point *is*?"

"You're her lesbian aunt!"

"So what! What do you expect me to do?"

Aimee uncrossed her arms, put her hands on her hips. "She's in trouble, Kate." She lowered her voice. "She needs help."

"Aimee. She's the daughter of a man who despises me. Us."

"I'm not talking about helping your brother. I'm talking about the young person who needs the help."

"Let's be reasonable, okay? He's in Red Bluff, she's maybe here, maybe in San Francisco, and I'm in the middle of a court case."

"You're always in the middle of something. You always have some excuse. Always."

Kate said angrily, "What exactly is that supposed to mean?"

"If this call had come in from the station instead of your brother, you'd be on it like paint."

Kate gave an impatient shrug. She'd heard this time and time and time again about the priorities of her work. A lesbian runaway hardly compared with a murder trial. "Till I'm done with this case, it comes first. It has to. My job is my job."

"No, your job is not your job. Your job is your *life*."

"Not true. You have *never* understood how it is to be a cop."

Aimee marched to the closet, yanked out her leather jacket. "After thirteen years I understand two things. Your job comes first. Then that drink in your hand. Everything else—forget it. Your niece would never have a chance with you under any circumstances. God help anything that comes between you and your two real loves." She flung on the jacket, picked up her shoulder bag. "To hell with anybody who needs your help who isn't dead to begin with."

Kate absorbed these blows unthinkingly to express her overriding concern: "Where are you going?"

"Out."

"Be careful."

Aimee tossed her a withering look and slammed the door behind her.

Kate settled back into her armchair. She had to testify tomorrow. She *had* to prepare—she had no choice but to prepare; she could leave nothing to chance, to the vagaries of memory. The night before her testimony in a high-stakes homicide case—how could Aimee be this irrational?

She picked up her scotch. The truth was, over their thirteen years together, despite the lip service, Aimee had truly never understood the pressures of working homicide, the massive personal expenditure required to be calmly authoritative at death scenes and with the grieving loved ones of a victim in the hours and days thereafter. The sheer detail that had to be absorbed in order to withstand the punishing rigors of a courtroom. Aimee had never understood the urgency, the necessity to put it all away in your few off-hours just so you could perform again the following day.

She took two deep swallows of her scotch, finishing it. Yes, she drank—it was medicinal and necessary, goddamn it. She'd never taken pills or drugs and she wasn't a drunk. And she'd given up smoking—not that she got any points for it from Aimee. All things considered, cigarettes had been enough to give up. More than enough.

She stalked into the kitchen and fixed herself another drink, then returned to her armchair. Hearing a faint scratching from the litter box in Aimee's study, she called out, "Come here, sweetie."

Miss Marple obediently appeared in the doorway of the living room and trotted with dignified eagerness over the carpet. Kate moved her stack of reports to the table beside her, and the cat leaped into her lap and began to ritually knead the flesh of her thighs, her claws almost puncturing the tough fabric of Kate's jeans.

"You're the only woman who's ever really understood me," Kate whispered to her, scratching the soft whitish-gray fur under her chin. Miss Marple purred, settled into a curl on her lap.

Kate picked up several pages from the file of forensic reports, sipped at her drink. She was not going to do one goddamned thing about her brother and his daughter. No matter what kind of guilt trip Aimee tried to lay on her. When Aimee cooled down, she'd understand. And come home.

BUT A DAY LATER AIMEE HADN'T COME HOME. Hadn't so much as called.

All around Kate, people were returning to Judge Terrell's courtroom. She turned off her cell phone and went in.

With court back in session and on the record, Alicia Marquez said, "Before the break I asked whether you obtained a search warrant for Victoria Talbot's house."

Kate seized the opportunity. "Since the victim's son informed us she held sole title to the house—"

"Objection, unresponsive," interrupted Quantrill.

"Sustained," Judge Jackson Terrell said and asked in a chastising tone, "Did you or did you not obtain a search warrant, Detective?"

"We did, your honor." Terrell did indeed run a tight courtroom.

But Marquez smoothly reinforced the point: "So you waited for a search warrant despite the fact that technically it was not required."

"Correct." In truth, search warrants had become a necessary safety measure. She could not take the slightest chance on leaving any aspect of a homicide case open to legal challenge, not in this day and age.

"Evidence was collected at the scene?"

"Yes. Some by the Scientific Investigation Division, and also by myself and Detective Cameron."

"As lead detective, were you the one to decide what would be collected and by whom?"

"Correct. The criminalists worked under the direction of Detective Cameron and myself."

She and Cameron had begun their evaluation even before that. While Patrol Officer Donna Moreno took down family contact information from Allan Talbot prior to escorting him off the premises, Kate had compared notes with Cameron.

"Under that load of grief," Cameron said, "the guy is big-time pissed."

A piece fell solidly into place. Cameron had identified the intensity burning through the grief in Talbot's eyes. "You're right, Joe. He's thinking maybe his father had something to do with this."

"Jewelry's gone to make it look like a robbery, but you saw that diamond on her hand. A real home invasion—they'd make her take it off or they'd pull it off her dead body. It sure as hell smells domestic, Kate." Cameron's eyes were as cold as his tone, and Kate knew this was personal. After three years of working with him, there were places in him still closed off from her and some of those comprised family history he alluded to but did not discuss. He said darkly, "A son's not going to finger his father even if he thinks he did the deed . . ." He kicked at a piece of the Talbot lawn as if it offended him.

Why not? Kate thought. If my father had shot my mother or had her shot . . . She dismissed the comparison. Such a thing happening in her family was too inconceivable.

"No sign of break-in, a half-assed robbery, no assault," Cameron said forcefully. "The wife gets a divorce the husband doesn't want. He brings in the family paycheck, thinks he's bought and paid for his wife and kids, can't stand anybody thinking any different. We've seen it, what, two million times? What do you figure?"

"I figure number two million and one," Kate said. Unlike TV mysteries, real-world murders were usually perpetrated by the most obvious suspect, usually someone the victim knew.

They reentered the Talbot residence. Until Coroner's Investigator Walt Everson arrived, they would not again approach the body, which they were forbidden to touch. It would remain there for hours until the scene was processed, the first of many indignities to be inflicted with efficient impersonality around and on the remains of Victoria Talbot.

Blue-clad criminalists had already assembled and begun work. Shapiro, the still photographer, slouched in the dining room making entries in his photographer's log with his usual air of wanting to be anywhere else. His lazy habits had improved not a whit over the years, but these days he was well aware of what she required in her homicide scenes and she was aggravated by him only on principle. Videographer Jill Edmonds more than made up for him with her competent thoroughness, and digital photos could be easily drawn from film. Kate had requested Baker to do the print collecting; from the nature of this crime scene, fingerprints would be the prime forensic evidence, with hair and fiber and ballistics the next best possibilities. Fingerprint technician par excellence, Baker took meticulous care in determining optimum techniques for each area of a crime scene.

She and Baker exchanged nods of wary, and mutual, respect. She began, "The back door—"

"You wanna tell me something I don't know? I can already tell I gotta start there. I can already tell I'm gonna end up printing the whole goddamn house." He stalked off. She smiled.

Cameron was consulting with the other criminalists on evidence collection strategy and needed no input from her on a scene that called for routine processing. After photography of the entire house was finished, hair and fiber would be gathered in the immediate vicinity of the body, and blood samples. After she and Cameron had finished their search of the house, the techs would spread out as Kate and Cameron dictated that they should.

In the courtroom, Alicia Marquez, having led Kate through a painstakingly detailed re-creation of all her steps at the crime scene, inquired of her, "What evidence did you yourself collect?"

"The victim's personal computer, her journals, and personal papers," she recited. "They were fingerprinted and collected for examination."

THE SEARCH WARRANT FOR THE HOUSE IN
Hancock Park had come speedily from the on-call judge. While

the team of criminalists proceeded with their slow and meticulous work around the body in the bedroom, she and Cameron, now able legally to look beyond the surface appearance of the house, had begun their inspection upstairs. Interviews of urgent priority needed to be initiated, but they first had to assess what was here.

Two traditionally furnished bedrooms fronted the street, each room aglow in sunlight; each had a separate bath tiled in patterns of maroon, dark green, and navy. On the walls of one bedroom were silent era movie posters in neat black frames; in the other, an entire wall of white shelving held stuffed animals arranged by category. Kate was somehow chilled by the stiff organization of these unused playthings for children, at least three dozen dolls rigidly lined along their own shelf, and a myriad of games still wrapped in their store plastic, and sporting goods and toys with the surface perfection and high gloss of newness.

"Not like my childhood," Cameron remarked.

"Mine either," she agreed.

At the rear of this upper floor, a large airy room with an expanse of multipaned windows overlooked the garden. Perhaps originally converted from a bedroom, it was a handsome study with shelves of books, a sophisticated-looking music system, and cream-colored leather armchairs and a rocker upholstered in sage-green corduroy. This floor of the house, although in full readiness for occupancy including plush towels and a plethora of toiletries in the bathrooms, seemed sterile, with a distinct air of disuse.

"I really like this house," Cameron said, surveying the well-cared-for beechwood floors protected by bright area rugs in the bedrooms and a deep maroon runner in the hallway. "Nothing elaborate but one of those places that make you wish you had money."

"A jewel," Kate agreed. Given her choice of rooms, she too would have chosen that ground-floor bedroom as Victoria Talbot had, would also have put a desk in its bay window and happily worked at home with that lovely garden in immediate view. "I have a feeling she's kept these upper bedrooms to lure the grandkids. Or maybe her own kids."

"Yeah, you can come home again, children. Doesn't feel like they do, though."

During their partnership Cameron had developed a good feel for assessing facts and following hunches, and she felt in sync with him on this case. "Feels like lots of dysfunction and misery in this perfect house."

"Yeah. Well, we know Allan is for sure devoted to his mom but we don't know about his sisters. Or whether Allan's ex-wives liked their ex-mother-in-law enough to let his own kids come here. Maybe this Hancock Park house . . ." Cameron gestured with clawing sweeps of both hands as if clearing away webs. "Maybe downstairs lies the corpse of Spider Woman."

"Maybe." Open to believing him, she sensed that the woman downstairs did not fit that picture. Surroundings reflected their occupants, and on the surface these surroundings did not fit a woman who had cannibalized her children. She said, "Let's see what we can find up here."

The closets contained off-season and formal clothes in plastic garment bags; the drawers were mostly empty except for a few perfectly folded children's pajamas with store tags still on them. Bookshelves in the study were overloaded with sets of classics, books on gardening and cooking; also quality modern fiction, mostly by women. Victoria Talbot was loyal to the writers she liked: A. S. Byatt, Alice Walker, Toni Morrison, Anne Tyler, Barbara Kingsolver, Dorothy Sayers, P. D. James, Joyce Carol Oates.

One of the shelves held six slim maroon volumes with JOUR-NAL stamped in gold on the spines. Eager to open one, she instead made a note to have Baker fingerprint them so she could collect all of them later. If they were personal diaries, they might hold a trove of information about this household. Next to the journals was a sturdy steel box, its lid propped open, the combination padlock for it visible within. "Wonder what she kept in here," Cameron said. They further examined the study with a care toward preserving fingerprints, then went back downstairs.

The criminalists were almost finished with collecting their swab samples of blood around the body. "Time to call Everson," Cameron said, and Kate reached into her shoulder bag for her cell phone.

A few minutes later they found Baker in the kitchen photographing a piece of tape on the doorjamb. "Get lots of hits?" Cameron inquired breezily.

"Nah," he said, lifting the tape and placing it in a labeled plastic bag, "not near what I should where I should. Somebody really cleaned up."

She and Cameron inspected the kitchen. It was pristine, the counters gleaming, not a mark on any of the appliances. She opened the refrigerator. Nothing unusual there, unless cleanliness and organization of foodstuffs on the shelves counted.

"What do you make of the cleanup job in this house?" Cameron asked her. "Especially when the son tells us Victoria Talbot didn't do any of it herself."

"At least not normally. Looks like somebody didn't want any trace evidence found—especially prints."

"Which leaves out the husband."

"Why, Joe?" she argued. "She's had the house for two and a half years. Maybe there's a restraining order—maybe he wasn't supposed to be here."

"Good thought. Let's run the husband, see about any priors or court orders."

Finished looking in the cupboards, he touched the tip of his shoe to the foot lever on a round silver garbage can artfully positioned in a nook between the Viking range and a cabinet, and prized up the lid. "Hey, check this out."

She peered around him, down into blooms of pure deep red exuding an ineffably sweet aroma like no other. "Roses. Recently cut. Have to be from her garden." She remembered that empty crystal flower vase on the table in the entryway.

"Yeah. Why would anybody throw out perfectly good roses?"

Rage, she thought. She made a note, *Roses,* and circled it. "We can't collect them, obviously. Baker?" she called.

Baker came over and peered into the garbage can. He snapped a photo and said, "I'll print the can. Shapiro should photograph this as is, then spread the flowers out on a white background and do it again. Okay with you?"

"Terrific," Cameron said.

STEPPING BACK FROM THE COURTROOM'S display board, Alicia Marquez said to Kate, "So you did not physically collect the roses you have just described, but People's Exhibits Forty-Six and -Seven, the two photographs I've just put up on the board, depict them as you saw them that morning?"

"Correct."

From there the investigation had gathered momentum, moved into high gear.

FOUR

"The husband?" Cameron inquired.

From the scant information they had, the ex-husband loomed large. But there was the location of this house to consider. It was on the corner of a wide street, with an adjacent neighbor only to its right. The occupants of the house to the rear, and across the corner, were far less likely to have witnessed anything or heard sounds from here. "Maybe the good friend next door first," Kate said.

If Marjorie Durant was a close friend, then information from the interview with her could better set up the interview with Douglas Talbot.

OUTSIDE, A WAGON TRAIN OF MEDIA VANS had moved into place and the audience across the street had swelled and become noisy. Patrol officers kept it all corralled and well at bay, but two camera operators began to walk along the periphery of the crowd, their shoulder-held equipment recording the progress she and Cameron made along the sidewalk to the house next door. The media circus and its onlookers would lose energy and disperse after the main event—the Coroner's attendants exiting with the body bag—and media relations would soon set up to answer questions from the press including those from her own personal pest, police reporter Corey Lanier from the *L.A. Times.*

She and Cameron trekked over a serpentine path through a vast expanse of manicured emerald grass and a mature, well-cultivated landscaping of flower gardens and palm and yucca trees toward an imposing white stucco Spanish-colonial house with arched windows and a gleaming terra-cotta roof. "Not a dead leaf anywhere," Cameron noted. "You need a gardener every day to keep lawns and gardens like this. Bet you could get arrested around here for driving while poor."

Kate nodded. She was conservatively dressed in a gray blazer and navy pants, but was conscious of a sag in one knee of her pants and tiny scuff marks on a shoe. The corner of a swimming pool came into view, an aquamarine glimmer against white tile. "Where's William Holden with the towel around his waist?" she muttered to Cameron as they approached a massive doorway of dark, highly polished, carved wood. From inside came the distant but sharp yapping of small dogs.

She rang the bell, then glanced to her right, to the Talbot house. A six-foot-high wrought-iron fence separated the two properties, but this house had a clear view through the fence to

the Talbot yard, and unlike the Talbot house with its conceal-
ing hedge, this one looked directly out onto the street.

The woman who answered the door, although older than
her deceased neighbor by perhaps five years, was no Norma
Desmond. On a slender, well-toned body she wore a long, sil-
very gray shapeless jacket with patch pockets over loose pants
tied with a drawstring. Her hair, skillfully tinted ash-brown to
minimize but not obliterate strands of gray, was cut to frame
her fine-boned face in a few soft waves. Although her dark
brown eyes were rimmed in red, she looked composed, if a little tremulous, an elegant older woman in an elegant house visibly willing herself into retaining her poise.

As Kate introduced herself and Cameron, the woman
looked them over, her gaze lingering briefly on Cameron. "I'm
Marjorie Durant," she said, a faint huskiness in her voice.
"One of the officers said some detectives would want to talk to
me." But she scrutinized their identification before inviting
them in. "You'll want coffee by now, I'm sure."

"Thank you," Cameron said with feeling. "We would."

As they went into the house, the yapping increased to a fran-
tic pitch. Apparently the dogs were being kept in a closed room
or perhaps in the rear yard of the house. "Three Scotties," Marjorie Durant explained. "They'll settle down once we do."

The cavernous living room smelled of cigarette smoke, and
Kate realized how seldom she noticed it in people's homes
these days. The house displayed every evidence of an interior
decorator's skills: an expanse of white carpeting and white
walls provided a gallery for impressionist paintings and an artfully composed arrangement of antique furnishings and bronze
sculptures of horses and dogs. The one divergent note was a
gleaming black grand piano on a carpeted platform near the

front window. A tapestry sofa and matching love seat, along with two ornate chairs upholstered in amber-brown, were grouped in front of a polished stone fireplace with family photos on its mantel. A circular coffee table had been set up with a bamboo tray holding a carafe warming over a votive candle, coffee mugs of white china rimmed in gold, and a dish of biscotti. "I have cream and sugar," she said, "but don't you police usually take it black?"

Cameron greeted this stereotype with an amused, "Yes we do."

He took one of the chairs and Kate seated herself on the unyielding love seat. Instinctively knowing that this woman would not welcome even being asked if using a tape recorder was permissible, Kate took her notebook from her shoulder bag. While Marjorie Durant poured coffee, Kate began formally: "Detective Cameron and I are very sorry for your loss. I understand you and Mrs. Talbot were friends. We appreciate the opportunity to talk to you—we know this must be very hard. We'll take as little of your time as possible." Actually, they needed to do an expeditious yet courteous interview and get out of here without offending or antagonizing this woman so that they could follow up with her if and when they needed to. "How long have you known Mrs. Talbot?"

Mrs. Durant handed steaming mugs around with a slightly trembling hand. "Since the day they moved into Hancock Park. All told, at least twenty years, I'd say. It was wonderful when Victoria was able to move in right next door."

"This was after the divorce," Cameron said.

"Of course."

Kate took a sip and was unsurprised that the brew was complex and delicious. She set down her mug on a small side table and flipped to a page in her notebook to verify Victoria Talbot's age: fifty-three. She would have been thirty-three back then. She asked, "So you would describe your relationship as close?"

"Very close." She offered the plate of biscotti, which Kate and Cameron declined with murmured thanks. "Every day—if I didn't go over there or vice versa, we talked by phone."

Kate waited until Mrs. Durant seated herself on the sofa, then asked her best open-ended question: "Can you shed any light on what's happened here?"

Marjorie Durant pulled a pack of Pall Malls from her jacket pocket. "I haven't smoked in ten years," she said, her voice quavering. A large cut-glass ashtray on the coffee table was strewn with more than a dozen long cigarette butts. "I had to beg a pack from Ella next door. My husband will be so furious . . ." She tapped the end of her unfiltered cigarette on the table with an expertise that belied her long abstinence. She looked up at Kate, then Cameron. "I don't know what's happened except she's been killed," she said. "Perhaps you can tell me."

"There's very little we can tell you at this point," Kate temporized.

Mrs. Durant scraped a match aflame and lit the cigarette. "Was there a break-in?" she asked. "We have a right to know that much. A robbery, a . . ." She did not finish.

"We're not really sure," Kate replied cautiously. "There appears to be no sexual assault but we're in the very preliminary stages of the investigation."

The yapping of the dogs had subsided but not ceased. Grimacing, Mrs. Durant nodded and took a deep drag from her cigarette. She looked toward Kate, yet past her, as if focused on a point in the distance. "I think it's best you talk to the family," she finally said.

Kate picked up her coffee mug, and Cameron took it as his cue to enter the conversation. "Anything you can say to enlighten us . . ."

"I think it's best you talk to the family," she repeated.

Kate tried an oblique angle. "According to my notes, when the Talbots originally moved in, Allan would have been thirteen, the two girls ten and eight."

Mrs. Durant exhaled smoke with her words: "That would be about right."

"Were you close to everyone, or just Mrs. Talbot?"

"Most everyone," she said in a quivering voice. She bounced the body of the cigarette on the edge of the ashtray.

"The children?"

"Most everyone," she repeated.

"What about the grandchildren?" Kate asked, remembering the sterile upstairs rooms next door. "Did you see them too?"

"In recent years only at Christmas," she said tersely, and Kate knew nothing more would be forthcoming on this topic.

"What can you tell us about this morning?" Cameron asked. "Did you see anything, hear anything unusual?"

"I've been thinking about that. I think . . . I think I heard it happen. They were gunshots I heard, I now realize."

"When was this?"

"I'm not sure, I—" She broke off with a sob, stubbed out her cigarette, pulled a crumpled tissue from her pocket, dabbed at her eyes.

"I'm sorry. I know this is very hard," Cameron said in a soft tone. "Perhaps you could just simply take us through this morning as you remember it."

"Yes. That would be good." Her voice was composed again. "I got up at six-thirty as usual—the dogs always get us up. Gene—that's my husband—we usually take them for their walk, but he had to finish packing, the limo was due at seven. It's not as bad as it was but you still have to get to airports early these days with all they put you through. He's in the air right now, to Philadelphia for his meeting, I've left a message for him to call. He doesn't even know . . ."

"What type of meeting?" Cameron inquired pleasantly.

"Finance," she said with a sharp look at him. "So I took the girls."

The girls. Kate stole a glance at the photos on the mantel, vacation shots of a husky man, presumably Eugene Durant, with Marjorie against European backgrounds. She wondered if the Durants' dogs, which had finally gone quiet, were substitutes for absent grown children. She finished her coffee, then asked, "Did you see anything unusual? Strangers? Cars in the neighborhood that aren't ordinarily here?"

She shook her head. "I can't tell you there wasn't something unusual. I was too busy with the girls. The three of them, they're quite active, quite a handful even on their leashes."

"I imagine," Kate said. "Do you—"

"Wait a minute. There was a black car. On the way back I noticed it was badly parked."

"Where?"

"Just down the street."

"What make?"

"A Mercedes, I think. Yes, it was. A brand-new one."

"Dealer plates?"

"Yes. But that's all I can tell you about it."

"Fine. Do you have any idea when you left or got back?"

"Well, I returned about five minutes before Gene left, so that would be about five to seven."

"What limo company do you use?"

"Liberty," Mrs. Durant responded, so quickly that Kate understood they used limos all the time. "The driver was Paul," she added.

Kate made a note to check with the limo driver; they usually arrived early for their assignments and perhaps he had seen something while he was waiting. "The gunshots," she said. "What time—"

"Well, that was the oddest thing," Mrs. Durant said, and shook another cigarette out of her pack. "It was about half an hour after Gene left and I was watching the *Today* show and they went to local news. I got up and was on my way to the kitchen for . . . I can't remember what. I heard this bang. One of the dogs barked from back there and that might have told me something, but they're hypersensitive you know, and she only barked once and I thought—or maybe assumed—it was on the news. I confess, I'm slightly hard of hearing and I keep the TV turned up a bit. And, I mean, you don't ever think of a shot actually being fired . . ."

Not around here, Kate thought. "So if the local news had come on, this would have been, what, about seven-thirty or so?"

"Yes, I suppose. But the odd thing is, I heard the other bang after that."

"Yes," Cameron said, "she was—"

"Mrs. Durant," Kate interrupted without looking at him. She was sure he had been about to reveal that Victoria Talbot had been shot more than once, a serious mistake. "That second bang sounded the same as the first one?"

She nodded. "Identical."

"But you describe it as odd?"

"Well . . . yes." She looked embarrassed. "Maybe it wasn't odd. Maybe all of us are too much influenced by the police shows we see on television, but you hear something that might be a shot and you think you might be mistaken if you don't hear more."

"I don't understand. You did hear another shot. Were there more than two?"

"No. But that second shot came sometime later."

"How much later?"

"I knew you were going to ask me that question and I've been thinking about it all morning. It might have been five minutes. Or even ten."

"As much as ten?"

The question came from Cameron, but Kate was just as intrigued as he. She was taking careful notes, as verbatim as possible.

"Yes. Or it could have been five, as I said. She *was* shot, isn't that—isn't that how it happened?"

"It is," Kate answered.

"Perhaps the first sound I heard was indeed on the news. Or . . . how many times was she—"

"We won't have all the facts until the medical examiner . . . uh, lets us know," Kate finished tactfully, skirting mention of the autopsy. "You remember the time of the first shot very clearly. Is there some reason you're unsure of the interval between the two sounds?"

"I was on the phone in the kitchen with my daughter and two of the dogs got to quarreling over their food dishes and barking and carrying on, and I lost track of the time. Or perhaps I'm just mistaken altogether—" She looked at them apologetically. "I'm just so upset, I may remember things incorrectly."

"We understand. We know you're doing your best. Do you think the second sound could have been sooner than five minutes?"

"No," she said decisively. "It was five minutes at least. But it might have been more, you see."

"You mean even more than ten minutes?"

"Maybe. Possibly."

"And you don't remember anything on television that might suggest the time—"

"No. It was on, but I was away from it and I wasn't paying a bit of attention to it by then."

"What do you remember happening next, Mrs. Durant?"

"The sirens. The police. Allan coming out of the house toward them, white as a sheet and looking like he could hardly walk. Paramedics going in. More police cars pulling up outside, blocking the whole street."

"How long after that second bang do you remember this happening?"

"It wasn't very long. A few minutes. I realized then that the sounds I'd heard meant something—they had to, with all those police arriving. I ran out but they just took my name and wouldn't tell me anything except a woman had been shot dead. But I knew that already, of course. Just as I knew when I walked into my mother's living room and she was sitting in her big armchair as usual, but . . ."

"Yes," Kate said with considerable sympathy, "sometimes you do just know." Like Allan Talbot had known.

"When I heard that first shot, I was just drinking my coffee and watching television and it never occurred to me that Vicki—" Saying the name released something; she lowered her head and sobbed.

Kate waited until she again composed herself, certain that she would; the woman's innate dignity was of tensile strength. "Mrs. Durant, did you realize at the time the direction the shots came from?"

"Not really. But yes, in retrospect, especially the second shot because I was in the kitchen and the windows were open. It came from the direction of Vicki's house, but at the time I thought it could have come from across the street from her, even the block behind us. I'm sorry, I still didn't realize what it meant—"

"Sure. Of course you wouldn't," Cameron said sympathetically. "Did you hear anything else? Loud voices? A car starting on the street?"

"No voices. Let me see . . ." She closed her eyes, pinched the bridge of her nose between thumb and forefinger, apparently her habit for concentrating. "No, but I wouldn't, you see. The front windows are double glazed."

"And you didn't see anything unusual from your windows anytime this morning."

"No."

They had gleaned all they apparently could from the interview, and Kate decided to push one more time. "Mrs. Talbot's ex-husband," she said. "Did you know him well?"

"At one time, yes. Not since the divorce."

"When was the last time you saw him?"

"I had no interest in seeing him at all. And I believe I've said all I want to say at this point," Mrs. Durant said. "I believe I've been as cooperative as I feel I can be."

"We very much appreciate your cooperation." Kate sensed that Marjorie Durant would be more forthcoming when they developed information and could ask her to confirm it. She produced a card, laid it on the coffee table. "We'll have more questions as the investigation proceeds. If there's anything else you remember, or want to add, please call us."

FIVE

"The evidence you and Detective Cameron collected at the Talbot residence," Alicia Marquez said to her from the podium, "did you seal and label it?"

"We did, except for the computer, the diaries, and personal letters and papers," Kate responded. "After they were finger-printed, I collected them for examination, with the appropriate chain-of-custody documentation . . ."

She answered her follow-up questions on automatic pilot; they related to the sealing and labeling of evidence, the chain of custody maintained for the integrity of evidence until it was presented in a courtroom—such well-traveled territory that her mind wandered toward Aimee even while she spoke to the jury.

How could Aimee do this to her, she fumed, especially when she was embroiled in a trial?

Finally Marquez changed topic: "At what time did the Coroner's investigator arrive?"

"If I may consult my notes . . ." Kate opened her folder.

"I SEE THIS PARTY'S ALREADY UNDER WAY," Walt Everson said from the doorway as Kate and Cameron searched the living room. The Coroner's assistant and Maria Phillips, his photographer, were ushered in by a grinning Fred Hansen. Everson's pencil-thin mustache twitched in the suggestion of a grin as he took in his surroundings. "I must say this place is less scuzzy than our usual rendezvous."

"Enjoyez vous," Cameron returned dryly.

Everson was already gowned, and Kate and Cameron followed him to the bedroom. Standing just outside the doorway, he pulled booties over his feet, then waited until the strobe lights of Phillips and Shapiro finished illuminating every angle of the body of Victoria Talbot.

Approaching, crouching a few feet away, his bag of instruments beside him, Everson snapped on double gloves as he contemplated the body. He edged his way forward, Kate and Cameron following in his crablike wake to lean over him. A gloved hand brushing back a lock of dark hair, he held a thermometer strip against her skin. "Good-looking house, good-looking corpse," he said. Delicately, he worked up a section of the tucked-in brick-colored shirt, selected a scalpel from his bag, made an incision. "She'll look good even in this." He sank a thermometer into her liver.

Cameron had already turned away. Everson's lacerating humor was clearly necessary self-protection in a profession in which he dealt every single day with corpses subjected to every manner of death and in every state of decomposition, but Cameron had not learned to tolerate Everson's patter. And he had yet to learn how to cope with the visceral realities of the Coroner's Office, especially the autopsy.

"Anything you can tell us yet, Walt?" Kate asked.

"Yes. It's nice to have a classy homicide scene like this one because it's my final curtain too. I'm retiring."

"No shit," Cameron uttered.

Kate experienced a momentary disorientation. "Are you serious?"

"Dead serious. Excuse the pun."

He had given no previous hint, nothing. "When did you decide this?" she asked.

"Couple of weeks ago. I heard you and Joe were the catching detectives on this one. So I asked to do my swan song with you two."

"I'm honored," Cameron said ironically. "But this is about you and Kate. You two go back a long way."

"To the Stone Age," Everson said. "Back to when I didn't have to wear a space suit to look at a body."

"Walt," Kate said, "retiring—to do what?" She judged Everson to be fifty years old, fifty-five, tops.

Sitting back on his haunches, he looked around at her, a reflection of the bedroom window on his glasses obscuring his eyes. "Run around the desert in my dune buggy with my grandkids. Go on the wagon yet again. Maybe keep a girlfriend around for more than a week or two."

"It's great you can afford to retire," Cameron contributed.

Again Everson's mustache twitched. "Couple of years ago all I heard was how dumb I was to put my retirement money in

T-Bills instead of the stock market. I don't look all that dumb now, do I?"

"You're a fucking genius," muttered Cameron.

Kate had listened ad nauseum to Cameron's wailing over his stock holdings and did not want it further injected into this conversation. She was focused on only one thing: "Walt—why?"

"I've run out of jokes, Kate."

She knew in her bones what he meant, but she bantered, "So you've repeated yourself a few times over twenty years."

"Twenty-two. Twenty-one and a half years longer than I should have. If I'd bailed after six months like my ex-wife said I should—it's the one thing the bitch got right. She warned me I needed to get out of this before I lost it."

She did not dare ask what "it" was that he had lost. Neither, apparently, did the silent Cameron. Walt Everson was a fixture in her career. Walt Everson with his fastidious personal manner, his understanding of how homicide detectives had to work.

Everson pulled the thermometer from the body's liver, glanced at it, and announced briskly, "TOD between seven and ten, take your pick."

His rote announcement. Time of death was always given as a three-hour window. "Can you do better," she said, also by rote.

"Between seven and eight."

The information, a confirmation of Marjorie Durant's statements, made all the difference for their area canvass, asking neighbors what they might have seen or heard within this narrower time frame.

"You might want to stand back," Everson said. "She's so heavy there could be compression."

Meaning blood as it settled had collected at the wound site and was being held in by the weight of the body. Cameron beat a hasty retreat to the doorway. Kate did not move. She was this woman's representative; she owed it to any victim violated by homicide who had come into her care not to turn away from anything until the case reached some form of disposition—hopefully, a measure of justice.

Grunting with effort, Everson lifted and turned the upper body. There was no further blood drain; the head had bled out and the bullet in the back had not exited the thick chest of Victoria Talbot. He eased the body back down.

"Nice one-two punch," he said. "Single shot to the head, single shot to the back. Redundant. Either one was fatal."

Redundancy borne of hatred, Kate thought.

Everson picked up his tape recorder and grinned at them. "So get out of here and let me finish. I'll check in with you later, Kate. You and Joe are welcome at my retirement festivities. I think they're planning on decorating the morgue and serving Bloody Marys."

She returned his grin. "Whatever. I'll be there."

WITH THE BODY OF VICTORIA TALBOT FINALLY gone, the criminalists continued to work. That Baker had finished in the bedroom was evident: Virtually every surface—furniture, mirrors, doorways, doorknobs—was glazed with gray fingerprint powder.

"Elimination prints," Cameron said, thinking aloud as he wrote in his notebook. "To begin with, from the family, the housekeeper, obviously. Mrs. Durant too," he said, grinning, "since she's admitted to being in here all the time."

After pulling on latex gloves, they began their search of the bedroom. "I'll take the desk," she said. Cameron nodded and opened the walk-in closet. Her practiced eye skimmed over the expensive accoutrements—the Mont Blanc pen set, the delicate

Lenox china boxes for paperclips and stamps—without interest. The Rolodex was automatic for collection, to establish the
victim's associates. Also the computer, for its potentially valuable cache of email.

She scrutinized the dozen small framed photos lined up
along the edge of the desk near the window. "Interesting, Joe,"
she said. "All the photos here seem to be of children. I don't see
a husband in any of them."

"Ditto on the dresser," he said.

The top drawer of the desk held only ballpoint pens and
rubber bands. In the right-hand drawer, among supplies of en-
velopes and writing pads, was a handsome maroon volume
with JOURNAL stenciled in gold on the front and on the spine.
Its heady smell of fine leather reached her. It was a match for
the set she had seen upstairs in the study, she realized. She
edged it open just enough to see handwriting, and made a note
to have it fingerprinted, then collected in a plastic bag. Perhaps
someone else had made themselves privy to Victoria Talbot's
personal thoughts, had read something motivating enough for
a rage killing.

In the bottom drawer a packet of letters was bound in an
elastic band, perhaps more grist. She collected those as well.
She moved from the desk to the dresser.

"A good haul, partner," Cameron said. "Look what I
found." He showed her two flat black velvet boxes. "Lots
more jewelry, looks to be very expensive stuff. I'll collect it—
maybe Allan can tell us what's missing."

IN THE COURTROOM, ALICIA MARQUEZ ASKED,
"Did you and Detective Cameron proceed to interview Douglas Talbot?"

"We did."

"When and where did the interview take place?"

"We arrived at his company offices at approximately one-thirty that afternoon."

"Did you tape-record your interview?"

"We did not."

"Was there a reason?"

"Objection," Gregory Quantrill said, his head jerking up from his note taking. "Prejudicial."

"Overruled," Judge Terrell said. "Cover it on cross, Mr. Quantrill."

She replied, "Mr. Talbot declined to be recorded."

THE OFFICES OF TALBOT & REESE, INCOR-porated, were on the thirteenth floor of a nondescript office building at Wilshire and Fairfax. Kate and Cameron had scarcely introduced themselves before the long-haired young receptionist leaped from her chair, came out from behind her desk, and beckoned for them to follow her. She led them in a rapid gait through a roomful of cubicles with dozens of people working intently at computer screens. "He's canceled every-thing," she said in hushed tones as she slowed before a closed office door, "just to wait for you police. He's really *upset*. A customer saw the story on TV and called him. He heard about it from a *customer*."

Kate wasn't sure if the receptionist was blaming them, the media, or the news-bearing customer for the method by which Douglas Talbot had first learned of his ex-wife's murder—cer-tainly a breech of common civility and decorum—but she did not ask or comment. Nothing could have been done to prevent it. Investigating officers had once had a span of control over a crime scene, the identification of the victim and dissemination of information, but in this era of immediate "breaking news" and hovering media helicopters with instant visual transmission, that span of control had all but vanished.

Douglas Talbot's office, a pleasant composition of browns and blues—walnut desk and credenza with three slate-blue chairs arranged in front—was standard issue except for its corner location and hazy western view of Beverly Hills and environs, and its large size and impeccable neatness. Two ficus trees, a photo montage of theater interiors, and a few family pictures and plaques were arranged along one wall; on the other a wide shelf displayed low pots of white daisies and cyclamen interspersed between what appeared to be electronics parts; a higher shelf held three television monitors.

Douglas Talbot looked to be in his mid- to late fifties, and wore his graying brown hair ultrashort in the current fashion of mature men with a receding hairline. Seated in a black leather chair, he was hunched over his desk, his buttoned navy-blue suit jacket straining across his broad chest, his tie tightly cinched, the flat features of his broad face clenched in a grimace.

After announcing, "The police are here, Mr. Talbot," the receptionist escaped. Kate introduced herself and Cameron. Talbot made no effort to acknowledge them. With a flip of his fingers, he closed the lid of his notebook computer, then took off his reading glasses and tossed them; they skittered along the expanse of his desk. Only then did he look up and contemplate them with green eyes as cold as winter.

"I wondered when you'd bother to turn up." He picked up a remote control and clicked it with angry jabs of his thumb, shutting off news broadcasts on all three TV monitors. "I guess thirty years of marriage doesn't rate notification from you people when something happens like the killing of a man's wife."

Cameron took a seat in one of the chairs without being asked, then responded, "We assumed your son or someone in the family would call you, sir. We assumed the news would more suitably come from someone close to you."

Kate admired Cameron's tact; LAPD regulations called for notification of next of kin, and ex-husbands as a general rule were not in that category.

Talbot was staring at him. "For God's sake, man, what the hell's going on? I don't know one goddamn thing except what the morons on TV are spouting."

Taking the chair beside Cameron, she said, "Your ex-wife was shot and killed this morning—"

"For God's sake, I *know* that." Talbot's clenched fists were white at the knuckles. "Jesus, everybody in *town* knows that much—"

"Your son found the body—"

"Allan found her?"

"—if not immediately afterward, within minutes."

"Allan?" He looked stricken.

Kate was doubly astonished: that no one from his family had called him, and that the news media had not discovered or disseminated the information that the victim's son had found the body. Most people in an area that had suddenly become a crime scene were hardly reticent about revealing what they knew, while expressing shock that "such a thing could happen in our neighborhood." If Marjorie Durant was representative of the neighbors in Hancock Park, the media would perhaps find slim pickings.

Shifting his gaze from them to his phone, Douglas Talbot stared at it as if it had betrayed him in some fundamental way. Kate scrutinized him. She remembered Allan saying he would call his sisters. Not his father. Whatever the animosity, whatever Allan's suspicions, why would he not call his father if even to confront him? Why would this father not have called his own son after the customer had told him about seeing the family home on the news? Why would this father not have called his daughters, or vice versa? What was the cause of so stark an estrangement in this family? She jotted a reminder in her notebook to check the answering machine tape at the Hancock Park house for its messages.

"How was she . . . Did she suffer?"

Kate said, "I can tell you that death was instantaneous."

Talbot's scowl had deepened; his face was dark with anger. She had learned over the years that anger was, for some people, their manifestation of grief. That he appeared distraught did not impress her. He could be a killer and still feel piercing anguish, if not remorse. Some murderers did not comprehend or concern themselves with the devastation they had wrought until after they had perpetrated it, especially when the fuel for killing was rage. She and Cameron already knew that Douglas Talbot was an ex-husband who had not wanted to be an ex-husband.

"Did somebody break in?" Talbot demanded. "Who the hell . . . Christ, this is unreal." His stare demanded an answer.

Kate gave her diplomatic response. "We don't have a suspect as yet. We've just begun our investigation and we're here to ask for your help."

Talbot nodded, looking somewhat mollified.

"We'd like to record the conversation if that's okay," Cameron said.

"Fucking forget it," Talbot snorted. "Do I look that stupid to you? You want tape, I want my lawyer."

Cameron raised his hands while Kate responded courteously, "Being recorded is your option—some people actually prefer an exact record of what they say. You're free to have a lawyer at any time, sir, but we're here simply looking for information." Even though he had substantive reasons for his bristling hostility, she disliked him. Cameron was busying himself with his notebook, but she could tell from the angle of his head and forward thrust of his shoulders his own animosity toward Talbot, and that he was trying to control it.

"I don't mind answering questions without a lawyer," Talbot conceded. "But I don't see how I can help."

Knowing they had scant chance of establishing rapport and would more likely reach a point of alienating this man with their questions, she decided to fill in some background. "What kind of business are you in, Mr. Talbot?" She gestured to the shelf display of electronics.

"Lighting. Basically, we supply key components for high-powered lights and lighting systems—klieg lights, theatrical lighting, spotlights for prisons, lighthouses, things like that."

"How large an operation are you?"

"Statewide mainly, locally pretty big, some national exposure that's expanding, even in a bad economy like this one."

She would need to verify his claim of prosperity in a recession but for now she could dismiss her probing for economic stress—a common impetus to murder. A person's occupation was usually neutral ground and like most people he was willing to discuss it, however warily, and the continuing discussion softened some of his hostility. Kate made only a few notes as he rambled on about beginning the business thirty-five years ago from his basement, the new plant that was going up in Folsom, the two hundred and fifteen employees that would staff this office and Folsom when it was finished, and the plant and warehouse in the Valley. That his business partner, James R. Reese, had come aboard ten years ago when the business needed a top-flight financial guy.

"Any family members involved?" Cameron inquired, writing in his notebook.

"Sure. My brother Larry's warehouse manager. A nephew's a service rep."

But none of his children or their spouses, Kate noted.

"About your ex-wife," Cameron changed topic. "When were you divorced?"

A shudder ran through him; he rubbed his eyes with both hands, ran them back over his stubble of hair. "She filed four years ago." He closed his eyes briefly. "The decree came through three years and a month ago. April twenty-ninth it was."

"What were her grounds?"

"Why?" he demanded, shoving his body forward. "What business is it of yours?"

"It's police business," Cameron returned sharply.

"Why? Are you insinuating I did this?"

"I wasn't, but let's get that over with. Did you?"

"Jesus Christ." Talbot looked up at the ceiling as if searching for the deity he had called upon. Then he spread his hands on the desk blotter. They were large, thick-fingered. "I'll be straight with you. We got divorced, so you can assume we had some problems. Everybody does, for chrissakes. There's no reason any stuff between Vicki and me has to come out—it's got nothing to do with this. What happened to her—this is one of those break-in home-invasion things, it has to be. Everybody loved Victoria. Everybody. The neighborhood's full of Mexicans—gardeners, laborers, you name it. The whole time we were together, she always liked to be out in her damn garden. Somebody got through the hedge—" He nodded vigorously as he warmed up to his scenario. "Yeah, it's got to be some Mexican asshole that followed her into the house or broke in and — what other explanation is there? That hedge wouldn't protect her, it'd just hide some asshole who'd have all the time and privacy in the world to—"

"Sir," Kate interrupted the ramble, "the problems between you and your ex-wife, how would you describe them?"

He glared at her. "I was a bastard," he said flatly. "That's all. Under pressure building my business, drinking a lot—you know how it is."

"Sure. You were stressed," she said in an effort at rapport. "So what brought on the divorce?"

He shrugged in irritation. "You know how it is. The stuff people do when they're on the sauce. I'm telling you, it's got nothing to do with this. Not one damn thing."

"We wish we could take your word for it," Cameron said. "You're smart enough to know we have to check everything out."

Kate looked at him. Cameron's body tension had eased and his words and tone were the right blend of empathy and firmness. She added in support of him, "We'll do all we can to protect your—"

"Which is flat nothing," Talbot snapped, sitting back in his leather chair. "Till you get the guy who did this, I'm fair game for the press." He made quotes in the air with two fingers: "Murder in Hancock Park, Ex-Husband Under Suspicion."

Sounds about right, Kate thought.

"Maybe we can take care of that right now," Cameron said, crossing an ankle over a knee. "Can you account for your whereabouts between last night and this morning?"

"Sure. Last night I was out in Lake View Terrace—" Talbot broke off, looking nonplussed.

"Okay," Cameron said, nodding encouragement. "Any-body see you?"

"Yeah. Tons of people. I was at the Angeles Shooting Range out on Little Tujunga."

Kate scarcely managed to keep from laughing. Cameron was not as successful: he emitted several short barks of mirth.

"Yeah," Talbot said dejectedly. "Shit. I can see the head-lines." Again he made quotes with two fingers: "Wife Dies, Husband Seen at Shooting Range."

No sane person wanted to find themselves in the maw of the media, Kate thought, but this man seemed inordinately ob-sessed.

"I've been going there for months," Talbot said. "I'm out two, three times a week if I can make it—there's good lighted night shooting."

"So, what do you shoot?" Cameron inquired.

"Paper targets mostly, some clay. Look—"

"I take it you own a gun?"

"Sure. Three of them. Legal, registered, locked away in a gun cabinet, just the way the left wing radicals want it."

Kate was no longer surprised at the arsenals people kept. "What kind of guns?"

"A Colt three-fifty-seven Python, a Beretta ninety-two FS nine, and a Remington rifle. Safari Grade," he added proudly.

Very expensive guns, she thought. She asked, "For target practice?"

"What am I, a Mafia don? Yes. All for target practice. And protection. The first one I bought, it was years ago to protect my family. Then I got interested, started collecting them." He looked sharply at them. "I left that first one with Vicki. In-sisted. She didn't want it, wouldn't take lessons or practice with it, but I still wanted her to keep it. Like I told her, even if you don't know how to use a gun, just pointing it at somebody can sometimes make them go away." He winced. "Did she at least try—did you find it?"

"No gun was readily apparent," Kate said, feeling a twinge of sympathy for him.

"Jesus, maybe she tried to use it and the guy got it away from her—" He looked stricken.

It was possible. People who owned a gun for protection frequently got themselves into more trouble than if they hadn't had one. But if Victoria Talbot had so disliked guns, she might have hidden hers away so carefully she and Cameron simply hadn't found it. "What make is it?"

"Smith and Wesson thirty-eight Special."

The same as her old service revolver. The one she'd carried before the mandated change to nine millimeter. She much preferred that old gun. Nines did have greater firepower but they were still peashooters compared with what was out on the street.

"Where did she keep it?" she inquired.

He looked suddenly uncomfortable. "I don't know," he muttered. "It was in a locked box the last time I saw it."

"Restraining order, Mr. Talbot?" Cameron asked, and added warningly, in the face of Talbot's glare, "We'll find out."

"She didn't need it," he said bitterly. "No way would I come near her if she didn't want me to—all she ever had to do was say so."

I'll just bet, Kate thought. "So when was the last time you saw her?"

"Two and a half years ago. If you don't count seeing each other at a distance at social events."

Kate checked a note. Allan Talbot had said Victoria Talbot

had moved into her new home approximately that long ago. "What about at her house?"

"That dump," he said derisively. "I work like a dog so we can get our great place on Rossmore to bring up our kids. She gets her divorce and turns right around and forces a sale so she can buy that other thing just to live next door to the Durants. No, she never invited me."

"Are you telling us you've never been in the house?"

"Jesus." He glared at her exasperation. "What do you think I'm telling you? No, I've never been there."

"So you don't know where she kept the gun you left with her."

"No. What a smart detective you are."

"We'll check thoroughly to see if it's there," she said, unperturbed by his sarcasm. She was remembering the open metal box upstairs in the study with the combination lock inside. Could that have been where Victoria Talbot had kept the gun? "We'd also like a look at your own gun collection."

"Fucking forget it," he spat. "You got no reason to pin this on me. Get out and find who really did it."

"You know," Cameron said conversationally, "maybe somebody had access to your collection and you're not aware of it."

"What crap. Forget it. You just stay the fuck away from me and my house."

Kate made a note to get a search warrant. Cameron asked, "What time did you get home from the shooting range?"

"I don't know—maybe ten-thirty."

"Anybody verify that?"

"Marta. Marta was there. My . . . housekeeper."

Cameron looked up, his pen poised over his notebook. "You have a housekeeper who works at ten-thirty at night?"

"Yes. I mean, she started out as my housekeeper—I mean, she still is, but . . ." He was waving a hand as if to wordlessly indicate what he meant, and Kate let him flounder, pleased that Cameron did as well.

"She's more than a housekeeper, of course. We have a . . . relationship."

"I see," Kate said.

"You don't see," Talbot snapped. "Don't give me your bullshit. A man can't just keep going along without meeting some needs, that's all."

"Does Marta have a last name?" Cameron inquired.

"Gonzalez," Talbot said, seemingly oblivious to the sarcasm. "Spelled with two z's."

"Mr. Talbot, we understand you live in Brentwood." They had gleaned little from Allan Talbot about his father, but he had shared this information. "What time did you leave your house this morning?"

Talbot stared at his desk blotter. Kate knew he had an idea, from when the news had broken on television, of when they had discovered the body.

"I'm trying to think whether I did anything out of the ordinary," Talbot said. "I didn't. So that means I left around eight-thirty, maybe a little after."

After Victoria Talbot was killed. "And you arrived here when?"

"Before nine, as I usually do unless there's a problem or a crisis that gets me here sooner."

"Can anyone vouch for those times?"

"Marta knows when I left. Bobbi—our receptionist—knows when I came in. So do other people in this office. Look, I didn't kill Victoria. I'm finding your insinuations very offensive."

"Sir, they're questions we need to ask."

"I loved her." His voice trembled with emotion. "She was my *wife*. Why would I kill my *wife*?"

His wife. Not his ex-wife. Knowing the interview was on the verge of termination, Kate plunged ahead. "Mr. Talbot, why were you not contacted by your son or daughters regarding the death of their mother?"

He impaled her with his cold green eyes. "I'll say this and only this: I have a daughter who's a snake. Who's poisoned everything."

"Which daughter?"

"That's it. I'm done. You can't claim I've been anything but cooperative. I have every right not to answer questions that are none of your goddamn business."

He would learn soon enough that a murder investigation removed everyone's privacy and that everything—and everyone—was their goddamn business. She asked, "Why do you consider this particular daughter a snake?"

"Jesus," he said, squeezing his eyes shut. "I can see it now. First you, then the media. My life has turned to shit."

Consulting her notes, she asked the question she was sure would be the final one: "Going back to your divorce, what exactly did you mean when you said you'd 'done stuff'?"

"Leave. Now." He swung his chair around to his city view.

"THE MAN YOU AND DETECTIVE CAMERON interviewed that day," Alicia Marquez said. "Do you see him in this courtroom today?"

"I do."

"Would you point him out and mention an item of clothing he's wearing?"

"He's seated at the defense table," she said. "Wearing a green suit."

"Let the record show," Marquez intoned, "that the witness has identified the defendant, Douglas Talbot."

"Proceed," said Judge Terrell.

"Now, this defendant claimed his live-in housekeeper could vouch for his whereabouts prior to eight-thirty the morning of Mrs. Talbot's murder—is that correct?"

"Correct," Kate responded.

"A housekeeper who is a foreign national?"

"Objection, no foundation," complained Gregory Quantrill.

"Sustained," said Judge Terrell, peering with narrowed eyes over his glasses at Marquez.

"A housekeeper with whom he was having a sexual—"

"*Objection—*"

"Sustained," snapped the judge. "Enough, Ms. Marquez. The jury will disregard this entire line of questioning."

Kate took a sip of water to conceal her smile, feeling a little happier with Alicia Marquez.

Marquez closed the legal pad with the notes she had been consulting, slid it to the bottom of her stack, opened the next one. "Detective," she said, "did you obtain a search warrant for the automobiles belonging to the defendant?"

"I did," Kate did, switching gears along with Marquez for this jump forward in the murder investigation. Marquez was limited by pretrial motions and the rules of evidence—especially the hearsay rule—as to what she could ask about Kate's interviews of witnesses. In any event, most of the key people she and Cameron had interviewed were on the prosecution's witness list and would testify as to their own direct knowledge.

Their next move had been in response to a call to her cell phone from Sergeant Fred Hansen as they wended their way back to Hancock Park. "You and Joe need to talk to a woman named

Alice Cathcart," Hansen had said in his usual no-pleasantries fashion. "She's the neighbor catty-corner from the victim."

"So what does she have for us, Fred?"

"Something good. She told Delgado about somebody getting out of a new black Mercedes early this morning. Might have gone into the Talbot residence."

"We're on our way, Fred. Thanks."

When Kate advised Cameron of Hansen's message, he pulled his own cell phone from inside his jacket. "That's the car Marjorie Durant saw. Time to run Doug Talbot through DMV."

ALICE CATHCART WORE AN EXPENSIVE OLIVE-green nylon jogging suit over her skeletal form. Pancake makeup only partly concealed an unnatural ruddiness of complexion and that signpost of hard drinking, broken veins. Standing in her doorway, brushing white-blond hair from her face, she breathed a "Hello" on them that contained the antiseptic smell of vodka. She nodded acknowledgment of Kate's introduction of herself and Cameron, then pulled the front door of her house shut behind her and came out onto the portico in so clear a message that they were not welcome in her imposing home that Kate did not bother to ask.

"Did you know Victoria Talbot well?" Kate inquired politely.

"Only enough to say hello, how are you," Alice Cathcart said in a huskily musical voice, her hands on her bony hips. "She hasn't been in the neighborhood all that long."

Amused that well over two years was not "all that long," Kate nodded her recognition of this typical Los Angeles behavior. Neighbors, if thrown into contact with one another, tended

to feign friendliness until they could once more completely ignore each other's existence. She herself was no different. In the
decade she and Aimee had lived in the condo, they knew virtually nothing about the people who lived a few reinforced walls
away.

"This is a horrible, shocking thing to happen in this neighborhood," Alice Cathcart said. "Reporters have come knock-
ing—can you imagine?"

She could well imagine. "Officer Delgado tells us you saw
something early this morning."

"Yes I did. I saw someone get out of a car across the street,
outside her house. About a quarter to seven."

"Are you usually up at that time?"

Alice Cathcart looked at her as if a tart response were on
the tip of her tongue, but restricted herself to a terse, "Sometimes."

"How did you happen to notice the car?"

"I went out to get my paper."

"Would you tell us what you saw?" Cameron said, busy
taking notes. Kate made a quick note of her own to check with
the newspaper carrier along this route.

"Sure," Alice Cathcart said, her slow, approving glance
moving from Cameron's bent head all the way down his lanky
body. "First of all those damned dogs were out with Marjorie,
yapping away like they do every damned morning. And then I
saw this shiny new black Mercedes—"

"Dealer plates?"

"Yes, dealer plates. Parked ass backwards—" She gestured
to the street, "the back end angled way out. Cars could get
around it, it's such a good wide street, but still, you know, it
only takes half a second longer to park properly."

"Had you ever seen this car before on the street?"

"Who knows?" she answered, and shrugged. "There's lots of Mercedes around here. You do tend to notice a new one all bright and shiny."

"Can you describe the person who got out?"

She shrugged again. "Wish I could. Had his back to me. Kind of big . . ."

"Tall? Short?"

"About average."

"Dark, light clothes?"

"Dark. A dark jacket, I think."

Douglas Talbot, Kate remembered, had worn a navy suit that morning. "A suit jacket?"

"I don't know, sorry."

"Hat?"

"No. No hat."

"His hair, light, dark, short, long?"

"I don't remember, except he didn't have much."

It was a sketchy description of Douglas Talbot, but consistent enough with his appearance. Alice Cathcart had seen Talbot—if the man in the Mercedes-Benz was indeed Talbot—within the same time frame as Marjorie Durant. The limo driver who'd arrived to pick up Gene Durant would probably also have seen the Mercedes. Kate asked, "He went into the Talbot residence?"

Cameron's cell phone rang; pulling it out of his pocket, he excused himself and backed down the walkway to take the call.

"He looked to be headed that way," Alice Cathcart said, watching Cameron with disapproval. "That's all I can tell you. I mean, I was getting my paper. I picked it up and went back into my house."

"Thank you, Mrs. Cathcart. Did you happen to hear anything unusual this morning?"

She raised hands that were thin to translucency, the finger-nails tinted with ivory polish. "Sorry. I know you mean gun-shots, but my bedroom suite's in the back of the house. It's designed to be quiet."

"Could anybody else in your house have—"

"There isn't anyone else."

Five thousand square feet, at a guess, for just this one woman. Closing her notebook, presenting Cathcart with one of her cards, Kate said, "If you happen to remember anything else, would you call us?"

"There is one other thing. I was up during the night. Saw lights on in the house over there."

Kate flipped open her notebook again. This was interesting. "Any idea what time?"

"After two, I think it was."

"The lights—this was unusual?"

"Indeed. She turns in early. That's why I noticed."

"Could you see anything else?"

"No, just the lights."

"If your bedroom is in the back of your home—" Kate broke off, the answer to her question occurring to her.

"Why did I come into my living room?" Alice Cathcart fin-ished the question. "I got up to go to the kitchen for a glass of water and I saw the lights through my living room windows."

She'd been drinking and passed out in the living room, Kate guessed. Probably not an infrequent happening. "Thank you, Mrs. Cathcart. We may have more questions."

"Of course. Any idea yet—"

"We're working as hard as we can."

After a slight raise of her eyebrows and a skeptical half-smile, Alice Cathcart turned and went into her huge Georgian house.

Tucking his phone back into his inside jacket pocket, Cameron walked toward her with a look of satisfaction on his face. "A Mercedes-Benz S430, a baby just two weeks old—registered to one Douglas Albert Talbot on Ashdale in Brentwood."

"Bingo." Kate smiled. "Since you now have the address of this brand-new baby, what do you say we drop by and say kitchy-coo?"

S I X

The major piece of evidence corroborating Talbot's presence in Hancock Park that morning had been easy to spot on the woodsy, country-like lane in the chic northern part of Brentwood, adjacent to the sprawling UCLA campus. The car was parked right in front of a Cape Cod–style cottage with large lattice windows, a house attractively landscaped and shaded with an assortment of deciduous trees—Kate readily recognized maple and elm from her native Michigan.

"This is too easy," Cameron said. "Let's impound it, get a search warrant."

"Sure." Kate grinned at him, exhilarated that pieces of this case were beginning to fit together. "You think he's left the gun in there for us? Victoria's blood? I don't like our chances. Plus, we still need to explain why any number of brand-new Mercedes couldn't be in an area of L.A. as affluent as Hancock Park at any given time."

"Yeah, okay," Cameron muttered. "One step at a time." He strolled over to the car. "Beverly Hills Limited," he said, writing down the name from the frame holding the dealer's plate.

The woman who answered the cottage door was small and pretty, with dark lively eyes. "Ms. Gonzalez?" Kate asked, offering identification.

"Marta is fine, please. Doug told me to expect you," she said, pronouncing the name "Doog." Smiling shyly, she beckoned for them to come in. "It is very terrible what's happened."

Marta seated herself on a white sofa in the living room and gestured vaguely to them to sit as well, saying, "Please." She was young, no more than twenty-five, girlish and demure. Knowing Douglas Talbot's relationship with this young woman and its power inequalities, Kate felt her dislike for him mounting. Marta's voice was soft, her English clearly enunciated; Kate could not identify the accent. Marta did not offer any hospitality, unusual for a Hispanic, and Kate wondered if Talbot had shared his animosity toward herself and Cameron, or if Marta felt too much the stranger in this house even though she was bedding down with its owner.

Kate led her through a series of innocuous, ice-breaker questions, learning that she and her mother had been working for a dozen Brentwood families over the past seven years; she herself had worked for Talbot the past eight months and became his full-time live-in housekeeper three months ago.

"This morning," Kate said. "When did Mr. Talbot leave the house?"

"His usual time," Marta said, meeting her eyes. "He left just about eight-thirty, like he usually does."

"Not before that?"

"No."

"Did he leave early and come back, leave again?"

"No. He left about eight-thirty."

"Are you quite sure?"

"Very sure," Marta said, her liquid, dark-eyed gaze unwavering.

"Has he been home today? Is he home now?"

"He has not come home."

"Why is his car out there?"

"He has another one. A BMW. He took that one this morning."

"Why?"

"He left this one for me to enjoy today."

"And did you?"

"I was too nervous to drive it. I was going to take it out on the Four-Oh-Five for a while," she said, referring to the nearby San Diego Freeway, "but then Doug called and said I should wait for you."

Kate wondered what else Talbot had instructed Marta to say. "What about last night? When did Mr. Talbot arrive home?"

"His usual time. Then he went to the shooting range. He was late coming back. I don't know what time—I was asleep."

"Let me say this," Kate said, choosing her words. "We're here on the matter of what's happened to Mrs. Talbot. Nothing else is of concern to us, we report to no other agency—"

"I am illegal, if that's what you're hinting," Marta said with quiet dignity, crossing her arms over her chest. "I am not a citizen, I have no papers. My parents brought me here from Guatemala when I was five."

"Thank you for telling us," Kate said, and shifted tactics. "It's very important you tell the truth beginning right now.

This is a very serious matter that will not go away, Marta. If you lie to the police, you can be charged with a crime. A serious crime. Obstruction of justice."

"I am telling the truth," Marta said coldly. She got up from the sofa, gestured toward the door. "If you would please leave now. Doug told me when you asked this question I should tell the truth and afterward say nothing more. I have answered your question and will say nothing more."

Outside the house, Cameron said, "The prick—he's got her all sewn up."

"Yes, well, he's hardly out of the woods, Joe." Despite her vow of objectivity, she was more and more despising the predatory Douglas Talbot. "If she's his only alibi witness, he's in big trouble. Her credibility ranks somewhere around zero. Do you buy him leaving the car here for her?"

"Nope. He did the deed, came back and got dressed for work, took his other car."

"Well, let's get his fancy new toy impounded."

IN THE COURTROOM, ALICIA MARQUEZ SAID, "The People would mark for evidence People's Exhibit Forty-Three, a registration record from the Department of Motor Vehicles—"

"No objection," Quantrill interrupted.

"So ordered," said the judge.

"The People would mark for evidence People's Number Forty-Four, the sales record from Beverly Hills Limited—"

"No objection," Quantrill said.

This part of the case was moving along, as well it should. No question that Talbot owned the car, and Paul Jankowitz at Liberty Limousine Service had been placed on the witness list to further confirm he, too, had seen the car outside Victoria Talbot's house while he waited to take Eugene Durant to the airport. Quantrill, knowing this evidence would be presented, had derided it in his opening statement, claiming that a new Mercedes with dealer plates would be one among hundreds sold each month in the city and county of Los Angeles, much less California. Marquez, in her close, would reiterate that the odds of such a coincidence were vanishingly small when no one on the block owned such a car, and why one would be parked on their street within so specific a period of time on the morning of the murder?

"Did you then interview the defendant's daughter, Lisa McDaniel?"

"Yes. Detective Cameron and I proceeded to her home in Studio City."

SHE AND CAMERON HAD LOCATED THE STUDIO City bungalow amid a line of similar houses on an elm-shaded block just off Laurelwood Drive. Uncomfortable in the San Fernando Valley's afternoon heat, the usual ten or so degrees warmer than on the other side of the Santa Monica Mountains, she pulled at the collar of her blouse, wishing for the thousandth time that she did not have to carry a gun that regulations required her to conceal in public; otherwise she could take off her jacket. At least her shoulder felt better in the sun, the tight muscles easing; they still ached from the bullet that had ruptured them four years ago in an arrest gone bad.

She looked at Lisa McDaniel's house with a smile. She had always marveled at the optimism of homes like this one, flimsy little stucco and glass squares endemic to southern California, so insubstantial that an inconveniently epicentered earthquake or freakish high wind would flatten them like a hand brushing down houses of cards. "These places—sturdy as blown bubbles," Cameron remarked as if reading her mind, and Kate smiled again, this time at the figure of speech.

On the way here, on the picturesque curving road through the mountains via Laurel Canyon to the Valley side, she had reviewed her notes and been immersed in her thoughts while Cameron drove. But he had interruped her thoughts to compare impressions with her.

"Estranged husband, a gun he claims was there—it all points to him, Kate. He goes there, argues, pops his cork, pops her. Empties a jewelry box, leaves the back door open, dumps the jewels and gun down a sewer."

She nodded to his profile as he navigated the road. "I'm guessing it's not his first visit, either. If there's a restraining order, this is a guy who doesn't take no for an answer. Remember Allan Talbot telling us how tidy the place was? Doug kills her, cleans up the place to get rid of his prints . . . But *tidy* is not the same as *clean*," she argued against her own scenario. "The place was immaculate. Somebody wanting to get rid of prints would just wipe surfaces clean, like everything was in the kitchen—"

"Hey, Kate, maybe she was expecting the guy. They have history together, maybe she was thinking—well, you never know. So she cleans the house. He kills her, wipes down his prints."

She nodded. It fit. It didn't feel right, but it fit.

"Kate, do you buy Marjorie Durant's story about the two shots all those minutes apart?"

"I'm not sure. We'll see what other neighbors say. It doesn't make sense."

"It does if you figure this: The guy wipes down his prints and maybe after that, with all this history they have together, he's still so pissed it's not good enough she's dead—he goes back and pumps one more into her for good measure." Cameron added, "I like it. When they do the post, won't they know for certain if one of the shots was postmortem?"

"Sure. But why the roses?" she wondered. "Why toss the roses?"

Cameron shrugged. "Who cares? Maybe he's allergic." His voice was eager as he put his hypothesis together. "So the SOB's trying to pin it on some poor Mexican gardener already out there cutting somebody's grass at seven-thirty in the morning. That business about going to a shooting range the night before—what a crock."

"A waste of time to run GSR tests on him or any of his clothes," Kate said disgustedly. "He's got a built-in excuse when gunshot residue shows up. Let's hope Baker finds a stray fingerprint Talbot missed."

"The bastard—he'll pay for that little trick about going to a shooting range. When we nail him, we'll have premeditation."

"We have a long way to go to prove it," Kate reminded him, returning to her notes but again taking notice of Cameron's animosity toward Douglas Talbot and reminding herself that she *had* to retain some objectivity or risk overlooking or dismissing evidence that led down other avenues.

The young woman who answered their knock on the door of the bungalow wore ragged cutoffs and a tank top. A cell phone pressed to her ear, she nodded emphatically, waving away their identification with a hand holding a cigarette, and stepped away from the door, gesturing for them to come in.

"Listen, Rikki," she said urgently into her phone. "Wait. Now just *wait*. *Listen* to me. It's the police, I'll call you back . . . Sure, I promise. Yes, yes the police are here . . . Yes.

Don't worry, I'll call the minute they leave. Yes I'll tell them. I'll tell them everything."

Heaving a sigh that was a combination of exhaustion and exasperation, she clicked off the phone and tossed it onto a well-worn beige tweed sofa. She smashed out her cigarette in a cheap tin ashtray overflowing with butts, ran taut fingers through straight brown hair. It fell attractively around a heart-shaped and pretty face with animated dark eyes and a sprinkling of freckles across a turned-up nose. "Jesus," she said, squeezing her eyes shut. "That was my sister. My hysterical sister. Not that I'm not. Hysterical, I mean. Look, you want coffee? Even if you don't, I need some, bad. Jesus," she said, and strode off toward, presumably, the kitchen. "Sit down," she tossed back over her shoulder.

Cameron sniffed the air and raised his eyebrows at Kate; the house reeked of cigarette smoke and an overtone of something that smelled like slowly burning rope—marijuana, Kate surmised. Cameron took a seat in an armchair whose seat cushion sagged discernibly under his weight. Kate remained standing, to glance around. There wasn't much to take in. The living room was pleasantly utilitarian with thin off-white carpeting and inexpensive Ikea-style furniture. Two large, bright, cheap prints of country scenes added color to a room awash with light from its large front windows.

On a faux marble mantel over a faux brick fireplace, amid snapshots of young children, were three similarly framed portrait photos, and Kate took in a teenage Allan Talbot, a female teenager she did not recognize, and the young woman who was now returning from the kitchen carrying a carafe of coffee in one hand, the fingers of the other twined through the handles of three mugs. She plopped them down on the pine coffee table, brushing aside dog-eared copies of *People* and issues of scandal magazines.

"Can we start over? Hello, I'm Lisa McDaniel. Welcome."

"Thank you," Kate said with as much of a smile as she deemed appropriate under the circumstances. "I'm Detective Delafield. My partner is Detective Cameron." Looking into dark eyes rimmed with red, she added, "We're very sorry about what brings us here, Ms. McDaniel. We're very sorry about your loss."

"Thanks. Call me Lisa. No offense," she said to Cameron, "but I'm glad they sent a woman besides you."

"I'm glad they did too," Cameron said gently. "But I'll do my best for you too."

Lisa poured coffee with a tremulous hand, almost missing the mug. "Cream, sugar?" There was a break in her voice, and Kate wondered if she had been holding herself together until now for the sake of her sister. "We take it black," she said. "Why don't you sit down and have your coffee, Lisa. We'll help ourselves. How's your sister doing?"

Looking grateful, Lisa sank into the sofa and took a gulp of her coffee. "You heard. Not good. We've been on the phone for hours, since Allan called. I'm trying to hold her together but she's really, really a mess."

"Does she have someone with her?" Kate poured and handed Cameron his coffee.

Lisa shook her head. "Not right now. Allan was there till a little while ago. She's got friends but her therapist is the only one that can help and she'll see Rikki tonight. Donna's gonna fit her in after her other appointments. Jesus, I'd *hope* so."

"It's good she's got professional help," Cameron said. He took a swallow of his coffee and his eyes widened; he placed the mug carefully down on the coffee table. "Sometimes it's the best way to go in circumstances like these. She been in therapy long?"

It was a crucially important question in gauging the sister's mental state and possible involvement in this homicide. Kate admired Cameron's smoothness in asking it.

"Forever," Lisa answered after another gulp of coffee. She shook a cigarette out of a pack of Marlboros. "Look, I have to smoke, hope it doesn't bother you. Years, Rikki's been in therapy for years. She's a mess. Right now she's even more of a mess. Donna's been real good with her but I'm sure she'll put her right back on the Prozac highway."

"How are you doing, Lisa?" Kate asked sympathetically. "Fine to take care of your sister, but—"

"I'm good. I'm okay." She dragged deeply on her cigarette. "I mean, not okay, but Larry took the kids—Larry's my turd of an ex, we share custody. He offered to leave work without my even asking. Pulled the kids out of school, helped me break the news to them. Says he'll keep them as long as I need him to. I guess even a turd can do something good once in a while."

She drained her coffee cup. "Please . . . I need to know, what's going on? I only know what Allan told me. He came right over after he called, then went to Rikki out in Granada Hills, and now he's seeing about funeral homes. He'll be back tonight."

Kate nodded. It would be a while before Victoria Talbot's body was released—the autopsy could be days away with the backlog in the Coroner's Office—but better the family find out one unpleasantness at a time how much this homicide would impact their lives. Funeral arrangements would keep Allan Talbot's mind occupied.

She took a sip of her coffee and barely managed not to choke. She was used to bad coffee, but this concoction could melt teeth. Looking up to meet Cameron's amused eyes, she swallowed to recover her voice, then said to Lisa, "You probably know as much as we do at this point."

"Have you talked to Douglas?"

Alerted by the cold tone of voice, Kate said cautiously, "You mean your father?"

"Yeah, who else would I mean?"

"Yes we have. You call your father by his first name?"

"I don't call him anything if I can help it. There's more to being a father than—well, you know. So what did he tell you?"

"About what, Lisa?"

"About *everything*. Anything. What did he tell you?"

"I'm sorry, we can't reveal the substance of any interview— regulations. But if there's something we should ask Mr. Talbot, we'd be glad to know what it is."

Her pretty face pinched with agitation, she said, "I'm just wondering where he was this morning."

"Do you think he had something to do with this?"

"Do you?"

"At this point we're considering everything. We absolutely assure you we'll check out every single avenue. Would you tell us why you think he may be involved?"

She replied with a shrug.

Kate placed her coffee gingerly on the table, thinking it might melt through the table and, for that matter, all the way to China. She pulled her recorder out of her shoulder bag. "We need to ask you some important questions, Lisa. Do you mind if we tape-record our conversation?"

"Hell yes. Put that damn thing away." She was not hostile like her father had been at the same overture; her tone conveyed simple aversion.

Kate obeyed, and opened her notebook. "We really need to

understand everything we can about your mother. Would you tell us about your family?"

"My fam-i-ly," Lisa said, enunciating each symbol as if dissecting the words. She sat back on the sofa, tucked her bare legs up under her, stared with distaste at the cigarette burning in the ashtray. "My family is a train wreck. No, a car wreck— that's way more like it." Her smile was brief and wry. "Five people in the car. One fatality. Three wounded, one critically."

Writing in his notebook, not looking up, Cameron asked easily, "Who was the driver?"

Lisa stared at him, her eyes widening. She gazed out the living room window, silent.

"Five people in the car," Cameron said, "but only three of them injured—"

"*Only,*" she repeated ironically.

"Lisa, was it the driver who escaped without injury?"

She nodded. "You know how it is with crashes. The guy that totals the car escapes without a scratch." Again she was silent. Then said softly, "The crash happened at the end of a long trip. One of us was at the wheel, too, besides him, along the way."

"Another driver, you need another one—that's usually how it is on a long trip," Cameron said in an equally quiet tone. "I take it you and Allan are the injured ones and Rikki's on the critical list."

"That would be right," Lisa said, and picked up her cigarette, drew deeply from it, replaced it in the ashtray.

Kate had stopped taking notes and was listening raptly to this metaphorical exchange, unmoving lest she somehow interfere.

Cameron, too, was motionless. "What happened, Lisa? Did the car hit another one, or—"

"It ran off the road."

"Was it forced off, was it—"

"Drunk driver," Lisa said succinctly, and crossed her arms tightly across her chest as if chilled in her tank top and cutoffs.

Cameron asked cautiously, "Did the driver happen to be an alcoholic?"

"Yeah."

"For how long?"

"A long time." She looked off to one side, thoughtful. "I guess . . . from when he was young, before I was born."

"Did he ever try to get treatment?"

"Yeah. Oh yeah, sure he did," she said with sudden animation. "But later. After the crash. It made things worse."

"Can you explain that?"

Lisa stared at the coffee table, reached for her cigarette. She jabbed it into the ashtray, stubbing it out as her words came in a staccato burst: "He did terrible things when he drank. Then he spends, like, twenty minutes at AA and claims he's sober now and we should all understand and accept he was a drunk and just write it off. Like it's one of the bad business deals he wipes off the books all the time. Like it's some different person who did all those things, not him." She flung the shredded butt into the ashtray.

Cameron seemed to choose his words as he approached this fertile territory: "What did your . . . what was Douglas like when he was drunk?"

"You mean, a happy drunk, a mean drunk?"

"Yeah, something like that."

"He drank all the time. If he didn't drink, he was asleep. So he was always the same. Vodka and tonic—way more vodka than tonic. Had a drink near him all the time. I mean, like you'd wear your wristwatch. At dinner, watching TV, downstairs in his woodworking shop. All the time."

"Okay, how was he . . . what was his temperament around all of you?"

"Mostly pretty even. Till something set him off. No matter how hard we tried, how much we tiptoed, did everything he wanted, something always set him off."

Cameron nodded, as familiar with this pattern as Kate. "What was he like when that happened?"

She looked up, but at Kate, not Cameron, and her eyes were those of a child—hurt, vulnerable, inconsolable. "He was horrible. We wouldn't have been half as scared if he just said something. But he never did, never said a thing, never yelled, nothing. He was a smasher. Smashed dishes, furniture. People."

Holding Lisa's gaze with difficulty, she asked quietly, "What people, Lisa?" When Lisa did not answer, she asked, "All of you?"

Lisa shook her head. "My mother," she whispered, "my brother."

"How bad?"

"Bad enough."

"Anybody ever report—"

"Not for years. It was like he was always smart enough to stop before . . . like, he knew how far not to go. Afterward he'd be the dad of your dreams," she said with acid contempt. Her next words came in a gush: "The best time to be around him. Get anything you want, didn't have to tiptoe, didn't have to do a thing. He couldn't be nice enough when he was trying to make it all right. Replace what he smashed, buy new stuff for us. But it got worse. Before, he did things like shove Allan up against a wall and slap his face, but then he started to punch. Shoved and slapped and slammed her too, pushed her into a wall so hard one time he broke her arm and wrist."

Kate asked into the silence, "Who knew about this?"

"Just us chickens," she said with an elaborate shrug. "He always said this time was the last time, absolutely it would never happen again. Mother always believed him—or said she did. Today I understand—Mrs. Douglas Talbot cared about appearances more than anything else. Mrs. Douglas Talbot couldn't have anybody ever suspect we weren't this ideal family. Nobody could ever know our rich, successful daddy was an abuser and a drunk, and our wonderful classy mother was this pretentious wuss who put up with it all."

Kate understood that Lisa's anger with her mother was a temporary palliative, that the reality of this death had not begun to penetrate the patina of shock. The day would come when grief would break through and incinerate the anger and uncover a bottomless depth of love and anguished regret. She said, "Tell me about when he broke her arm. Did she consider pressing charges?"

"Nope, not even then. Threatened him but didn't do a thing. But that time the police did come. Rikki broke ranks. She ran to a pay phone and called them."

Kate and Cameron exchanged a brief, exultant glance. "What did the police do?"

"Nothing. My mother and Douglas talked them into believing Rikki'd misinterpreted what went on. Allan wouldn't talk and the cops decided to pretend they didn't notice he could hardly stand up with the pain in his ribs. I wasn't there," she said bitterly.

Kate nodded. They had already learned that a restraining order was on file. From what Lisa had just told them, there would also be a police report. Divorce records. Maybe other records . . . The case was building.

"I assume she went to a hospital?"

"Yeah, Cedars. Swore up and down she fell."

Kate nodded. It was so familiar, this story of domestic battery with one spouse enabling his or her abuser, and contrary to popular belief, it did not correlate with economic status. She felt a weary heaviness as she made a brief note to get a subpoena for the hospital's records. "You said he hurt Allan."

"Yeah. For a while. You met Allan so you know he's not a big guy but one day he picked up a baseball bat and told Douglas to never touch him again. That was the end of it. For Allan," she amended.

"What about you?"

"Never touched me."

"What about Rikki?"

"Rikki . . . she's a whole other story."

IN THE COURTROOM, ALICIA MARQUEZ PHRASED her question with a slowness that denoted her care: "Is it correct to say that Lisa McDaniel's statements led you to a domestic battery police report involving the defendant?"

"That is correct."

"A domestic battery report alleging battery on the victim and the victim's son by the defendant?"

"That is correct."

Admissibility of this report had been a hard-fought battle, and out of the corner of her eye, Kate could see Gregory Quantrill watching Marquez, his dark eyes narrowed.

"Did you discuss her sister, Rikki Talbot?"

"Objection!" Quantrill was on his feet. "Hearsay."

"Your honor," Marquez said in a polite, injured tone, "the question requires only a yes or no response."

"Mr. Marquez is correct, Mr. Quantrill," said Judge Terrell. "Overruled."

"Sidebar, your honor," Quantrill said before Kate could respond, "I request a sidebar."

"Approach." Judge Terrell beckoned to them, and Quantrill and Marquez and the court reporter went to the bench for a meeting out of the hearing of Kate and the jury.

She knew what the sidebar involved. In pretrial rulings, any information relating to Rikki Talbot had been deemed unproved, prejudicial, and inadmissible. Quantrill did not want any insinuations from Marquez, any skirting around the edges of what Lisa had said about Rikki . . .

"YEAH," LISA MCDANIEL HAD RESPONDED TO Kate's question, her lips thinning and turning downward. "Yeah, he touched Rikki, all right."

Clearly, this abuse had gone beyond the emotional and physical battering meted out to Talbot's wife and son, and Kate chose not to put Lisa through a series of feeling-out questions. She asked bluntly, "You mean sexually?"

"What else would I mean?"

"From when?"

"From always."

"Always?" Surely she couldn't mean . . .

"Rikki says she can't remember when he didn't."

"Would you mind telling us what he—"

"What he did to her? Yeah. Yeah I would mind. She wouldn't want me to. Even under these circumstances. Isn't it enough for you to know he's all but destroyed her?"

"Yes it is," Kate said. "It's enough." For some children, she thought, the monsters other children conjured up actually existed. She gestured to the mantel. "The picture—is that her?"

Lisa nodded, uncurled her legs, and got up. She took down the photo, handed it to Kate. Surveying their full coffee mugs, Lisa picked up the carafe and refilled her own mug.

Kate studied the headshot of a teenager far less conventionally attractive than her pert, bright-eyed older sister. Rikki had the same light brown hair as Lisa but hers was thin and stringy; her skin was sallow, with dark shadows under the eyes, and her expression was melancholy. Kate handed the photo to Cameron, saying to Lisa, "You seem very close to Rikki."

"Yeah. Don't let that picture fool you. She's the best. The nicest, sweetest—my sweet baby sister. Alan and me—we talk to her every single day, look after her the best we can."

"The sexual abuse, Lisa. You said it was ongoing. How did you find out? And when?"

"Four years ago. Donna helped Rikki enough that she could finally tell me."

Four years ago. When Victoria Talbot filed for divorce. "Your mother—when did she know?"

"Well, that's a good question, isn't it." Her tone was so cold that Kate could fathom some of the depth and pain of this wound. Lisa slammed the mug down on the coffee table. "Rikki says she told her when she was eight. Mother claims she didn't really know. Not till the day I made all of us confront what happened."

Kate was not surprised that Lisa would be the one to galvanize the family into action. "You don't believe your mother didn't know?"

She shook her head. "Rikki told her. Mother didn't believe her." Pain gathered on Lisa's face in a narrowing of her eyes, a distinct deepening of the line between her eyebrows. "Allan like usual tried to see both sides."

How Allan saw this wasn't important, Kate decided. "Do I have this right?" she asked gently. "You're saying Rikki told your mother but your mother didn't believe her?"

"Not exactly." Lisa squeezed her eyes shut as if to shut out images. "It was horrible. It was like this. Rikki did tell her but Mother asked *me* about it, see? Didn't investigate, didn't ask her husband, didn't talk to anybody else—she asked *me*. When I was ten. That's how I know Rikki's telling the truth—she said she was eight, and I'm two years older, and I remember this weird conversation with my mother this day when I was ten. She pussyfoots around wanting to know how Rikki and I get on with him, is he okay as our dad, is there anything I want to tell her and I can come to her and tell her anything, anything at all, I can trust her." She shook her head. "How the hell am I supposed to know what she's talking about? I mean, she *knew* he was a lousy father, she *knew* he was brutal, a drunk . . . What was I supposed to think? What else was I supposed to read into—"

"Lisa, do I understand this right? He sexually abused your sister, she tells your mother, and your mother comes to *you* about it?"

"Yeah, can you *believe* it? All these years later she claims she thought Rikki made it up. Okay, Rikki always had this vivid imagination, imaginary playmates, all that stuff. But Christ, what else was she supposed to do? Where else could she live except in her head—thanks to her mother? Where the hell else do you live when thanks to your mother you can't live in the real world?"

"Maybe this is a dumb question from a dumb male," Cameron said softly, "but maybe your mother thought your sister told you?"

Lisa looked at him as if she fully agreed with his self-assessment. "Wrong. My mother figured if he was doing it to Rikki, he was doing it to me too. 'You're the pretty one,' she tells me all these years later—*right in front of Rikki*—'so if he wasn't touching you . . .'"

Kate looked back over her pages as if searching for a note, but she was collecting herself. Maybe in some enlightened future century, she thought, children would no longer be possessions and parents would be prosecuted for their aiding and abetting role in the crimes against their own children. Douglas Talbot had not touched his pretty, confident, firstborn daughter. Instead he had selected the less likely one, the deniable one. After all, if he were going to enjoy a daughter sexually, wouldn't he have chosen pretty Lisa? Lisa had been more valuable as a shield.

Kate glanced at Cameron. Tight-lipped, he stared at the photo of Rikki Talbot in his hands. At this moment she fully shared Cameron's loathing for a monster of a man who had turned one daughter into an emotional wasteland and given the other the devastating permanent scars of survivor's guilt.

Lisa said, "You know what our mother told us? If she'd asked him and it wasn't true, he might have beaten her to death."

"Do you think she really thought that?"

Her eyes dark with rage, Lisa flung both hands up. "What does it matter? Who the fuck cares? I mean, did she for chrissakes have to be alone with him when she asked him? I mean, couldn't she ask him in a restaurant? On the street?" She stared at Kate with smoldering eyes. "The bottom line is, she wanted fancy clothes and jewels and a fancy house. The bottom line is, she didn't protect us. Why the fuck didn't she protect us?"

Why indeed. Victoria Talbot had given her daughters material comfort while abdicating responsibility for the most basic protection a mother should give a child. Marjorie Durant, in response to Kate's question as to whether she had seen Victoria Talbot's grandchildren, had replied, "Only at Christmas." The sterile upstairs rooms of that house in Hancock Park, those rooms hungrily awaiting the visits of children . . . Except for Allan Talbot, who remained devoted to his mother, children had been removed from Victoria and Douglas Talbot's lives. Their own children, and their children's children.

"You said all of you confronted your father, too. What was his reaction?"

"He said he couldn't remember," Lisa sneered, and made circles around her head with her fingers as she continued, "He had all these blackouts, these blank spots in his memory. Isn't that just too convenient? I said it was funny how he didn't seem to have any when it came to business. He said he did. I don't believe him."

"So he wouldn't admit it?"

"Not exactly. He said it *might* have happened in a blackout. After the divorce, after he spent his twenty minutes at AA, he claimed there wasn't a minute when he wasn't stoned and it was never the real him that did those things to us. So we should just all get over it, right?"

"Did your sister consider pressing charges?"

"Uh-uh. No way would she ever live through anything like that. Rikki's had three divorces, barely holds it together day to day. She's great with her kids, though."

"Lisa, let me ask you about something else. We understand your mother had a gun in the house."

"Right. Yeah, she did. Kept it in a locked box." Smiling faintly, she added, "That was after Rikki found it and took a shot at us." Studying their faces, she said, "Oops, guess I shouldn't have mentioned that."

"Relax, we'd have found out," Cameron lied with an easy smile. "Tell us about it."

"It was an accident, okay? Rikki was maybe sixteen. She's in our parents' bedroom looking for God knows what, finds the gun in my . . . in Douglas's nightstand. We're all sitting in the living room watching some detective show. She comes downstairs waving it around—exactly the kind of stunt she'd pull. My mother leaps up, shrieking at the top of her lungs. The gun goes off, we all dive for the floor, even Douglas." Lisa was telling the story with relish, her slim shoulders shaking with mirth. "It was funny as hell. She said Mother scared her when she screamed—that's why her finger jerked on the trigger. The shot went wild."

"The first time you fire a handgun you're always surprised at the kick," Kate said, smiling at her.

"Yeah. We finally spotted the bullet hole in the corner of the ceiling."

Kate knew Cameron was thinking the same thing she was: Had the firing of that gun been a true accident or had Rikki Talbot tried to kill her father? Or mother?

"That's when they put the gun in that steel box with a combination lock and only the two of them ever knew what it was."

Kate exchanged a glance with Cameron.

"Douglas bitched and bitched about it," Lisa continued, waving a hand. "You know the deal—by the time he works the combination and gets the gun out of the box, we'd all be murdered, yadda yadda. But it was the only way she'd have a gun in the house—about the only time she ever put her foot down."

Kate made several quick notes. To have Douglas Talbot's computers added to the search warrant for his house. If child porn was present, they'd find it. In Victoria Talbot's house, get that steel box upstairs printed along with the lock. Douglas Talbot's fingerprints could have been left on the box years ago, but if they were on the lock . . .

"We'll need to talk to Rikki," she said.

"Talk to Donna first," Lisa said quickly. "I'll give you her number—"

"She won't give us any information," Cameron protested. "Therapists can't—"

"I know," Lisa said. "But she'll need to organize when and how it can happen, trust me. You're not going to get one rational word out of Rikki right now. She'll be on heavy drugs till Donna can get her to face this."

Again Kate exchanged glances with Cameron. They indeed had questions for Rikki, and the key one was: Where had she been this morning when her mother was killed?

"Lisa," Kate said, "when did you last see your mother?"

She bent her head in thought. "Marjorie Durant's seventieth birthday party. That would be . . . back in April."

"And before that?"

"Christmas."

"How often did you speak to your mother by phone?"

Lisa shrugged. "She calls . . ." Her voice broke and her eyes teared up. She picked up her coffee mug and gulped down much of the contents.

Kate watched her with sympathy. The death of Victoria Talbot would inflict on this family fresh new wounds. So many people carried bitter animosities with little regard to the possibility that death could intervene and extinguish all opportunity for healing, reconciliation, forgiveness.

"Mother called all the time," Lisa finally said in a choked voice.

"You didn't call her?"

"Didn't have to. She called every Tuesday, all day long, filled up my answering machine with messages."

"Which you didn't return?"

She dabbed at her eyes. "Yeah I did, once in a great while. I couldn't forgive her. I tried—I just couldn't . . ."

"What about Rikki?"

"Never. Rikki never talked to her. Changed her phone number again last week so she wouldn't have to hear her voice on the answering machine."

"But Allan saw your mother, talked to her."

"All the time. He talked to all three of us all the time. Allan's a peacemaker, you know. Always trying to fix things between us."

"Does 'us' include Douglas?"

"No," she said flatly. "It does not include Douglas."

"Lisa, do you know of anyone else we should check out? Besides your father," she added.

"No. No one. Nobody in the world had a reason to hurt my mother. Including Douglas, even if he deluded himself into thinking he did."

"The neighborhood," Kate said. "It's been suggested maybe this was an attempted robbery gone wrong. Did your mother ever mention any burglaries or anything like that close by?"

"Hell no. Anybody break into one of those places, burglar alarms would go off from there to the moon."

Kate smiled. "I didn't notice one in your mother's house."

"She figured there were plenty enough without her having to get one. I don't think a burglar did this."

"Thank you, Lisa," Cameron said. "We'll have more questions later."

"Okay." Lisa took a swallow of coffee, made a face "Jesus," she said, "this stuff tastes like camel piss."

SEVEN

"Detective Delafield," said Alicia Marquez, then paused to leaf through her notes. Kate could tell she was winding down her direct examination from the formal use of Kate's name and because she had exhausted most of the areas where Kate was allowed to testify. "Detective Delafield, was jewelry taken from Mrs. Talbot's residence?"

"Yes there was. I made a list of items reported by the son of the victim and the victim's close friend, Marjorie Durant."

"What were the items?"

Receiving permission to consult her notes, Kate enumerated the missing jewelry: three gold chains, two pair of diamond earrings, two bracelets, four gold rings.

"And the approximate value?" Marquez asked.

"The total estimation is between five and ten thousand dollars."

"Did you find other jewelry in the house?"

"Yes, we did." Consulting her inventory list, she read, "Two diamond rings, two diamond and emerald bracelets, four necklaces of diamond, emerald, ruby, and sapphire."

"And their approximate value?"

"In excess of a hundred thousand dollars, according to Allan—"

"Objection. This is well beyond the scope," complained Quantrill.

"Sustained," said Judge Terrell.

Kate was pleased; the jury knew that what had been left was of far greater value than the items taken.

"Detective, is it true that the victim was wearing a diamond ring?"

"That's correct. And a Patek Phillipe eighteen-carat-gold watch."

"Thank you. Did you have the criminalists examine the defendant's Mercedes-Benz?"

"We did."

She volunteered no further information and there would be no other questions on this topic; Criminalist Nancy Browner would testify that she had found gunshot residue on the steering wheel, on the passenger seat, and in the glove compartment.

"Did you subpoena telephone records for the victim and the defendant?"

"We did. For the previous two years." Those records would be entered into evidence.

"Did you find phone contact initiated by the victim to the defendant?"

"We did not."

"Did you determine that there were phone calls from the defendant to the victim?"

"We did."

"How would you describe this contact?"

"At the beginning of the time frame, one or two calls per day. During the six months prior to the victim's death, frequency had escalated to three or four a day. Without exception these calls were of a few seconds' duration."

"In your experience, what does this represent?"

"Objection," Quantrill said forcefully. "The witness is hardly an expert."

"Overruled. The witness can express an opinion. You may answer the question," the judge said, peering over his glasses at Kate.

"In my opinion, each connection was too brief to be anything but a hang-up," Kate replied.

"Did you examine the victim's computer and email—"

"Objection!"

"Sustained. Rephrase, Ms. Marquez."

"Was a forensic examination performed on the victim's computer?"

"It was." A computer forensics expert would testify about the number of email messages from Douglas Talbot that had been found in Victoria Talbot's recycle bin, which, unfortunately for the defense, had never been emptied by the dead woman. In pretrial motions the content of these unopened messages had been deemed inadmissible, but what was admissible was the fact that they existed, the number of them, and that their frequency had escalated over time.

Marquez turned a page of her notes. "Did you attend the autopsy of Victoria Talbot?"

"Yes. Along with Detective Cameron."

The autopsy had been the usual test of endurance, made more gruesome by the grievous wounds on the victim, especially the one to the head. Afterward Cameron had thrown up in the parking lot, and Kate, as was her habit, had immediately gone home to inhale from a bag of pepper while pulling off clothes that seemed corrosively contaminated with the chemicals and death smells of the autopsy room. But this autopsy had been worth the discomfort, had been unusually productive.

"During the autopsy," said Marquez, "was a thirty-eight-caliber bullet retrieved intact from the chest of the victim?"

"It was." Thanks to the fleshiness of Victoria Talbot's chest and the sheer chance that the bullet's velocity had been further diminished by hitting bone at an oblique angle, the pathologist had extracted a virtually intact thirty-eight-caliber bullet. Which would be entered into evidence when firearms expert Harvey Gaviland testified.

"Did you then obtain permission to search an address on Rossmore Drive where the victim and the defendant had once resided?"

"We did."

"Without going into the results, was this for the purpose of seeking a bullet that had been fired some years earlier within that house?"

"It was," Kate said and looked down to be sure she would conceal her surge of elation at this crown jewel in their trove of evidence.

She vividly remembered the handsome colonial house on Rossmore Drive, and the consensual search permitted by the Hartfields, the elderly retired couple who had taken ownership from Douglas and Victoria Talbot. The Hartfields had been co-operative, indeed thrilled by the opportunity to be part of a police investigation, and were amazed and even more thrilled when Gaviland dug a bullet out of their living room ceiling. It was the bullet fired by Rikki Talbot fourteen years ago, buried in the soft plaster of the molding, in exactly the place where Lisa McDaniel had claimed it would be. Harvey Gaviland would testify that the thirty-eight-caliber bullet was, in his gleeful words, "a dead bang match" to the one found in Victoria Talbot. She had been shot with the gun from that box upstairs in the study, the gun to which only she and Douglas Talbot had had access.

Other equally damning evidence had not been allowed into the trial, not even its existence. The court had ruled for the defense in its motion to bar Victoria Talbot's written journals as unverifiable and prejudicial—and prejudicial they were, a veritable indictment of Talbot's obsessive-possessive behavior and escalating pattern of harassment and stalking. Victoria Talbot had written in a maelstrom of emotion, her handwriting streaking across the page in repetitious fury at her ex-husband and at herself, endless anger and anguish over the rejection she suffered from her two daughters, their withholding of themselves and her grandchildren from her life.

The journals had been painful to read. To Kate's mind, the grievous loss for this trial was the last journal, the one she had found in Victoria Talbot's desk, a powerful piece of circumstantial evidence. The page dated the day of the homicide had been ripped out and the journal's smooth leather cover, an ideal surface for recovering prints, had been clean. Kate held no doubt the journal had been open on the desk when Victoria Talbot was killed, that the page contained incriminating information about Talbot, perhaps about him coming to the house. He had torn it out and taken it with him.

The court had also ruled inadmissible Talbot's railing letters to his wife that Kate had collected, as well as the contents of the emails he had sent virtually on a daily basis. Adverse court rulings were to be expected; they were part and parcel of the court system. When Douglas Talbot had entered a not-guilty plea and refused to enter plea bargain negotiations, the District Attorney's Office judged that they had more than enough evidence to proceed on a first-degree murder charge, and the losses resulting from pretrial motions had whittled down but inflicted no mortal damage to an already circumstantial case.

"Detective, without going into detail, did you interview Patrol Officers Paula Woodson and Felix Litrell regarding a domestic disturbance call to the Talbot residence on June fifteenth, nineteen ninety-six?"

"I did." The two patrol officers were on the prosecution's witness list.

"Without going into detail, did you obtain hospital records relating to the physical condition of Victoria Talbot on the same date?"

"I did." The ER doctor on duty had been subpoenaed to testify.

"Prior to the death of Victoria Talbot, was a court order— a restraining order—on file against the defendant regarding contact with the victim?"

"There was."

Marquez's voice rose as she asked, "As a result of the evidence you accumulated from your interviews and from all of these other sources of evidence, did you seek and obtain an arrest warrant for the defendant?"

"Yes we did. On June ninth we proceeded to place the defendant under arrest."

"Was the defendant given his rights under the Miranda rule?"

"Yes. Detective Cameron read Mr. Talbot his rights, and we proceeded to take him into custody."

The arrest had not been nearly as surgical as she had described, and she sent a swift glance at Talbot. He instantly shifted his baleful gaze from her; he was remembering, too.

The receptionist at Talbot and Reece, Inc., had yelled "Hey, wait a minute!" as she and Cameron marched their way past her and through the office cubicles and into Douglas Talbot's office. Three gray-suited men gathered around Talbot's desk looked up in astonishment, as had Talbot.

"I have a warrant for your arrest for the murder of Victoria Talbot," Kate informed him. "Please stand and turn around."

As Cameron approached, handcuffs ready, Talbot shot up from his chair. "Get the hell out of here! You're fucking crazy!"

Cameron rushed him, grabbed him, whirled him around, and ran him to the wall, slamming him into it so hard that four plaques fell off. Cameron yanked Talbot's arms behind him and handcuffed him as Talbot struggled and yelped in pain, astonishment, rage. The three men seated in front of the desk remained frozen as Cameron shoved Talbot toward the door.

All the clattering sounds of commerce had come to a halt and phones rang unanswered while the employees of Talbot and Reece, including the open-mouthed receptionist, watched their boss being frog-marched through his own company while Cameron loudly recited the Miranda warning. It had all been very gratifying, and she'd enjoyed arresting the child-molesting, wife-beating son of a bitch every bit as much as Cameron had.

Alicia Marquez closed her legal pad and favored Kate with a slight smile. "Thank you, Detective. No further questions."

"Mr. Quantrill," said the judge. "Do you have questions for this witness?"

"Yes, thank you, your honor," Quantrill responded. "May we have a brief recess?"

"We'll take a ten-minute recess," the judge intoned.

To let me stew a little longer, Kate thought, watching him finish a note as the judge cautioned the jury. Well, she could use a break, for more than one reason. As could Marquez, apparently; she immediately left the courtroom.

In the hallway, Kate keyed on her cell phone, waited for it to find service, then checked her incoming log. No messages. She called the house again, thinking she had next to no time to talk if Aimee answered. Well, no problem in that regard, Kate thought wryly as the answering machine clicked in. She could not think about Aimee. Not while Quantrill had her up on his roasting spit.

TOUCHING THE NECK OF HIS BLUE-PATTERNED tie, getting to his feet, and buttoning the jacket of his pearl gray suit, Gregory Quantrill approached the podium. He brought a single notepad with him.

Kate's shoulder had begun to ache, and she took the opportunity to shift in her chair and settle herself so that it would be unnecessary to do so under Quantrill's questioning, when it might be misinterpreted as unease. She had observed Quantrill throughout the opening days of the trial, especially during his opening statement, and as he placed his notepad down, she scrutinized him again. Unlike Marquez, Quantrill drew and held attention with his confident mannerisms, his air of certainty. A further advantage was his distinctive handsomeness: thick-textured, dark wavy hair and large dark eyes in a lightly tanned face. A hint of flabbiness around his midsection managed to escape concealment under his expensively tailored silk-blend suit, but he still projected an impression of fitness, a well-built man who worked out diligently and took good care of his body. There was no hint of disorganization about him; his every movement was contained and purposeful, like the crisp, tight economy of an athlete.

"I have a few questions, Detective," he said in a mellifluous voice that projected easily in the courtroom. He directed a smile at her and then at the jury.

She did not react in any way, and was not deceived by this attempt to relax her with the carrot-on-a-stick promise that if there was to be a grilling, the pain would end in good time. She had taken the witness stand expecting a punishing cross-examination, and she held no doubt it would happen.

"You worked very hard on this case," he said, and again directed a smile at her.

She knew better than to reply to comments that were not questions, to let defense attorneys, rather than herself, open doors. But she had a safe reply, and she said politely, "I work hard on all my cases."

"And that's very commendable. With three decades of experience I'm sure you know all the ropes."

The statement was not meant as a compliment; it was intended to suggest that she was a law enforcement hack who performed her work by rote. She did not respond.

"So, do you know all the ropes, Detective?"

"I do my job as well as I possibly can." She directed her reply to the jury, reminding herself of her method: Look to Quantrill for the question, and if appropriate, address the jury with the answer.

"Do you know all the ropes," he repeated.

"I know what my experience and training have taught me."

"Would it be fair to say that you settled on Mr. Talbot fairly quickly as a suspect?"

The old rush-to-judgment ploy, a favorite with defense lawyers. "He was not arrested until two weeks after the murder," Kate pointed out.

"Would you say that that's not fairly quickly?"

"It depends on what you mean by 'quickly.'"

"What would your own definition be in the context of a homicide investigation?"

"Objection," Marquez said. "Irrelevant."

"Overruled. You may answer the question, Detective."

"'Quickly' could mean," Kate told the jury slowly, carefully, "that evidence at the scene of the crime was so obvious and compelling that it would point directly to someone we could immediately take into custody."

"Would it be fair to say that there was no such evidence found at the scene of Mrs. Talbot's death?"

"It would be more fair to say that the evidence at the scene was of a nature that needed to be evaluated and combined with other evidence, and it took time and care to do that."

"I see." He leaned over the podium and asked genially, "Did you consider other suspects besides Mr. Talbot?"

"Certainly," she said. For the fifteen minutes, she thought, before she and Cameron talked to his son.

"Who?"

"We looked at everyone." Just looked at them—Talbot was obviously their man.

"Did you tape or otherwise make an exact record of all your interviews?"

"We tape-recorded those who consented."

"And how many of those interview subjects consented?"

"Perhaps half," Kate said.

"So the fact that Mr. Talbot did not agree to be recorded was not unusual, isn't that true?"

"Yes."

"And he was well within his rights to decline, isn't that true?"

"Yes."

"Thank you." Quantrill consulted his notes. "As I understand it, you and Detective Cameron conducted important interviews with Mr. Talbot's son, next-door neighbor Marjorie Durant, another neighbor named Alice Cathcart, and Lisa McDaniel, Mr. Talbot's daughter. Would that be correct?"

"It would not. We interviewed dozens of other people."

"Fair enough. Would you characterize those interviews of other people as important interviews?"

"Every single interview is important."

"Wouldn't it be fair to say that some interviews are more important than others?"

"All of them form a mosaic in putting together evidence," Kate said doggedly. She knew what Quantrill was doing, and she was not going to give him a sliver of daylight. The real battle was, which of them would look more credible to a jury raptly watching this fencing match?

"Your interview with Marta Gonzalez, Mr. Talbot's housekeeper, on the same day as the murder," Quantrill said, "and the subsequent ones with the neighbors all along Mrs. Talbot's street, the people at Mr. Talbot's company—weren't those to support a theory you had already formulated as to Mr. Talbot's guilt?"

"In a homicide investigation, all possibilities have to be considered."

"Yes. Of course. But isn't it true that you very quickly decided that Mr. Talbot was your man, Detective?"

"I keep an open mind. On any investigation. My job is to

gather all the information I can." She bit down hard, as if she could somehow take the words back, because she knew she had said too much even before the next question emerged from Quantrill:

"And did you gather all the information you could?"

"We gathered sufficient information to justify . . ." She re-phrased her answer. "The District Attorney's Office judged from the facts of the case that probable cause justified an arrest warrant."

"Did you interview every neighbor on Mrs. Talbot's block?"

"We interviewed every neighbor who would talk to us."

"Did you do follow-up interviews for those who wouldn't talk to you?"

"Of course. We followed up on those people, and we rein-terviewed many of the people who had already talked to us."

"Would it be fair to say you conducted your interviews only up until the time Mr. Talbot was arrested?"

"No. It wouldn't."

"The additional interviews—were they done for weeks af-terward? Or months? At a guess," he added as she reached for her folder of reports.

"Months," she said.

"More than two months but less than three?"

She thought, and then nodded. "Yes, that would be ap-proximately right."

"Would it be correct to say you're satisfied you interviewed everyone with any possible information regarding this case?"

"No sir. I'm satisfied only that we interviewed everyone we could find."

"You testified that jewelry was missing from Mrs. Talbot's bedroom."

"That's correct."

"Did you seek interviews with gardeners who worked in the neighborhood?"

"Yes."

"Did you interview construction workers?"

"Yes."

"Let's talk about those particular interviews."

So much for his "few questions." She knew he was establishing groundwork for what prosecutors derisively referred to as the SODDI defense—Some Other Dude Did It. The same defense the "Dream Team" had so famously claimed in the trial of O. J. Simpson.

Twenty minutes later, he had wrung concessions that no, she and Cameron had not interviewed all possible gardeners working in the neighborhood, nor had they interviewed all possible construction workers involved in the renovation of a house on the block behind the Talbot house.

"Thank you, Detective. Let me ask you something else," Quantrill said pleasantly, hands clasped as he leaned over the lectern. "Did you review reports of crime in the neighborhood?"

"Yes I did."

Quantrill quizzed her closely about crime reports and she answered confidently. She had indeed gone over all the neighborhood reports, the 211s first. Only one armed robbery had occurred in the previous six months, a purse and jewelry taken at gunpoint from a woman getting out of her Lexus SUV who had obeyed her assailant's instructions not to look around for five minutes, and therefore could offer no description other than his Southern accent. Nothing in the 459s looked unusual—plus, burglars stole, they rarely killed. After many years of investigations she had an instinct for what stood out in these reports, but did not come close to hinting at this to Quantrill, who would use her admission to launch a withering attack.

"Now, Detective, you ordered tests on Mr. Talbot's new vehicle."

"His new Mercedes, correct." He would not be pleased with her reminding the jury that Talbot drove an eighty-thousand-dollar car. "Also his other car."

"Gunshot residue was found on the steering wheel, passenger seat, and glove compartment, is that—"

"Objection," Marquez said.

Quantrill turned around and looked at her in surprise as did Kate. Quantrill had asked a question about a fact not yet in evidence, nor had it been covered in the direct examination of Kate, but she could not understand why Marquez would object—it was to their advantage whenever it came into evidence. "Grounds, Ms. Marquez?" the judge said.

"Withdrawn," Marquez said sheepishly.

"We did find gunshot residue, that's correct," Kate said, smothering her exasperation.

"Evidence that my client had discharged a firearm, is that correct?"

"Correct."

"Did you also find gunshot residue in Mr. Talbot's other car, his BMW?"

"We did."

"Does the test have any way of telling you on what day my client discharged this firearm?"

"No, it doesn't."

"Can it tell you what kind of firearm it was?"

"No."

"Thank you, Detective. Did you perform gunshot residue tests on anyone else besides my client?"

"No."

"Did you perform GSR tests on Mr. Allan Talbot?"

"No we did not."

"On Lisa McDaniel or Rikki Talbot?"

"No."

"No one else?"

"No one else."

"Thank you, Detective. Now, is it fair to say that you checked to see if there might be other brand-new cars of make and model and color similar to Mr. Talbot's owned by anyone in the neighborhood, and found none?"

"Correct."

"Okay. Getting back to the forensic tests you ordered to be performed in the course of your investigation, is it fair to say that Mrs. Talbot's house was extensively fingerprinted?"

"Yes it was." More extensively than he knew—hair and fiber as well as fingerprinting. Baker had spent the better part of three days dusting every surface, inside and out, that could remotely hold a print, including books and magazines, glassware and cutlery, the contents of the refrigerator and the cupboards. All they needed was one usable print of Talbot's. Just one.

Quantrill smiled and asked genially, "Did you find any fingerprints that could not be identified?"

"Yes. But only three," she said pointedly.

"Did you find any fingerprints that matched my client's?"

"No," Kate said.

"My client has agreed to a stipulation that a steel box with a combination lock in Mrs. Talbot's study contained the gun that the Talbots once owned together. Were there fingerprints found on that box?"

"Yes there were."

"Whose prints, Detective?"

"Mrs. Talbot's."

"Not my client's?"

"No."

"What about on the combination lock?"

"The partial print found on the lock was not identifiable."

"Did you in fact find any evidence whatever—hair, prints, or fiber—that Douglas Talbot had ever been in that house?"

"No."

"Did you conduct a search of Mr. Talbot's home?"

"In accordance with the terms of a search warrant, yes."

"Did you seize evidence from this residence?"

She paused, casting a deliberately contemptuous glance at Talbot to give whatever message she could to the jury. During the search of the Talbot residence they had found no computers, an impossibility for the head of a business enterprise. There had been noticeable gaps in the shelves containing books, tapes, and DVDs. Child porn, Cameron had contended, and she believed he was right and that Talbot, no fool, had hurriedly removed and destroyed all traces of it before they could obtain and serve a search warrant.

"No," she said.

"Thank you, Detective. Has the murder weapon ever been found?"

"It has not."

"Douglas and Victoria Talbot had gone through a protracted divorce. Isn't it true that restraining orders are quite frequently a part of divorce proceedings?"

"I wouldn't know the frequency of when restraining orders are issued."

He nodded. "That's fair. In the interviews you conducted of Mrs. Talbot's neighbors, did you conclude that any of them had seen Mr. Talbot on foot in the vicinity of the house?"

"On foot?" she said pointedly. "Not on foot." Alice Cathcart's observations had not been definitive enough for a positive identification of Douglas Talbot.

"On the morning of the murder, Detective, did anyone see Mr. Talbot on foot anywhere in the neighborhood?"

"Not on foot, no."

"In fact, Detective, isn't it true that no one has ever seen Mr. Talbot on foot near Mrs. Talbot's residence in the entire time that Mrs. Talbot owned the house?"

"Yes." Lawyers loved these rhetorical questions, loved to gain an advantage where they could hammer a point into the ground. Further, Quantrill's thanking her when he felt he had scored a point had registered by now with the jury. She looked over at Marquez. She was taking rapid notes, her head bent. If she didn't clean some of this up on cross-examination, Kate vowed she would take that pen of hers and . . .

"So no one has ever seen Mr. Talbot on foot—"

"Objection. Asked and answered," said Marquez.

"Sustained," said the judge with undisguised impatience.

Finally, Kate thought.

"Thank you, Detective. The phone calls between Mr. and Mrs. Talbot," said Quantrill. "You characterized them as hangups, correct?"

"Correct."

"Did they come in at the same time of day, or at various times?"

"Various times. There was no pattern. Except escalation," she added before he could get in his next question, and she did not miss his fleeting reaction: irritation.

He asked, "Do you have any way of knowing who hung up on whom?"

She found the question ludicrous. But she answered simply, "I do not."

"Isn't it possible that Mr. Talbot hung up on his ex-wife?"

She did not try to hide her derision as she answered, "It's possible. Anything is possible."

"Isn't it in fact possible that all Mr. Talbot was doing was checking to see if his wife of thirty years was okay?"

"Objection," said Marquez. "Calls for speculation."

"Sustained," said the judge.

"Detective, did you interview Mr. Talbot's daughter, Rikki?"

"No," she said. All attempts to interview the young woman by anyone had been fruitless, with Rikki Talbot first expressing her cooperation, then breaking into uncontrollable shaking, followed by sustained bouts of hysterical tears at the first question. Kate was certain that similar attempts by the defense had met the same fate—she was not on their witness list either.

"Thank you, Detective." Quantrill smiled at Kate, a full-toothed smile conveying the message that her every answer had been exactly the answer he had expected, had been exactly what he'd been looking for. "No further questions."

Kate was surprised, but then realized that Quantrill would resume his questioning after Marquez's redirect.

"Ms. Marquez," said the judge. "Redirect?"

"Yes, your honor," Marquez said, sounding taken aback. Hastily, she picked up her legal pad, gathered up a few extraneous Post-Its, and went to the podium.

After clearing her throat several times and fussing with her notes, she said, "Detective Delafield, in general terms, how do you approach the investigation of a homicide case?"

Kate knew where Marquez was going with this question and she answered with the ease of practice. "The immediate priority is to take every precaution at the crime scene to preserve, photograph, and collect evidence. Then talk to anyone who had contact with the victim in the hours immediately prior to the crime and can help us reconstruct those final hours. Then talk to everyone indicated by those people as further potential witnesses. Beyond that, anyone we can find who may have any knowledge of the victim, any knowledge helpful to the solution of the crime. We attend the autopsy, review test results from the criminalists, collect all the information we can find."

"How often do you place someone under immediate arrest?"

"I can't recall ever having done so."

"And you've had over twenty years of experience in homicide investigations—"

"Asked and answered," Quantrill said.

"Withdrawn," Marquez said, her objective accomplished; she had reminded the jury of Kate's extensive experience. "So it usually takes some amount of time, measured in at least days, to conduct an investigation?"

"Correct," Kate replied.

"Detective, did you rush to judgment in your investigation of this murder?"

"I did not," Kate said. Was it a rush to judgment when a mountain of evidence pointed to Douglas Talbot as the only logical suspect?

Marquez asked, "How do you determine who is a suspect?"

The question was a softball right down the middle, and Kate hit it squarely: "Everyone initially is a suspect."

"Everyone?"

"Everyone. Until facts and evidence tell us otherwise."

"And after that?"

"It's a winnowing process—we go where the evidence leads us."

"Did you and Detective Cameron find any evidence whatever that led you to Allan Talbot as a viable suspect?"

"We did not."

"Did you find any evidence that led you to the defendant's daughter, Lisa McDaniel, as a suspect?"

"No." If she were to kill anyone, Kate thought, it would be her father.

"Did you find any evidence that led you to the defendant's daughter, Rikki Talbot, as a suspect?"

She had been the next best possibility, with no alibi other than being with her three small children. But why kill her mother and not her father? Or both? "No," Kate answered firmly.

"Did any evidence lead you to any relative, friend, or acquaintance of Victoria Talbot?"

"No." Victoria Talbot did have two brothers and a sister, all of whom lived in West Virginia and had had only rare contact with their sister. None had come to her funeral, nor to this trial.

"Did any evidence lead you to any of the men and women day workers performing services around the neighborhood?"

"No."

"Is it true that unidentifiable fingerprints are frequently found at crime scenes?"

"Yes, quite frequently. It's why we take elimination prints—fingerprints of everyone who would normally be at the scene so we can eliminate known prints. But compared to the general population, relatively few fingerprints are in the automated fingerprint identification system, which is law enforcement's national data bank."

"Could the unidentified prints you found be those of a friend or relative for whom you don't have elimination prints?"

"They could be."

"When you first entered the victim's house, was there anything about its appearance that immediately struck you?"

"I, uh—" she fumbled, then understood what Marquez meant. "It was very neat," she said.

"And did anything strike you when you conducted your search of the house?"

"I noticed that the surfaces were unusually clean—"

"Objection. Vague, irrelevant," said Quantrill. "Not covered on cross."

"Your honor, Mr. Quantrill's questions regarding fingerprints have opened this line of questioning."

"I agree," said the judge. "Proceed."

"The kitchen was gleaming," Kate said, remembering those shiny surfaces, the smell of cleaning products when she and Cameron had first entered the house. "Everything looked freshly cleaned."

"So this would substantially narrow the chance for the defendant's fingerprints to be—"

"Objection! Your honor—"

"Sustained," said the judge. "Ms. Marquez, this is improper and you know it."

"Sorry, your honor," Marquez said without a trace of penitence. "Now, the defense asked if you had collected any evidence of anyone seeing Mr. Talbot on foot. Was there evidence of Mr. Talbot being seen other than on foot?"

Several witnesses were on tap to give this testimony, but Kate was glad to introduce it to this jury. "Yes. Mr. Talbot was seen driving down the victim's street on numerous occasions."

Even though Quantrill knew this evidence was coming in, she was amazed that he had not objected to this hearsay testimony. He was looking on in polite interest, arms crossed.

"Now, is it correct that the defendant is the chief executive officer of his own company?"

"Correct."

"The warrant you executed in accordance with your search of the defendant's premises, did it include his computers?"

"Yes it did."

"Did you locate any?"

"We did not."

"Thank you, Detective," Marquez said. "I have no further questions."

"Mr. Quantrill?" the judge inquired.

"Subject to recall, nothing further, your honor," Quantrill said with a smile.

Kate stared at him in amazement. She had expected worse. It should have been worse. Much worse. What did this man have up his sleeve?

"You may step down, Detective," said Judge Terrell. As Kate gathered up her papers, he spoke to the jury: "We'll adjourn for the day," and proceeded to lecture them on their sworn responsibility not to discuss the case with anyone until it was officially assigned to them.

Five minutes later the courtroom was emptied of everyone except herself and the prosecution team.

She sat down beside Marquez and her second chair, Martha Dicter, at the prosecution table. "Where the hell do you think Quantrill's going with this?" she asked Marquez.

"I have no idea. But somewhere," she replied ominously.

"He give you any discovery?"

"Hell no. When do they ever?" Martha Dicter snorted as she stuffed papers into an already bulging briefcase.

Kate nodded. Under California law, ambushes were not allowed in criminal court proceedings and each side was duty bound to furnish the other with information, but this burden always fell primarily on the prosecution. All police reports, documents, tapes—everything had been turned over to the defense. The defense had in turn furnished a few innocuous and uninformative reports from its own investigator, contending they had come into the case late and were "still developing information" as the trial proceeded. The contention was bullshit, and understood by everyone to be bullshit.

"Can I look at their witness list?"

"Sure, for what it's worth."

There were about twenty names—not uncommon; defense lawyers usually listed everyone they could think of, then called only those who were most strategic. "I don't know half a dozen of these names," Kate said, pointing them out.

Marquez peered at the list. "They're friends of Talbot."

"Why are Jerome and Judith Steinberg on here?"

"They're neighbors, right? Didn't you talk to them?"

"Yes. Of course we did. They left on a trip to New Orleans shortly after seven that morning and didn't see or hear a thing. They don't own a Mercedes—we checked."

"Well, we've got three people who say they saw Talbot's Mercedes there. So are these people on the list going to say it wasn't?" Marquez looked at Kate searchingly. "Is there something I don't know, Kate?"

She had given voice to the lingering fear of all attorneys: that they would be blindsided by some key fact that someone deemed unimportant or, conversely, had chosen to conceal. "Alicia," Kate said, "believe me—you know everything I know, everything there is to know."

"Then I don't see what we have to worry about, and let's not worry if we don't have to. You were really good up there, Kate," Marquez added. Admiration was in her cocoa-brown eyes. "You tell the truth, and yet you do it with great judgment about how you answer questions."

"You were good too," Kate said, and she meant it. Yes, she could nitpick a few things but basically Marquez had protected her well enough; and her preparation had been thorough and meticulous, her direct examination and redirect better than Kate had expected.

As she walked from the courtroom, Kate decided that Marquez was right—they shouldn't worry until there was something to worry about. She had enough anxiety on her plate with Aimee. Still, there had to be some reason why she hadn't been tested by Quantrill.

E I G H T

A s Kate opened the door to the condo, a small furry face appeared at the edge of the kitchen doorway. She whispered to the cat, "Is your other mother home?"

Miss Marple stared at her with unblinking jade eyes, then abruptly withdrew into the kitchen. "Easy to see whose side you're on," Kate muttered.

Closing the door quietly, she stood motionless, listening, then went into the kitchen to check on Miss Marple's food and water dishes. They were full. A note lay on the counter:

> *Am at Marcie's. Please don't call me there or at work.*
> *I need you to give me some time to think things through.*

The note was signed, *A.*

Think what things through? How much time was "some time"? Kate raced into the bedroom. The bed, which she had hurriedly abandoned that morning, was in the same state of disarray, a sign of either an enormous act of will on Aimee's part—she was a compulsive tidier—or enormous anger. Kate flung open the closet door. A two-foot-wide cavity gaped amid the clothes hanging on Aimee's side of the closet. Another gap was evident in Aimee's shoe tree. Kate checked the dresser: Drawers were depleted and Aimee's lingerie drawer was empty.

Shit. She's taken enough for a trip to Europe. She could be gone for weeks. Months . . .

She stripped off her clothes and flung them into a corner, pulled on sweatpants and a T-shirt. Went back into the kitchen and yanked a bottle of scotch from the cupboard. Bottle in hand, she studied the note and the upright letters of Aimee's handwriting. This is serious, she thought, this is really serious.

That Aimee had gone to stay with Marcie Grissom added insult to injury. This was the very same Marcie Grissom that she, Kate, had not only helped to get a stalker-husband out of her life but had put her career on the line to do it. Kate poured a drink, replaced the bottle, and slammed the cupboard door shut. So much for the repayment of good deeds.

In the living room she took a deep gulp of her drink, put it down on the coffee table, and flung herself into her armchair. The balm of the scotch beginning its welcome work, she clicked on the TV and stared morosely at the news, thoughts of Aimee and the day in court swirling through her head.

Maggie. She should call Maggie. If she ever needed a best friend, it was now.

The phone rang. *Aimee.* Maybe it was Aimee. Kate leaped

up and snatched the portable on the bookcase before the second ring began.

"Hello, is this Kate Delafield? It's Nancy Harrison."

Crushed with disappointment, Kate snarled, "Look, your husband—"

"I know. Please give me one minute." The voice was trembling with urgency. "Please—just one minute."

Would there be any end to the awfulness of this day? What else could conceivably happen? Clenching the receiver, Kate closed her eyes. "One minute," she said. "Not a second more."

"Dale speaks before he thinks. I wish—"

"You're wasting your minute."

"Please—Dylan is sixteen years old. *Sixteen.*"

"I know that. What I don't know is why you or your homophobe husband think—Look, even if I found her, why would I return her to people who—"

"I understand. I realize she'd only run away again the first moment she could. I simply need to know she's safe. That she knows she can call me, come to me for help, come to me anytime for anything without . . . interference."

"Are you telling me you have no interest in curing her?"

The sigh coming over the phone reverberated with pain. "Try to understand. We do blame ourselves. Dale wanted a son. From the time she was born, he loved her as a daughter but treated her like a son and she just loved it. We didn't know what we'd done till the first time we almost had to tie her down to get a dress on her. Is it so wrong to think we confused her?"

"Yes, it's wrong," Kate stated, memory encroaching of her own excruciating adolescence. "She didn't run away because she's confused. She ran because she *knows.*" How could she even begin to educate this woman about the vast spectrum of lesbian experience? "Your minute is almost up," she said firmly. "I think a private detective could best deliver your message."

"Wait, wait please. I've already considered that. I know my daughter—"

"Do you," Kate said, and sipped her scotch.

"Enough to know she's had to be alone with this, completely isolated. I'm just sick over her thinking she had to leave home and it was the only answer she had. I realize we've given her every message she couldn't come to us, couldn't tell me—"

"Let me say this," Kate said in a softer tone. "She probably wouldn't have told you about her sexuality under any circumstances." As a teenager she would never ever have gone to either of her parents with her secret. Times had changed, society was light-years more accepting of sexual diversity, but religion kept homophobia solidly entrenched and the desperate wish of adolescents to believe that differentness was transitory had changed not a whit. Nor had the hope that they would somehow grow out of this and manage to belong to the larger culture, manage to somehow live up to everyone's traditional expectations, especially those of parents. Kate added, "Her secrecy had everything to do with how she felt about herself and nothing to do with you or her relationship with you."

"Please help her. She's sixteen and on the streets. You're the best and only real hope I have."

Kate quashed what she had been about to say. As worried as Nan Harrison was, she could not imagine how dangerous the streets were today for a teenager, especially a female. "Mrs. Harrison—"

"Nan. Call me Nan."

"Nan, I have no idea what I could do."

"She's in Los Angeles. We're—I feel reasonably sure of that.

It's so much bigger than San Francisco and farther away from us. It's logically where she would go to disappear and to . . . to . . ."

"To find her own," Kate said, remembering the forays she had made all those years ago to the lesbian bars in what was then her nearest big city, Detroit. "Why me? Why would she listen to anything I say?"

"You're a police officer."

Kate managed not to laugh. Authority was exactly what Dylan had fled. "What does she know about me? Does she even know my name?"

"Yes. Dale knew his birth name before he met you—"

"Of course," Kate said. "What exactly did he say about me?"

"Only that you're a police detective and somebody immoral. I'm sorry, but you asked."

Kate smiled. By using that code word, Dale had given the strongest possible clue to his daughter. Perhaps she had indeed come to L.A.

"Dylan's very curious by nature," Nan said, "and she never stopped pestering him. He wouldn't say another word except he regretted ever searching for you."

Dale and Nan Harrison probably knew the truth about their daughter all along, Kate thought. From all the coming-out anecdotes she'd heard from gay and lesbian acquaintances, most parents did suspect, and often said so years after they had given the most punishing and hurtful messages of condemnation to their children in the futile attempt to prevent suspicions from becoming truth. Her own parents had been no exception in the message department, with their pained disapproval of her boyish ways, but both had died before their fears became officially confirmed.

"A folder we found on her computer had articles from the *L.A. Times,*" Nan told her, "articles on women in the LAPD—

she must have run a search through their archives. One was a case you were involved in at the La Brea Tar Pits. I think she'd respect anything you have to say. Besides, it would be easier for you to find her than anyone else—you know what she looks like."

"I do have a photo of you and your daughter," Kate admitted.

"Yes, Dale mentioned he was sorry he'd ever given it to you. He also told me anyone would know in a second she was your niece."

Smiling wryly, Kate asked, "What resources does she have?"

"Her savings—"

"How much? Hundreds? Thousands?"

"Several hundreds, I suspect, but I honestly don't know. It's from doing odd jobs around the neighborhood. She had her own bank account and we made it a point not to inquire, thinking it would be good to respect her independence that way. She's very industrious."

And resourceful, Kate thought. She might only be sixteen but she's been planning this.

"Other than that," Nan said, "she didn't take anything else except a sleeping bag and a few basics in her backpack. From what I've been able to learn, some organizations in your community can maybe help her, is that true?"

She told Nan Harrison what she knew: "The community has organizations and centers here and in San Francisco. I'll make no promises but I'll see what I can do." Her mind already involved with the problem, she thought: The youngster may very well have stopped in San Francisco before coming here. She could take advantage of professional courtesy among police agencies and enlist the aid of SFPD, get them to keep an eye out for her, get the name of somebody up there to use as follow-up. "But only if you'll agree this stays between you and me. I want nothing to do with Dale. If he finds out, I'm done with this."

"Agreed, Kate—may I call you Kate?"

"Yes, of course."

"Let me give you my cell phone number."

She reached for a notepad. "Fine. I'll give you mine."

Afterward, Kate sat for a few minutes finishing her drink, then went back into the kitchen for a refill. Miss Marple was busy at her food dish. "Miss Marple," Kate addressed her, "Aimee walked out because I refused to help a niece I've never met. I've just agreed to help her."

The cat looked at her with her head cocked to one side. "So," Kate said, "I've done a classic 'lock the barn door after the horse has gone.' Because no matter how good a job I do with finding Dylan, this particular horse named Aimee could decide never to come back . . ."

She dumped scotch liberally over ice cubes, thinking that the issue of Dylan Harrison was actually only a factor in what had happened. Aimee might enjoy her taste of being unpartnered. Might even prefer it. On the plus side, over the past thirteen years she and Aimee had settled into domesticity and Aimee had given her no reason to be jealous. The plus side was also the minus side. The risk had always been there, came with the territory. Having a partner whose looks drew double takes and suggested to most people a brunette Candice Bergen was only part of that risk. Aimee being fifteen years younger was what exponentially increased it. Maybe she would decide that their thirteen years together was enough, and sharing the unpredictable life of a cop had gone on long enough.

Maggie, she'd call Maggie. Fear was surrounding her, threatening to become a rising tide. She gulped more scotch. And felt the fear begin to recede. One more drink to fortify her a little more and she'd definitely call Maggie.

NINE

A ringing phone intruded into her dream, a summons she couldn't muster up enough will or interest to answer. The house phone. Her cell phone. I'm asleep in bed, she told the caller, I don't care who the hell you are. But why, why did they keep calling back?

A pounding intruded. So insistent that consciousness surfaced, try as she might to hold it at bay in the blissful oblivion of her dream world. The gunshot-like reports hammered in counterpoint to a sudden painful thudding in her head. Groggily awake, she was surprised to discover she was not in bed; she was sitting up in her recliner in the living room and was still wearing her clothes. She struggled to her feet, reeling as she stood. Something brushed her ankles: Miss Marple, winding herself around Kate's feet, peering up at her in agitation.

The source of pounding was the door. What maniac could be making such a ruckus at this late hour? "Go away!" she shouted. Then she saw that the light in the room was not from a lamp but daylight.

"It's Joe! Kate, open the goddamn door!"

Cameron. Why was Cameron . . . Her head throbbed with each beat of her heart. Must be a migraine. Pain this bad—had to be a migraine if it wasn't a brain hemorrhage. Sick and dizzy, she looked at her watch through a field of vision that seemed fractured at the edges. Almost ten . . .

"Shit shit *shit*!" She rushed to the door, flung it open.

Cameron, impeccable in his best navy-blue suit, froze in midknock. "Fuck, Kate, why didn't you answer the damn phone? I called last night, called all this morning. You scared—" He broke off, staring at her wide-eyed. "You look like—what's going on?" He gripped her shoulders. "Are you okay? What's going on?"

"Nothing. I'm okay, all right?" She yanked his hands away; he was making her head hurt ferociously. "My head—I just need some aspirin."

He peered past her, closed the door behind him, walked into the living room, looked around. "Where's Aimee?"

"Not here," she said succinctly. Nausea was rising in her throat.

"Okay," he said, and asked with evident care, "Will she be back?"

"Sure," she said, and headed quickly for the bathroom. Leaning over the toilet, she retched repeatedly, but nothing came up. She took a bottle of aspirin from the cabinet, shook some into her palm heedless of quantity, downed them with a Dixie cup of water.

Realization dawned. She was supposed to have called Cameron last night and bring him up to date—he was working on open cases and had not been in court, relying on her for accounts of the trial. The two of them were supposed to meet early this morning to go over his testimony. He was supposed to be in court . . . *Jesus*. Cameron was supposed to testify . . . Cameron was supposed to be on the stand right *now*. How could she have done this? How could she have been so self-indulgent, so fucking *stupid*?

She came back into the living room in a stumbling run, holding her head. This was the worst, worst headache of her life. "Joe, my God I'm so sorry—"

"Get in the shower, Kate. Marquez's got us covered. She's as worried as I was. She's got other witnesses, they'll go out of order till we get there. We'll talk on the way."

"Look, I was just . . . sick. I sort of heard the phone ringing but I just couldn't—I couldn't wake up . . ."

He gathered up an empty Cutty Sark bottle near her armchair, used it to point to the bathroom. "Get in the shower," he repeated.

Utterly exposed, utterly humiliated, she did not know what to say, other than, "Yeah, okay."

"Make it cold, Kate. Cold as you can stand, long as you can stand it. I know whereof I speak. Get in there."

"Joe," she began, then said lamely, "Feed Miss Marple, will you?"

Twenty-five minutes later Cameron was driving her Saturn down Wilshire Boulevard toward downtown and the Criminal Courts Building, the windows of the car open for the benefit of

Kate's head and also her hair, which she had not taken the time to blow-dry. They had been talking about the case since she got out of the shower; he'd stood outside the bathroom while she was toweling off her goose-bump-laden skin, and then outside the bedroom while she dressed and did her best through her pounding head to fill him in on what had happened the day before, desperately trying to ignore how sick she felt, physically and emotionally.

"I got you covered with the lieutenant," he told her. "Marquez's covered for me with the judge. We'll talk about this other stuff later, Kate, but right now—"

"Right now our priority is the case," she said, nodding carefully around her pain. "I've never done this before, Joe."

"Goes without saying, Kate."

"Never pulled a stunt like this in my entire life." At least not her professional life. She'd get lit up from time to time, enough so that Aimee or Maggie had to take care of her, but Aimee usually got after her when she'd had more than a few drinks. Aimee had become more of a safety valve on her booze intake than she'd ever realized . . . Right now she couldn't remember anything beyond pouring a fourth drink and thinking she'd call Maggie afterward.

"Anything I can do for you?" Cameron inquired, throwing a sideways glance at her as he drove.

Bring back the person I love most in the world, she thought. "Just get us to the courthouse," she replied.

"Done," he said. "As early as I called this morning, Aimee would have answered the phone—I know she never goes to work that soon. This is about her, isn't it?"

After a moment, she admitted: "Yes."

"Anything you want to tell me, Kate?"

"Yeah, probably," she said. "But not right now."

"I'm here for you, Kate. Like you were here for me when Janine . . . happened."

Kate nodded, the knifelike pain making her instantly regret it, and she remembered a line from a song in which a mournful Kris Kristofferson woke up one Sunday morning with no way to hold his head that didn't hurt. She knew Cameron was alluding to the end of his fourteen-year marriage, when he'd found out that his wife, an instructor at the Police Academy, had been conducting a clandestine six-year affair with another instructor. There had always been an indefinable air of dark tension around Janine Cameron that Kate never liked, and so it had been easy for her to be angry on Cameron's behalf. After he learned of the betrayal, for the next four days, when he and Kate finished their shift together, she confiscated his service revolver and then went drinking with him, commiserating with his drunken rants. Each night she took him home with her and put him to bed on the sofa. She told Cameron now, "The priority is to talk about Quantrill. He's got something big up his sleeve. There's a reason he didn't even try to tear me limb from limb yesterday."

"He's waiting for me to take the stand, the sexist pig," Cameron offered with a grin, weaving his way aggressively through traffic.

Careful not to nod, she mustered a smile. "Right." If anything, Quantrill would be easier on Cameron. The lead detective—in this case, herself—made most of the key decisions in a homicide investigation.

"His every question was a setup," she said. "For what? I think we need to go over the defense witness list with a fine-tooth comb. There's probably somebody on it we should talk to."

"Maybe. Maybe he's just going through the motions," Cameron suggested. "Putting on a competent defense to get himself under the radar of anybody thinking he didn't put in a good effort, then take the money and run."

"Not him," she said. "He has a rep. He takes cases to win. He expects to win."

Peering at her, he said, "That aspirin helping? You still look a little green around the gills."

If I felt any worse I'd be dead. "I'm okay," she said. She needed to be in court to consult on ongoing strategy with Marquez, to hear the witnesses and most especially cross-examination, to discern where Quantrill was going and whether witnesses should be added or could be dropped from their own list. Short of passing out, she'd hang in there.

When they entered the courtroom, Quantrill was concluding his cross-examination of Dr. Gerald Green. Obviously, Marquez had taken enough time with the medical examiner that he had been the only witness thus far. Kate was disappointed to have missed him. Along with the fact that the back wound was postmortem, delivered after life had been extinguished by the first shot to the head, Green would also have presented X rays revealing healed fractures in Victoria Talbot's ribs along with the broken bones in her arm and wrist, a gallery of Douglas Talbot's domestic violence over time. Quantrill would not have accomplished much on cross-examination; medical facts were rarely subject to major challenge.

Marquez called Cameron next. He presented an attractive presence and was well spoken, but after an hour and a half of him the jury was visibly restless, several members not bothering to conceal their yawns at questions that elicited nothing new; and it was all Kate could do not to join them. The tedious testimony was required substantiation that Cameron's perceptions of the development of the investigation and the evidence matched her own account.

Kate listened intently to Quantrill's cross-examination, making notes; his areas of inquiry overlapped those he had focused on with her: whether there had been a rush to judgment; the range and extent of the witness interviews; and what had been determined about the scene by the investigating detectives the morning of the murder. Cameron was finally dismissed, and as he left the courtroom she gave him a thumbs-up sign. As prearranged, she would call him on her cell phone and he would pick her up when court was adjourned, take her back to her house, and get his own car.

Allan Talbot was next to be called. The last time she had seen him, more than six months ago, his heavy beard and shaggy hair and rumpled clothes suggested someone who had just staggered in from the desert. He had since returned to work, and today he was clean-shaven, the tight curls of his hair neatly barbered, and he wore a tan polo shirt under a navy jacket. But he made his way to the witness stand as if his feet hurt him, took the oath, and sat down and concentrated on hitching up the knees of his perfectly pressed tan pants, not lifting his head until Alicia Marquez addressed him: "Sir, the victim in this case—was Victoria Talbot related to you?"

"Yes, she was my mother," he replied in an even, calm tone, and answered Marquez's ensuing questions in the same detached manner, his gaze occasionally floating over his father but never descending on him. Kate thought he looked just as gaunt as he had the morning of the murder, still hollow-eyed with grief.

He recounted not reaching his mother by phone the night before or that morning. Coming over to the house at approximately eight o'clock, going around to the garden when she did not answer the door—none of the detail deviating from what he had told Kate. Finding the back door ajar, coming into the house: "And then I found my mother . . ." His control, and his voice, broke.

Marquez waited while Allan composed himself and finished his account. She asked, "From purely your own observations, Mr. Talbot, what were your impressions of your mother's marriage to your father?"

"It was constantly abusive," he said, his voice firming.

"In what way?"

"Objec—"

Douglas Talbot put his hand on his attorney's arm.

"Mr. Quantrill?" the judge said.

"Withdrawn, your honor."

Allan said, "Douglas beat my mother and me."

"How often?"

"Intermittently. He finally stopped punching me, but not her. It was an escalating pattern over their marriage. From as early as I can remember. It was happening virtually every few weeks before she filed for divorce."

"Did she at one point suffer a broken arm and wrist as a result of his assault?"

"Yes she did."

"Did she ever make a police report?"

"My sister Rikki called the police. Once."

"Sir, did your mother swear out a complaint?"

Allan Talbot looked directly at the jury. "As usual, she chose to believe Douglas's promises each time that this would be the last time."

"Sir, when the marriage ended, did you make attempts to convince your father that he should accept the divorce and an ending of his contact with your mother?"

"I did. Numerous times."

"And what was his response?"

"It was always the same: that what God had joined together, no man should put asunder."

Kate was watching the jury. Several of the women, and the man who looked like a Marine, did not try to conceal their expressions of disgust. She could only imagine Gregory Quantrill's frustration at having to allow this testimony to run unchecked, on the instructions of his client.

"When your mother was murdered, Mr. Talbot, whom did you immediately notify of her death?"

"I notified my two sisters, Lisa and Rikki."

"But not your father?"

"No. I did not call Douglas," Allan replied.

Kate was flooded with a mixture of feelings: triumph at the eloquence and power of Allan's testimony; rage at Douglas Talbot; inchoate sorrow for Victoria Talbot. Victoria had paid a grievous price for the trappings of her family life, sacrificing her entire self to provide comfort and safety for her children, only to have it result in the ultimate deprivation—estrangement. And then death. Allan's testimony could not have conveyed more effectively that he was a son convinced of his father's guilt, and so loathed him for the act that he had chosen, like Lisa, to use his first name rather than acknowledge him as his father.

Marquez asked gently, "What kind of person was your mother?"

"She was . . . wonderful. Incredibly generous. She wanted the best for us, urged all three of us to go to college, have all the opportunities she never had. Her own childhood in the South was hard, so her whole dream was that her children would never want for the things she did." His voice was trembling and his face was wet with tears, but he continued heedlessly, "She was warm, she was bright, she was funny, she was intelligent, she loved books and music and nature. She had this sweet sense of humor. She was a sweet, tender person, and if she even thought she hurt anybody, she felt terrible grief because she couldn't bear to hurt anybody. She didn't have a cruel or hateful bone in her body. I—I loved her very much."

Kate heard sobs from behind her and knew they came from Lisa McDaniel. Allan wiped his face with the back of his hand, then touched the neck of his polo shirt as if to button it across his throat. He threw a glance at his father, and as his lips tightened, his face hardened into a mask of loathing. Kate wished she could see Douglas Talbot, his reaction. The jury had seen it—which was all that mattered.

"Thank you, sir," Marquez said. "I have no further questions."

"Mr. Quantrill," said Judge Terrell.

Quantrill rose. "Thank you, your honor."

Talbot had again put a hand on the sleeve of his attorney, but Quantrill said, "One question, only one, Mr. Talbot. When you came into the house, the back door was open, is that correct?"

"Yes it was." His face was frozen in antagonism.

"Was it customary that your mother would leave that door open?"

"No. It wasn't."

"Thank you, sir. I have no further questions."

Typical lawyer—promise one question and ask two, Kate thought. There would have been many others except for orders from his client. Questions to open up other possibilities for the murder, such as what kind of life Victoria Talbot had lived after her marriage. Quantrill could not ask them, however gently. Douglas Talbot had elected not to have his son cross-examined, no matter what it cost him.

Marjorie Durant came next to the witness stand, sitting

erect on the edge of the chair, prim and dignified in her gray silk jacket and skirt, bestowing not a glance on Douglas Talbot other than to identify him to the jury as someone she knew. She testified with barely suppressed emotion to her long-standing friendship with the dead woman, then: "Yes, I heard two shots that morning," the first one around seven-thirty, the second an indeterminate time later, but at least five minutes. Yes, she had seen a new black Mercedes-Benz parked outside the Talbot residence that morning while walking her dogs. Yes, she had seen Douglas Talbot on numerous occasions driving slowly down the street, "who knows how often but at least once a day and I don't look out at the street that much." Yes, she had been in Victoria Talbot's house "dozens and dozens" of times when calls had come in, calls Victoria had either hung up on or they had gone to the answering machine with messages from Douglas Talbot that he was calling to see how she was, and would she call him.

The cross-examination from Quantrill was so courtly, so genteel that Kate could only admire his skill. Marjorie Durant relaxed and exchanged frequent smiles with him and confirmed that yes, undocumented workers were quite common in the neighborhood; and yes, regardless of any history she knew regarding the Talbots, her knowledge of what she had seen and heard that morning around the time of the murder was limited only to the car and the shots. No, she had never seen Douglas Talbot in Victoria Talbot's house or on foot in the neighborhood.

Eugene Durant, a powerfully built man wearing a gray suit at least as well tailored and expensive as Quantrill's, brusquely confirmed that he, too, had seen the Mercedes-Benz, but on cross-examination agreed that he knew "next to nothing" about the Talbots in recent years except "what Marjorie tells me." Limo driver Paul Jankowski, a small, nervous man in his fifties, shyly confirmed that he, too, had seen the black Mercedes. Alice Cathcart mumbled her testimony of seeing the car despite constant admonishments to speak up, staring all the while in unconcealed contempt at Douglas Talbot. Quantrill had a few questions for her.

"Mrs. Cathcart, did you see anything else unusual relating to the victim's house early that morning?"

"Yes, I think around two o'clock. I happened to get up around that time. I saw lights on."

"Where did you see these lights?"

"Both upstairs and downstairs."

"And this was unusual?"

Cathcart shrugged. "From what I knew of her, yes."

It was a detail that seemed to help neither attorney, and Marquez had no follow-up questions about it. With her raspy drinker's voice and bleary-eyed visage, Cathcart was the least presentable witness thus far, and Kate was not pleased with the thought that she herself had spent the night in the same condition as this virtual stumblebum of a woman. My drinking doesn't compare with hers, she consoled herself. Or with Douglas Talbot's. At least I'm not a drunk like either of them.

Forensic testimony by the crime scene technicians and the unsealing of evidence and the firearms analyst came after lunch, the questioning conducted by second chair Martha Dicter. It occupied the afternoon and would go on into tomorrow, evidence so cut and dried that Kate distracted herself from her misery by observing and making notes about the jury that Marquez might find helpful when she made her closing arguments.

Racial composition—six Caucasian, three African-American, and three Hispanic—was not as significant in this case as gender breakdown: five men and seven women. The preponderance of women might seem to favor the prosecution, but the defense had the decided advantage of needing only one vote to hang the jury if it did not come back with an acquittal. As a general rule, Kate knew, hung juries consisted of more than one holdout; it took rare fortitude for a lone juror to resist the pressure exerted by eleven unanimous opinions. A far more likely scenario was that two jurors could join forces and support each other. Since the laden issue of domestic violence presumably would unite and predispose the women toward a guilty vote, Kate looked to the men for the potential of opposing votes, men who might be swayed by affinity with the defendant, plus an effectively presented defense and a potent closing argument. There were no obvious candidates. Juror number nine reminded her of an officer she had known in the Marine Corps, and she would put her money on him, or possibly the matriarchal-appearing juror number two, to end up as the jury foreperson.

Finally the long day ended with adjournment. A day that scored very well on the prosecution side from what she could see, although virtually every case looked that way until the defense mounted its part of the trial. Still, Alicia Marquez had done a thorough and workmanlike job. Other testimony remained: more forensics, and the technician from Cedars with further X-ray proof of the broken bones sustained by Victoria Talbot when Rikki had called 911 and breached the wall of silence around Talbot's brutalization of his wife and children. Psychologist Dr. Sylvia Fernandez would be an additional important witness, testifying to the escalating pattern present in spousal abuse, and the lethal potential of stalking.

"This man fits the profile of a borderline personality," she had told Kate and Marquez in a pretrial meeting. "Like the Glenn Close character in *Fatal Attraction*. Once a person with this type of disorder attaches themselves to someone, if they begin to lose their span of control they become more and more obsessive. You get someone in your life who's a borderline, you might as well pack up and move to Siberia. You'd think the defense would have a better chance using Talbot's mental condition."

"Juries aren't impressed, Sylvia," Marquez had informed her. "They recognize that people can have severe emotional problems, but if they think you know right from wrong when you pull the trigger, that's all they see."

Kate had agreed. Talbot's best chance was a not-guilty plea.

The final witness in the prosecution case would be Lisa Mc-Daniel. Her testimony might not have the dramatic impact of Allan's because she had not had his horrific experience of discovering the body of her mother, but it promised to be effective nonetheless. Whatever her previous estrangement from her mother, in the ten months since her death the reality of that permanent separation had set in, as had a purity of grief that infused Lisa's face and drained the vitality from her. Continuous counseling had improved Rikki's emotional status over the months since the murder, but since her recovery was still too tenuous for the stress of a courtroom, Lisa would conclude what appeared to be a very strong prosecution case.

Kate scrutinized Gregory Quantrill as he strode from the courtroom, his briefcase swinging. He looked too comfortable, too confident. Some way, somehow, somewhere, he had set up an ambush.

TEN

"The Steinbergs," Cameron said. Sitting across from Kate at the homicide table in Wilshire Division, shirtsleeves rolled up, he was poring over the witness list provided to the prosecution by the defense team.

"Yeah, I noticed them too," Kate told him. "Marquez and I talked about them."

"So tell me why the hell they're on the defense list. You got an FI?"

"Sure." Kate checked back through her folder of notes for her copy of the field interview. "Here it is. Pedersen talked to them first—June fifteenth—three weeks later. We'd already run a DMV—they own a Cadillac Eldorado and a Honda Accord. I did a phone follow-up with Jerome and Judith Steinberg when they got back. They didn't see or hear a single thing that morning, too busy with packing and closing up the house. They left at five after seven—Steinberg claimed he looked at his watch when they left the house."

"Did they know Victoria Talbot?"

"Hardly at all."

"Do they know Douglas Talbot?"

"Only by name," Kate said.

"I fucking don't get it," muttered Cameron. "Everybody else on the defense list belongs here. Their prime witness—Marta Gonzalez—she's his alibi. Bobbi Phillips the receptionist—she'll say he got to work at his usual time and," he added sarcastically, "will provide the useful information that he didn't look to her like he'd just killed somebody. Jason Jenks from the Angeles Shooting Range—he'll confirm Talbot was there the night before to explain the GSR in his car. Anderson, Houston, Stanley, Jacobs, and Steele—they're fellow corporate crooks and drinking buddies who'll say what a fine upstanding sober citizen he's become. His sister, his aunt—"

"Maybe the Steinbergs remembered something after they talked to me."

He grinned. "Like what? They saw Talbot's Mercedes out there? Or maybe they remembered they didn't see it, which doesn't hurt us—we still have them outnumbered—" He broke off, looking up.

"Hello, you two gumshoes," Lieutenant Carolina Walcott said from behind Kate. "Trying to match wits with the bottom feeders?"

"You got it," Kate replied, swiveling her chair around, smiling. She was always happy to see Walcott. During the last three pressure-laden years at Wilshire, she had remained high on

Kate's most admired list. With all the changes at LAPD—yet another new police chief had come into office amid full-press coverage in the national as well as the local media—Walcott had provided a buffer zone of calm competence at Wilshire Division. As an African-American, she had been upset over the volatile and bitter politics surrounding the departure of Chief Bernard Parks and his replacement by William Bratton, but had kept her opinions to herself except for one incisive statement: "You don't want to come close to hearing what I think."

"You feeling okay, Kate?" Walcott asked, coming toward her to look more closely. "You look a little under the weather."

"Touch of intestinal flu," Kate offered sheepishly, aware of Cameron. She had made the same excuse to Marquez. She told Walcott, "I was just thinking the same thing about you."

"Just weary, bone-tired." Walcott rubbed her face. "The crap level never goes down so much as an inch. How's Marquez doing with the trial?"

"Better than I expected. Our part went well. We think Quantrill's got something up his sleeve."

"Yeah, well, we're covered, right?"

Meaning, if something blew this case, would it be counted against courtroom events and attorney warfare and not back to the investigation and police error?

"We're covered," Cameron said.

"Good. Go home, Kate," Walcott said, "take it easy. The both of you."

"Talked us into it," Cameron said, pulling his jacket off the back of his chair.

Fine with me, Kate thought, gathering her notes together. Cameron could pick up his car, she'd change clothes, go see Maggie. And have no drinks at all tonight.

———

house, Maggie said to Kate, "This isn't about your niece."

Sitting on the living room carpet, her back up against the
sofa, Kate picked up her glass of wine. Wine wasn't the same as
scotch; wine hardly counted as a drink, not in her book and
not when it tasted as ghastly as the stuff Maggie kept on hand.
"Okay," Kate said, "then what the hell is it about?"

"Everything. The only time it's about one thing is when she
finds you in bed with somebody else." As she voiced this opinion, a knowing, reminiscent smile creased Maggie's face.
"Look, anybody can walk away from a fight, leave the house.
When she stays away—it's about everything. Whatever the lat-
est thing is, it's just the final straw."

"You make sense," Kate conceded. "If this was just about
Dylan Harrison, we'd have done our shouting, made peace,
and I'd end up doing some version of what she wanted—that
would be the end of it."

"So you're the one who always gives in."

"What, you don't know that? Always." She could stand
Aimee's unhappiness with her only so long, usually no more
than a day.

"I wonder if she sees it that way. There's this couple that
comes into the bar. Connie's big bitch is how she's compromised
so much for Jinx. Poor Jinx just smiles. One look at Connie and
you know she aims to control everything, even sunrise."

"Are you telling me—"

"Hey. All I'm saying is, we look at things our way. Did you
have an idea problems were brewing?"

"Sometimes I wondered . . ." She shrugged. "Basically I
thought everything was . . . well, you know, okay. Not fine all

the time—nothing is. But still, things seemed pretty good . . ." The leaping fire from the environmentally treated log was soundless, virtually odorless. An imitation log, a mirage, she thought, like her relationship with Aimee. "I guess all this time I was too dumb to see the elephant shit piling up around me."

"It may not be piled too high yet, Kate."

The comment had been offered in Maggie's usual soft husky tones, and Kate rested her gaze on her. Maggie sat in her worn plaid armchair, Nike-shod feet up on the battered leather ottoman, drinking tea out of the huge, faded ceramic mug she'd owned for the better part of half a century. She was always the same, the same old loyal, humorously philosophical Maggie no matter what the calamity.

Maggie was gold. That Aimee could meet somebody else, could leave—that was always possible. Real friends like Maggie, there was that special trust. Joe Cameron too; there was a firm, unshakable bond between them now. People like Maggie and Joe judged you right off the bat, and if they accepted you, they managed to forgive pretty much anything. Maggie, come hell or high water, would be here. Like tonight. Pick up the phone: "Maggie, I need to come over," and here she was, the one unchanging, dependable person in her life. Always in one of two places, the Nightwood Bar or this tiny one-bedroom house on this nondescript street in Pacoima, with the laughably minuscule swimming pool in the backyard and the brick barbecue in use virtually every night except weekends when she was in town running the bar. Maggie's loves were constant: her friends, the bar, and the San Fernando Valley with its blistering hot summer days and balmy nights.

Maggie, her best friend—her finite best friend, Kate thought with a sliver of fear. In her customary shorts and T-shirt and year-round tan, Maggie looked healthy enough, but she had never paid much attention to the strong body she'd been given, never exercised, and her burly muscularity had softened into a Jell-O-like bulk, her face into a road map of deep seams. She had tried and succeeded in quitting cigarettes, had tried and failed to quit drinking. The bill had come due: She looked every day of her seventy years of age.

Kate drained her glass of wine, poured another from the bottle on the coffee table. She returned her gaze to the fire. Why, really, was she here? Aside from a few minor liaisons she could count on one hand, there had been two all-consuming relationships in her life—the twelve years with Anne, these thirteen with Aimee—while Maggie had had dozens of partnerships, their duration measured in months. Unlike Kate, she did have many friends and some were close, but lovers were different, and Maggie had no clue about sustaining long-term love relationships.

"You're figuring I know from nothing," Maggie said, peering sagely at her. "When I had the bar open full time, I saw women every night of my life in every stage of love and divorce, heard chapter and verse ad nauseam about their breakups, and some of them were together twenty, thirty years. All the stories I told you over the years about the bar—that's not a fraction of what I saw."

Kate nodded. Bartenders did see and hear it all, in astonishing candor from people with inhibitions loosed by alcohol, blurting their secrets as if in a confessional.

"Unless you're a saint or a Siamese twin," Maggie continued, "nobody gets along with their partner all the time. What were the beefs with Aimee?"

Kate said reflectively, "You know, I don't think I actually had any with her. But as for her with me . . ." She ticked off points with extensions of her fingers. "I don't talk to her about the right things. I drink too much. I get more paranoid every day. I'm in the closet. I'm too narrow-minded . . ." She held up the other hand to use those fingers. "I'm insensitive, selfish—"

"You hardly deserve to live," Maggie said. "For starters, how don't you talk to her?"

"Jesus, Maggie." Another lawyer cross-examining her. "I'm no different from anybody else. A really tough day, I don't want to relive it, I don't want to even open my mouth but I make an effort. I always ask about her day."

"Come on, Kate, what are these so-called 'right things' you don't talk about?"

"My feelings," she said in exasperation. "The job. She doesn't understand the job. No one does except another cop."

"You talk to me about it, Kate. What exactly aren't you telling her about this priesthood you belong to?"

Kate quaffed a good slug of wine, thinking this was the first time she'd felt decent all day. Nothing like the hair of the dog that bit you, albeit an inferior breed of dog. She said, "I can talk to you because you don't third-degree me about how I feel. For chrissakes, what is there to feel when you see a murder except sick to your soul? When I talk to you, you're okay with it, you don't get all upset, you just let me talk. I don't have to worry about you pitching a fit over what you hear, you don't give me a hard time about why I keep doing my job."

"I have an advantage, Kate. I don't see you every single day. She does. She sees what the job is doing to you. So why do you keep doing it? It's a question you should be able to answer."

"Maggie, I'm good at what I do. That's the answer." *What else would I do? It's all I know how to do.*

Maggie said, "So what you're telling me is, this job stuff isn't about her, it's about you deciding to shut her off from it."

"Whose side are you on here?" She was only half joking.

"Your side. Don't doubt it. The drinking. You do drink too much, in case you hadn't noticed."

"So do you."

"You think I don't know it? Ever take any of those 'Do you have a drinking problem' tests?"

"Not for a while," she lied. She took them every time she saw one. She always failed, by a mile. She was sure that all cops would fail.

"Think you have a problem with booze, Kate? Think you could give it up?"

"Why should I?"

"Because," Maggie said lightly, "it's maybe costing you your relationship with Aimee and with yourself?"

"That's a good reason," Kate said with a grin. She added seriously, "I can't imagine coming home and not being able to relax with a drink. What the hell would I do?"

"How relaxed do you get?"

She hesitated. Sometimes too relaxed. Sometimes she came home thinking only about making love with Aimee, but if she proceeded to have more than a drink or two . . . Yet simply the sight of Aimee never failed to arouse her, and if anything, when they did make love, alcohol slowed down the pace of their lovemaking and their sex life was better than that of most women she knew. It wasn't just her opinion; Aimee made the same claim. "I don't think I have a problem I can't handle," Kate said.

"Remember when Audie stopped drinking after all those years? I'll never forget what she told me: 'It took me a long time to get into trouble with alcohol, but alcohol is patient,' she said. 'Alcohol will wait for you.' Poor Audie," she added.

"Is she worse?"

"She's tidying up, giving stuff away, getting ready to die."

Kate shook her head. Audie was her friend too. Not a close friend like she was to Maggie, but a friend. "I could get breast cancer tomorrow. A lot of good it did her to quit drinking."

Maggie cast her a disgusted look. Then asked, "So what about this paranoid business? You think somebody's following you?"

Kate chuckled, relieved at the change in topic. "Somebody often is. A *Times* reporter, usually. One of them's been after me to give an interview about being a lesbian cop."

"I suppose Aimee wanted you to do it."

"I didn't even ask her. My personal life splashed all over the newspaper? Forget it, no discussion required."

"Not when you won't even have it splashed all over LAPD," Maggie pointed out.

"Have you been talking to Aimee?" Kate said jokingly. "That's exactly what she would say."

"That you're not out at work—it really bothers her, Kate."

"That's because of her definition of 'out.' The LAPD rumor mill figured it out long ago," she said. "Without my having to make a public address announcement."

"So do you ever talk about your female partner with your fellow cops?"

"It's not my style to talk about any personal stuff. The cops I work with respect my privacy."

"Ever go out with them?"

"Sometimes." These days she turned up at retirements mostly, and briefly when she did so. The boozy back-slapping conviviality of off-hours cop activities had always made her uncomfortable.

"Ever bring one of them home?"

"Joe Cameron," she said. "When Janine walked out on him. He was with us for four nights." He was more close-mouthed than she was, and so descriptions of her home life did not get spread all over LAPD. She had not mentioned his visit of this morning nor the circumstances that had brought him over.

Maggie said, "The only reason you're not fully out at work is habit. You're like a bird that's always lived in a cage—the door's sprung open but you won't fly out. If you don't mind my saying so."

She did mind. Intensely. Easy for people to judge when they didn't have her job, her life, her demons.

"Why wouldn't Aimee feel justified in believing you don't respect her feelings about this?" Maggie demanded. "She's right out there, she talks freely about you, her life, everything she wants to when she's at work. You hardly ever bring anyone home, never bring her to any police functions—what she sees is that she's a secret."

"She's not a secret," Kate said heatedly. "I'm telling you, everyone knows."

"Knowing isn't the same as telling, Kate, and you damn well know it. You close off an entire part of your life from your partner, from the people you work with, you're sending a message. It means you think there's something wrong—"

"Give it a rest," Kate snapped. "I've heard it and heard it. I'm telling you it's too much of a distraction. You don't understand, I don't expect you to understand." The job was brutal enough without having to undergo inquisitive poking around in her personal life by her peers. What she did in her off time was none of their goddamned business. She was not about to turn her workplace into gossip central. Especially after all these years. Case closed.

"Far be it from me or anybody to try and come between

you and your homophobia," Maggie said, waving a hand in dismissal. "We were talking before about you being paranoid."

"She threw that one at me when I suggested we might consider moving out where it's safer."

Maggie sat straight up in her chair. "Out of the *city*? You're not serious. Like where? Please tell me you don't mean Simi Valley."

Kate gestured vaguely. "Just . . . away." In fact, she had meant Simi Valley and would have pushed for it had Aimee not said with instant and withering finality, "I'd rather be dead than leave West Hollywood for some stupid boring place in the 'burbs." Simi Valley had been given a bad name by the Rodney King jury, but lots of cops lived out there and for good reason. It was less dangerous. "All I want is to keep her safe. The same reason I insisted on dead bolts and window locks for this Swiss cheese of a house you live in."

"Yeah, well, a homicide down the block was pretty good incentive too. I make it a point to own nothing worth stealing," Maggie observed, glancing around her modest living room with satisfaction.

"The bad guys don't know what you've got in here," Kate returned. "Sometimes they break in for reasons that aren't theft." And beat to death older women like you just for the hell of it, she thought, remembering last year's homicide on Hauser Avenue of an eighty-three-year-old woman whose face and body had been unrecognizable pulp. She continued, "We had a grand theft auto in our own condo garage and I still can't get Aimee to look around whenever she goes in there." Her voice rose. "You and her—you're like these people who become supporters of causes only when something happens, when it's too late. Monsters are out there, Maggie, far more dangerous, far more immediate than any terrorist—but you won't believe it. You don't see the things I see."

"No I don't—thank the goddess. But I do believe you. I know every day could bring Armageddon. I just don't want to live that way. Neither does Aimee."

I have to, Kate thought. I know what can happen and it goes beyond what I see every day. It's knowing how a car can veer out of a lane and one second later Anne's car has flipped over, is on fire, and she's dead. It's knowing the only time I can be sure Aimee's safe is when I'm curled around her at night holding her in my arms. I *have* to do what I can to protect people I love.

Kate managed a grin. "Whose side did you say you were on again?"

"Like I said before—your side."

"Then tell me what I should do about this."

"Wait. All you can do for now is wait. And do some soul-searching."

"About what?" Maggie's look was so castigating that Kate held up her hands. "Hey. Just kidding."

"Were you? Kate, listen to me. Listen carefully. I have yet to hear anything out of your mouth so far tonight except self-justification and rationalizations. You say you don't have any beefs with her—doesn't that give you a clue? She feels she's living your life and she's served notice she doesn't want to do it anymore. Whether you think she's right or wrong about things doesn't matter anymore. You better decide what you want to do about it."

"If anything," Kate said defiantly.

"Right. If anything. I'm sure you can just march right out there and get yourself another Aimee."

"What makes you think I'd want to get anybody at all? The way you live looks pretty good to me right now."

"God, you're dumb. You're even dumber than I thought," Maggie said, and drank more tea.

Kate smiled and drank more wine.

Maggie finally said, "So what are you going to do about Dylan?"

"Find her. I'm the police, remember?"

ELEVEN

Kate sat restlessly in the courtroom, waiting for a pretrial conference in Judge Terrell's chambers to end and the trial to resume. On this Monday morning frustration and anxiety were prime components of her impatience. No Aimee—not even a phone call or email message over the entire weekend. And there was the continuing Dylan Harrison problem. She had not as yet become worrisome, but Kate could feel an edge of suspicion that soon she might be, that any news for Nan Harrison might be bad news.

The weekend had not been entirely unproductive. She had contacted the Family and Juvenile Services Division of San Francisco PD, had been referred to an investigator who invited Kate to call her Monica and then asked crisp questions and issued crisp instructions about faxing Kate's photo of Dylan. When Kate explained the circumstances surrounding Dylan's voluntary disappearance, Monica's tone changed: "I'll look after this one personally. You know we have a lot of homeless, many of them runaway kids."

"We do too," Kate said. "More every day."

"Nobody wants to deal with the truth—most of the kids are gay or lesbian. Where's the Amber Alert program for them? All the propaganda in this country about protecting children, they don't count, they're throwaways—" She broke off with a bitter chuckle. "Okay, you got me started. We'll do our best to find her, Kate. If we do, I'll call before we do anything else." She gave Kate her pager number. "Call me anytime. And I mean anytime."

Kate had also enlisted Maggie's aid. But the collegial reception in San Francisco stood in stark contrast to Maggie's endless carping, beginning with when they were walking up North Schrader in Hollywood. Kate had remarked, craning her neck as she looked over the angular, modernistic façade of the Los Angeles Gay and Lesbian Services Center, "This is a really handsome, impressive building."

"You've never been here before," Maggie said, the statement made as if Kate had just discovered ice cream.

Kate answered in irritation, "Obviously not."

"This impressive building is merely the center of the gay and lesbian community in Los Angeles. The Center's existed for over thirty years. It's just over the line from Wilshire Division. Odds are you'd drive by it just by accident if for no other reason."

In no mood for Maggie's constant hectoring, Kate snapped, "If you'll lay off till after I find this girl, I'll turn in my lesbian membership card, okay?"

"Turn it in? The whole point is, you need to *activate* it."

They had made inquiries from a friendly and efficient young man at the reception desk, visited various youth activities offices throughout the Center, where Kate left flyers showing Dylan's picture along with her LAPD business card. No one recognized Dylan from the flyer. Same procedure at the Gay and Lesbian Adolescent Social Services on North Robertson. Afterward they prowled West Hollywood and Hollywood Boulevard by car and then on foot, visiting bars and bookstores and any establishment displaying the gay pride flag until Maggie expressed confidence that Kate had done a sufficient saturation job in distributing the flyer and the dozens of cards on which she had written, *Call me. I can help.*

"Maybe she's in San Francisco. Hell, she might be in Mexico," Kate had grumbed to Maggie. "She might be catching rays and laughing it up on a beach in Hawaii." But at least the search was under way.

Aside from the time she'd spent with Maggie, the weekend had been utter misery. In all her time with Aimee she could count on one hand their nights apart. She missed the daily routine and ritual of their lives together, beginning with Aimee's custom of bringing coffee to her in the morning. Nights were equally agonizing. She missed the nightly body contact so acutely she had abandoned the bed and now slept on the sofa. She had vowed to limit her drinking but had not been able to resist the simple, easy relief offered by that glass of lovely amber liquid, not when she was lacerated by loneliness and heartache. Adding to her depression was the certain knowledge, as if a hand held her by the neck forcing her to see, how insidiously her need, her dependency on alcohol had grown over the years. *No wonder she left me . . .*

L.A. Times reporter Corey Lanier, nattily attired in jeans and a denim blazer, came down the aisle of the courtroom and leaned over Kate, surveying her with cool gray-blue eyes. "Hello, Detective," she said in the throaty voice that always reminded Kate of Demi Moore, "how's it going?"

"Couldn't be better, Corey," Kate replied.

"That bad, eh? You ready to give me that interview?"

"What interview would that be?"

Grinning, Lanier peered at her over the top of her dark-rimmed glasses. "That would be the one with the headline, 'Lesbian Cop Tells All.'"

Kate returned her grin. "Ah, that one. Have pigs flown yet?"

"I know better than to ask about the case," Lanier said, nodding toward Quantrill, who had just entered the back door of the courtroom along with Judge Terrell and Alicia Marquez and Martha Dicter, "but he wouldn't be here if he didn't expect to pin your ears back."

"No comment, Corey."

"Ah, the Kate Delafield we all know and love." Lanier aimed a pretend punch at her shoulder, then sat in the aisle seat across from her, pulling a pen and notebook from her jacket pocket.

What indeed, Kate wondered, would this day bring? Neither of the Talbot offspring was in court today and she doubted that either would return except, perhaps, for the closings and/or the verdict. Lisa had testified on Friday, the final witness before the prosecution rested, and her brother had been here to support her. Not so transparently hostile toward her father as Allan had been, she was in her own way as chillingly effective. Wearing a black suit, her demeanor steely calm, she was nothing like the spirited young woman Kate and Cameron had seen the day of Victoria Talbot's murder. In an objective, remote tone, she answered Marquez's questions about the years leading up to the murder as if her father were not present, as if she were testifying in a case involving people in whom she had no emotional investment. She too referred to him distantly as "Douglas." But like her brother, when she was asked to describe the kind of person her mother was, she too broke down as she stammered out an answer. She left the courtroom looking neither right nor left, followed by her brother, and Kate watched with profound sympathy as they departed. This murder had taken its usual toll of emotional devastation, as murder always did. Lisa and Allan Talbot were the personification of what made homicide the ultimate crime.

Compared to most murder trials, which inevitably extended beyond the best estimate of their duration, this one was moving along toward assignment to the jury in the eight to ten days projected for it. One reason was not having to install and remove exhibits; thus far there had been few beyond the usual display of evidence: a schematic of the house, photos of the body and crime scene, and a time line chart listing the distances and travel time between Douglas Talbot's house, his company, and Victoria Talbot's house. The primary reason for speed was Quantrill himself and his method of cross-examination: on-point questioning to clarify testimony.

He apparently was not interested in the customary defense tactic of obfuscation, of trying to muddy every fact of the murder to produce reasonable doubt, especially in his questioning of the forensic witnesses. Only one issue was belabored at every opportunity: the lack of direct physical evidence placing Talbot at the scene, a very good tactic in this day and age when juries, influenced by TV shows, had reversed course in their suspicion of DNA and forensic evidence and now embraced and expected it.

Quantrill's speedy trial strategy had included declining the offer to adjourn when Marquez rested the prosecution's case mid-Friday afternoon. Leaving her scant opportunity to switch mental gears into the role of cross-examiner, Quantrill had begun his defense of Douglas Talbot by calling Marta Gonzalez as his first witness.

Efficiently establishing the circumstances under which she had met Talbot and the months she had known him, and that she was a resident in his home, Quantrill brought her to the morning of the murder. According to her simply told narrative, Douglas Talbot had departed for work at his usual time and left the Mercedes for her use during the day. He returned home at his usual time and not before.

"So is it your truthful testimony that Mr. Talbot left the house at eight-thirty that morning?" Quantrill asked.

"Yes," said Marta Gonzalez.

"And it's your truthful testimony that he did not take his Mercedes-Benz?"

"Yes."

"No further questions," Quantrill said, striding back to his table.

At the podium, Marquez began, "How old are you, Ms. Gonzalez?"

"Objection. Irrelevant."

"Sustained," said Judge Terrell.

Kate nodded. Marquez had drawn attention to the fact that the pretty, girlish-looking female on the stand was three decades younger than Talbot.

"You stated you had use of the defendant's Mercedes-Benz the day of the murder, Ms. Gonzalez." Marquez's tone was polite, even friendly; she was being initially circumspect with this witness even though her own heritage would serve her well in not alienating Hispanic members of the jury. "When did he decide to leave the car with you?"

Marta looked momentarily confused. "Ah, it was, ah, that morning. When he went into the garage to get his car. He came back and said he was taking my—his other car, his BMW. And I was to use the Mercedes."

"And where was the Mercedes at that time?"

"In the garage."

"Do you recall where it was when the detectives interviewed you the day of the murder?"

"Yes, it was parked on the road outside the house."

"Why was it out of the garage, Ms. Gonzalez?"

"I had taken it out to take a drive but Douglas called me on my cell phone and said the police would be talking to me, and to wait. So I left it there while I was waiting for them."

"I see," Marquez said, favoring the jury with a glance of clear skepticism. "Are you still residing in Mr. Talbot's house during these proceedings?"

"Yes."

"How long have you been a resident in this country?"

"Objection," Quantrill said, as Kate had been sure he would. "Irrelevant. Beyond the scope."

Marquez said, "The question goes directly to motivation, your honor."

"Overruled," said Terrell. "Please answer the question."

"Twenty-two years. Since I was five."

"Isn't it true that you are not a lawful resident of this country?"

"I am working on it," she said softly.

"Please answer the question. Are you a legal resident?"

"I am trying to be."

"Ms. Gonzalez, I'm asking you questions that require a simple yes or no answer. After you give that answer, you can then explain. In the twenty-two years you've been here, have you ever before *tried* to be?"

"This is my first good chance," she said.

"Is your answer yes or no?"

"Objection," complained Gregory Quantrill. "Badgering the witness."

"Overruled," the judge said.

Marta Gonzalez was much savvier than the impression she gave, Kate thought. She was making Marquez look like a bully.

Marquez asked sarcastically, "When did you first *try* to become a lawful resident, when did this *first good chance* happen?"

"The last year," she admitted after a moment.

"Isn't it true that you've only *tried* to become a lawful resident because this defendant—"

"*Objection!* Your honor, this is inflammatory—"

With an air of resignation, Judge Terrell beckoned to both attorneys. After a brief, heated bench conference, Marquez walked calmly back to the prosecution table saying, "I have no further questions." But she had gotten her questions in, the damage had been done to Maria Gonzalez's motivation for offering an alibi for Talbot, and Quantrill's redirect that Friday afternoon could do nothing to repair it.

If last week was the nadir for the defense, this was a new week, the defense's week, and along with her own misgivings, Kate shared Corey Lanier's curiosity about what rabbit Quantrill would pull out of a hat to turn this case.

With the jury finally in place and the preliminaries accomplished of going back on the record in the matter of the People versus Douglas Albert Talbot, Quantrill strode to the podium.

The day proceeded swiftly, the witnesses consisting of employees from Talbot's company, business associates, and character witnesses including his sister and an aunt. They were on and off the stand quickly; Marquez had few questions on cross-examination other than to wring concessions that they knew little or nothing about Talbot's personal history with his ex-wife and children.

There was little here of interest to Kate, and she spent time in the corridor during much of this testimony, reviewing by phone with Cameron their other open homicide cases, conferring in the endless requirement for organizing repeat interviews, completing reports and assorted other paperwork.

Late in the afternoon, Quantrill finally announced the first witness of interest: "The defense calls Jerome Steinberg."

As the bailiff walked to the courtroom door to summon the witness from the hallway, Marquez used the excuse of following this process to turn and exchange a glance with Kate, her expression saying: Should I request a recess? Do you know anything new? Anything I don't? Kate replied with a minimal shrug and equally minimal headshake.

An old man, bent from the waist at a forty-five-degree angle, shuffled into the courtroom assisted by a sturdy cane. Beige pants flapping against skeletal hips and legs, he hobbled his way through the courtroom to the witness stand with a stiff dignity that forbade any attempt to assist him. A shapeless V-neck gray sweater hung from his bony shoulders, over a lemon-colored shirt adorned by a bright yellow polka dot bow tie. He stated and spelled his name, then, raising a liver-spotted, shaking hand, took the oath, and lowered himself gingerly into the chair, placing his cane beside him. Pulling the microphone toward him, he favored the jury with a yellow-toothed smile.

"Good morning, Mr. Steinberg," said Gregory Quantrill, smiling at him.

"Not so good a morning. I haven't been down here in years

and you've got all this traffic and smog now and the parking is terrible."

There were titters in the courtroom. The judge smiled. Across from Kate, Corey Lanier put her notepad away and leaned back in her seat to enjoy this testimony. Steinberg would not be an easy witness for either Quantrill or Marquez; mavericks never were. However amusing he might be, the essential question remained: what did he have to offer?

"Mr. Steinberg, where were you on the morning of May twenty-ninth of last year?"

"Was that the day that poor woman was murdered just two doors down?"

"Yes it was, sir."

"Then I was home."

"Would you tell the court and this jury what happened that morning?"

"Yes sir. Not much in our house, thank God. The wife and I finished packing up and we went off to New Orleans to visit my daughter."

"When did you leave the house, sir?"

"It was five minutes after seven."

"How do you know it was that exact time?"

"Because I looked at my watch."

Kate was listening tensely. Thus far, there was no deviation from anything either of the Steinbergs had told her.

"Besides, we were late," Steinberg added. "My son-in-law was late."

Son-in-law? He had made no mention of any son-in-law.

"What time was your son-in-law supposed to be there, sir?"

"At six-thirty. We weren't flying to New Orleans, it's not so much fun on planes these days," he said with a knowing look at the jury, "but there's all the traffic and we wanted to—"

"Yes sir. Did you see or hear anything unusual before you left your house?"

"Nothing. No gunshots or anything like that. Neither did the wife."

"Objection, hearsay," Marquez said, only because it was expected; Steinberg could only testify for himself, not his wife. Leaning back in her chair, taking no notes, Marquez was watching Steinberg intently.

"Sustained," said Terrell.

Steinberg turned to the judge. "What does that mean?"

"It means—" Pushing his glasses up on his nose, the judge replied, "It means Mr. Quantrill will ask you another question, Mr. Steinberg."

"What a rigamarole," Steinberg said.

"Mr. Steinberg," Quantrill said, "did you look out at the street?"

"Sure. I was watching for Lenny. He's always late. You know how it is," he said directly to the jury. "With family he figures he can always be late, what can we do?"

The jury sat relaxed, all of them smiling at him.

"Lenny, your son-in-law, what is his full name, sir?"

"That's Leonard David Berman."

"And where was he coming from, sir?"

"From some hotel out by Pomona, I think. They had to stop there because they got away so late the night before."

"He was coming in from out of town?"

No, please no, thought Kate. If she could see her own face, she knew it would have gone pale.

"Sure he was coming in from out of town," Steinberg said. "Why else would he be staying in some burg like Pomona?"

"Where do your son-in-law and daughter live, Mr. Steinberg?"

"Las Vegas. Lenny sells real estate there."

"What kind of car was your son-in-law driving, sir?"

Kate braced herself for what she knew was coming.

"Your honor," Alicia Marquez said, rising to her feet, "the People object. The People object to what is clearly ambush tactics by the defense. The People have received absolutely no discovery related to this witness—"

"Your honor," Quantrill said, "that's ridiculous. The People know that we came late into this case. The People had the same access to this witness we did, the People—"

"Approach," snapped the judge, glaring at Quantrill.

Amid the general commotion of the two lawyers and the court reporter making their way toward the judge, Corey Lanier whispered, "What's that smell, Detective? Never mind, I recognize it—it's a smoking gun."

Kate did not look at her or respond. Coincidence, she thought. What would be the odds against such a coincidence? But then, as her father had often said, there's really no such thing as coincidence because when you think about the randomness of life, it's all coincidence.

Some minutes later, her face impassive but her posture rigid, Marquez returned to the defense table.

"Mr. Steinberg," the judge said, casting a glance of undisguised displeasure at Quantrill, "you may answer the question."

"What kind of car, you wanted to know," Steinberg said. "He's doing real good with his real estate," he said, turning to the jury. "A real chip off the old block even though he's gone off to such a place to do it. It was a Mercedes-Benz. Brand-new, a lovely car. His first trip in it, and Lenny and Deborah were driving us to New Orleans to visit my other daughter, Leah."

There was a low murmur in the courtroom, a stirring, the

shuffling of feet. Kate looked at Marquez. To her credit, she remained expressionless.

"What color, Mr. Steinberg?" Quantrill asked.

"Black. The classy color."

"Did it have a license plate yet, sir?"

"Nope. It was so new it still had the paper gizmo the dealer puts on there."

She had checked the sales records for the state of California. Had this son-in-law resided in the state, she might have had a chance. Out of state, with a different name, no chance. Nonetheless, this was all her fault; she could not use the excuse of having no way of knowing about an out-of-state car registered to Leonard Berman. Every interview hung on asking the right questions. Neither she nor the District Attorney's investigator had asked the right questions of the Steinbergs. Quantrill's investigator had.

"Were you looking out the window when Lenny parked, sir?" Quantrill asked, smiling at him.

"Sure was."

"So you saw him park the car."

"Sure did. He parked it like it was a donkey driving. He was in a hurry, he was late, he knew I'd be mad."

"Was your daughter in the car?"

"Nope, she was waiting at the hotel in Pomona for us to get her on the way back out of town. My Deborah, she's a smart girl."

"Did Lenny come into the house?"

"Yeah. He came in." Steinberg shook his head. "The wife, she insists he has to have coffee and a bagel and cream cheese, she's got it all ready for him. I keep looking at my watch, wanting him to hurry up and eat. So that's how I know we left at five after seven."

Kate slumped in her seat. So much for their best evidence in placing Douglas Talbot at the scene. Events in a courtroom were all theater, and she did not need to look at the jury to gauge the impact Steinberg had made.

"The man wearing the brown suit sitting at that table," Quantrill said, pointing. "He's Mr. Talbot, the defendant. Mr. Steinberg, do you know him?"

Steinberg looked over at the defense table. "I've never laid eyes on him till this minute."

"Thank you, sir, I have no further questions."

Steinberg reached for his cane. "Just one moment, sir," Judge Terrell said. "The other attorney may have some questions for you."

Marquez said grimly, "I have no questions for this witness."

Steinberg gripped his cane. "Such a rigamarole," he said.

"Your honor," Gregory Quantrill said, "we have no further witnesses. The defense rests."

CHAPTER

TWELVE

"The bastard!" Alicia Marquez fumed as she stalked into her office ahead of Kate. "He's been sitting on this, planning his strategy around the Steinbergs the whole time. Not giving us his investigator's report—what a crock. The judge said as much right to his face and on the record. But Terrell's got no choice, Kate—this is eyewitness testimony, he's got his eye on the Appellate Court, he had to let it in. The fifteen hundred bucks or whatever Terrell comes up with for a sanction— Quantrill's gonna pay it with a great big smile on his smug face." She slammed a hand on her desk as she went behind it.

"I'm really sorry, Alicia," Kate said disconsolately, sinking into a chair across from Marquez in her tiny cluttered office in the Criminal Courts Building.

"Bag that. I'm just blowing off steam." Kicking off her shoes, Marquez pulled off her suit jacket and tossed it over the credenza. She poured two glasses of water from a carafe. "It happens all the time, maybe not as big a yank on the rug under me like this one, but it happens. You should see the garbage cases I've been handed and expected to win. This case—it's professionally investigated, well documented, clean, all there—one of the best I've ever prosecuted. You and Joe are real pros. This was and still is a great case."

Kate nodded, accepted the glass of water, and drank a little of it. If only she could add scotch.

Marquez sat down at her desk and contemplated Kate. "We're still in a very strong position. My sons would call this case primo. Look at this defendant, this piece of excrement. You think the jury can't see how his own children won't even look at him? Here's a man who's a stalker, a wife beater, a child beater—"

"Worst of all, a child molester," Kate finished. "And we can't bring so much as a sniff of it into evidence. They get in everything on their side, but we can't."

"Yes, but that's the game we have to play, Kate, you've always known that. The monster he is—it's there in plain sight for the jury. The more character witnesses Quantrill puts on, the more he tries to perfume his skunk of a client—I mean, what does that show? He's had this all schemed out for timing, but there's still my closing argument. I get to put it all back in perspective. I get to remind them all about Douglas Talbot. Whatever Quantrill counters with, I still get the last word. I know you didn't have much confidence in me going in—"

"Alicia, I have nothing but respect for you," Kate said, meaning it. "I don't see how anyone could have prosecuted this case with greater determination. Or feeling."

Marquez looked momentarily flustered, then gratified. "Believe me, I appreciate that. I have an idea of how we can turn Steinberg's testimony right back on Quantrill. If you'll trust me a little further, I promise you we'll nail this bastard."

Smiling, Kate got up; Marquez reached to her; they clasped hands.

"You're a good prosecutor and a good person, Alicia."

"Kate, you're a great cop."

Walking down the hallway past the warren of ADA offices, Kate wished she could shake her dread and somehow absorb Alicia Marquez's confidence and believe her promise of victory. She wished she could cast off the premonition that after tomorrow's closing arguments, when all was said and done, when the jury came back, Talbot was going to walk. And it would be all her fault.

DRIVING THE SANTA MONICA FREEWAY IN rush-hour traffic, she tried to decide between going to the station, where she would have to bring both Cameron and Lieutenant Walcott up to date, face to face, on her role in the setback in the Talbot trial, or to do it from home, where there would be no Aimee. Maggie was at the Nightwood Bar, and Kate did not want to go anywhere near a bar. If she went home, she would drink. So . . . the station was it.

Her cell phone rang. Maneuvering into the slow lane while she dug it out of her jacket, she flipped it open and glanced at the caller ID. She did not recognize the number. Aimee, maybe it was Aimee. "Kate Delafield," she answered.

"I hear you're looking for me." The voice was low, and held an odd, indefinable familiarity. Kate could hear traffic noise on the line: the call was coming from a pay phone. "This is Dylan Harrison."

Kate blinked in surprise. And relief. At least she would not have to confirm to the Harrisons their worst fear, that their missing daughter was dead. "I'm glad to hear from you," she said.

"Why?"

"I'm glad to know you're all right."

"You don't even know me."

No I don't, Kate thought, and so far you've been nothing but a royal pain in the neck. "Where are you?"

"What do you want with me?"

There was firmness to the voice; she didn't sound like a typical sixteen-year-old. Except of course for the rudeness. Kate wanted to say: nothing, you little snot, and hang up. "Look," she said. "I'm on the freeway. Give me a second to pull over."

She put the phone down, took the La Cienega off-ramp. Parked at the curb, she said to Dylan, "I have a message from your mother."

"I figured as much. I've had all the messages from my parents I need to hear. Ever."

"I understand that. But—"

"No way do you understand that."

"I definitely do understand that," Kate said. "In case you don't know, I'm your lesbian aunt."

"Yeah, I figured that, too. From how my dad acted. You'd think he met Hitler. Doesn't that tell you anything?"

"Sure it does. Your mother wants you to know you can come to her for help. Without strings, without interference from your father."

"That's how she is. Stepping in to fix things only after they're broken. You don't know my mother. Or my father."

"No I don't. I do know this. I'm a cop and the streets here—"

"—are better than my home life. Less risky than up north."

The "less risky" business didn't make sense. Being a lesbian teen anywhere was no picnic, but small California towns were hardly the hellholes they used to be, and L.A. had more predators than the jungles of Brazil. "Why don't we meet and talk for a few minutes," Kate said. "Where are you?"

"Forget it. You'll just pick me up and have me shipped home in handcuffs. Message received, okay?"

"Wait. Don't hang up. I promise I won't ship you anywhere." She was a cop—she was allowed to lie—but damned if she knew what she would or should do with Dylan Harrison. *Maggie's right. I don't know enough about my own community. I haven't a clue what a good alternative might be.* "I give you my word, all I want is a meeting."

"Where? When?"

"Right now. Wherever you say. I'm on La Cienega, where are you?"

"West Hollywood. Santa Monica Boulevard."

At least it wasn't Hollywood or Venice. "I'll come straight up La Cienega and look for you on the corner of Santa Monica, should be no more than ten minutes. Okay? Watch for a Saturn. Blue."

"A Saturn," Dylan repeated, disdain in her tone, presumably at so uncool a car.

FIFTEEN MINUTES LATER, CIRCLING THE block for the second time, an aggravating task on this part of La Cienega, Kate peered at the young jean-clad males clustered on the corner and snarled, "Where the hell are you?" No sign of Dylan this time either, only these hustlers who once more stared into her car as she slowed down to drift past.

One of them gestured vigorously to her and pointed to himself. Kate rolled down the window.

"Kate Delafield?" the young man called.

Kate recognized the voice. "Dylan?" she said incredulously. She keyed the electronic lock of the passenger door. *Holy shit. No wonder nobody knew her from the flyer.*

"Yeah, it's me. The real me," Dylan said, and opened the door and folded her lanky self into the car.

Taking a long look at her as she pulled slowly away from the curb, Kate did not speak, absorbing what she saw. A slender, bony, flat-chested figure with dark hair in a mannish cut no more than an inch in length. Low-slung jeans over narrow hips, with a wide belt and large silver belt buckle. A white shirt open at the throat, sleeves rolled to the elbows of sinewy arms, a tattoo visible on the left forearm. She had seen a spectrum of lesbians in her time, ranging from ultrafeminine to bull dyke, and Dylan Harrison was at the farthest end of bull dyke: she could not look more masculine unless she exposed a penis.

"Fooled you, didn't I," Dylan said, looking pleased with herself.

Kate looked up from the body, to the face. The in-person resemblance to herself was jarring, far more evident than it was in the photograph Kate owned. Dylan Harrison's eyes were her eyes—the same light blue color. She had her nose. Her lips, the shape and set of them. Her chin, her head. Her hairline. Her ears. Masculine, Kate thought. I never dreamed I could look so masculine . . .

Behind them, a car honked. Kate pulled over to the first open space she saw on Santa Monica Boulevard so that she could frankly stare at her without causing an accident. "How tall are you?" she asked faintly.

"Five-nine. Same as you, I bet." Dylan was conducting her own candid scrutiny of Kate.

"Right. Same as me." Had she ever had that same slim figure at Dylan's age?

Dylan grinned. Kate's grin. "My father can blame you for the pervert gene. That should make him feel better."

Spotting a car moving out of a parking place, Kate pulled into it. "How about we get something to drink," she said.

They settled on an open-air coffeehouse on Santa Monica and took a front table at Dylan's request. An ankle crossed over a knee, she sat back, her hungry gaze following same-sex couples sauntering along the street in the warm late afternoon. She looked, Kate thought, for all the world like a teenage boy. As Dylan picked up her coffee mug, Kate saw that the tattoo was an interlocked design of male and female symbols.

"I can't get used to being here," Dylan said wonderingly. "This is the happiest I've ever been in my whole life."

Surprised, saddened by the comment, but believing it, Kate asked, "Was it really that tough at home? No chance they'd ever come around? Your mother seems . . ."

She trailed off as Dylan fixed her light blue eyes on her. They held anger and defiance; but Kate could also see a depth of vulnerability. And pain. Dylan said, "You don't understand."

"You keep saying that. I don't know what it is you think I don't understand. When I grew up, it was the inner circle of hell. We didn't dare be out, we never had places like this—" She gestured around her to the obviously nonheterosexual clientele of this coffeehouse.

"I know all that. I really do. I've read about it. What my parents won't accept is, I'm not female. Never have been. I tried to tell them and they won't even begin to hear it." Studying Kate's face, she added, "I see they're not alone."

Kate knew she had not changed expression—she'd had too many years of practice in interview rooms. Dylan's interpretation was based on hyperacuteness to the absence of response. "Give me a chance here. Why do you think you're not female?"

"My body—it's a mistake," Dylan said intensely, her shoulders hunching, her hand tightening around her coffee mug. "I've known it as long as I can remember."

The newest thing, Kate thought. The transgender, transsexual trend. Dylan was certainly young enough to be affected by it. Looking at the tattoo on Dylan's arm, she remembered a discussion with Aimee and her own contention that tattoos had been part of the origin for the transgender issue, the urge to redecorate and somehow claim your own body.

Nothing was ever good enough for some people, especially kids. As per usual, some of them took body transformation too far, turned it into a crusade and demanded their beliefs be considered rights, be tolerated and accepted. Self-mutilation to the point of gender bending was simply the newest test of society's sufferance, girls wanting to be accepted as males, or boys who thought they could act like women. The exaggerated, cartoon femininity of male to female transsexuals was particularly ridiculous, she had argued to Aimee, even offensive, their notion of femininity an insult to women.

Aimee had disagreed: "Why aren't they in the same boat as we are? Down through the ages we've all had to hide our difference. Like us, they don't hurt or threaten anyone—except with their difference. This isn't anything new, Kate. These people have become visible, that's all—just like we did."

Keeping her face and her tone impartial, Kate said to Dylan, "You're attracted to women, though, is that right?"

Dylan smiled. "That, too, as long as I can remember."

"Me, too, as long as I can remember. It took me a while to be comfortable that I was lesbian . . ." *Like, most of my life.* "So I can understand that maybe you feel your gender isn't—"

"Did you ever want to be a boy?"

"Sure."

"No, I mean did you really *want* to be a *boy.*"

The forcefulness of the words told Kate this was a crucial question, and she took time to sip coffee and give Dylan a considered answer. "I envied boys," she finally said. "Envied that sense of entitlement they have, that superiority they just assume is theirs, the freedom that gets handed to them on a silver platter. I grew up wanting their freedom. Actually, I guess what I really wanted was for society's expectations of boys to apply to me." She indicated Dylan's jeans and shirt. "I wanted to wear their clothes—they give your body total freedom. Skirts, dresses—they've never seemed anything but straitjackets. So hell yes, I wanted to be a boy."

"Okay. But did you want a boy's body?"

Again she reflected. "I like men's bodies. They're . . . simple, efficient. For a while I bought into that whole propaganda thing about nature designing male and female bodies to fit together, so if having a penis meant I could please a woman better, then I wanted one. Then I found out lesbians don't need a penis at all—we're better lovers than most men."

"You still haven't answered the question," Dylan said with a faint smile, pointing a finger at her.

Kate contemplated her. Sixteen, she thought. Either she was
remarkably bright or she had been thinking about this issue for
a very long time, or both. She said to Dylan: "Maybe I can't.
You know, you might have a chance of your parents coming
around about you being a lesbian. Transgender—" She shook
her head. "What I don't understand is why it's not good enough
for you to be a lesbian."

"Because I'm not. Let me ask you this: Did you ever hate
your body?"

"Hate it?" Kate answered. "Put off by it sometimes, yeah. I
wanted smaller breasts, flatter hips. I always could do without
the periods. But basically I'm okay, I've always been okay with
my woman's body."

"I hate mine," Dylan said vehemently. "Having periods
makes me want to puke. I hate having breasts, don't want
them—"

"Where are these so-called breasts, what did you do with
them?" Kate inquired mischievously. Dylan's chest looked perfectly flat.

"They're wrapped down tight. Ace bandage."

"Must be uncomfortable."

"Yeah. It will be till I get rid of them."

"You want surgery?"

"I want everything. Hormones, everything. The minute I
can. The minute I'm old enough. I wish I could slice them off
right now. They feel like a birth defect."

Vaguely offended by Dylan's fervor, Kate reminded herself:
She's sixteen. A memory of Aimee intruded, her mouth and the
fierce pleasure of it on Kate's breasts. Yes, she liked being a
woman. She asked, "Have you been with someone yet, made
love?"

"Yeah, I had a girlfriend. Not for long." Hunched over, Dylan gazed into her coffee mug.

"For someone who claims to be attracted to women," Kate said carefully, "what you say about our bodies sounds like you hate us."

Dylan jerked her gaze up to her. "I love women, love their bodies. I just don't want one for myself. You heard of babies being switched at birth, ending up with the wrong parents? I'm a male whose body got switched. I figure there's somebody out there with a male body who's just as damn unhappy having the body that belongs to me."

Was I ever so self-possessed? Kate wondered. Was I ever so sure about anything when I was sixteen? No, not till I was twenty-five and met Anne. Kate switched topics. "Tell me your personal situation."

"I take it you're all done with what we were talking about, it's all you need to know to make up your mind, right?"

Kate allowed a trace of impatience to show. "No, I'm just asking a question."

Dylan shrugged. "Fine. I'm staying with some people like me."

"You mean, transgender?"

"And transsexual."

"Where? Who are these people?"

"I'm not telling you. How you feel about this, I don't trust you. I'm not telling you one damn thing about my personal situation."

"Look at it this way. I'm the police." Kate smiled at her. "It's to your advantage to get along with me. It's up to you whether you let me think about you, see what I can do about you, or whether I call right now for backup and take you in."

"You promised," Dylan said, shock spreading over her face.

Suddenly she looked all of sixteen. And far too naive to be out on the streets. "It's moot, Dylan. You know what that means? It means any promise is worthless if I can leave here and issue an all-points, state-wide bulletin with your current physical description. What difference does it make if I pick you up now or have you picked up tomorrow or the next day?"

Dylan stared at her in hostility. "Okay, there's a household of us. A dozen. We live in a house in Hollywood."

"How big is the house?"

"Small, couple of bedrooms. We use sleeping bags, we manage."

"How did you find this place?"

"The Internet. A TG chat room. I don't know what I'd have done without the Internet and chat rooms and Instant Messaging. I found all the lesbian and gay stuff, but when I found transgender, I knew I'd found home. Where I needed to be."

"When did this happen?"

"It started . . . maybe two years ago."

"You were fourteen?" Kate asked faintly. What had the Internet wrought?

"Going on fifteen. From the stories I heard, I knew I had to figure out what I needed to do, how to get away and not let my parents get a clue about my plans. My dad was nagging me every minute that I had to dress in female drag, nagging about boyfriends and proms—I knew I had to get out, I couldn't stand staying home much longer."

"What about money? How much do you have?"

"Lots. I saved nearly two thousand bucks," she said proudly.

It was a lot, but long term, not much. "Are you carrying it?" At Dylan's head shake she asked, "Where is it?"

"Didn't dare get a bank account so I buried it. Two places."

Kate nodded. "What are you doing about school?"

"School?" Dylan looked at her as if the word were an absurdity.

Dylan had to go to school. Kate knew not to say anything. "School been rough for you?"

"Bad enough. Could have been worse. I wasn't like Russell—he's a femmy gay boy. Or Leroy—he'll be an MTF as sure as I'm sitting here."

"MTF?" queried Kate.

"Male to female. I'm an FTM, female to male. The MTFs, they're the transgenders with trouble. Getting-killed-type trouble, like Gwen Araujo up near San Francisco."

"True," Kate said, remembering the case of the male youngster up north in Newark who had been beaten to death by four young males for dressing as a woman. "When your two grand runs out—"

"That'll take forever, the way I'm living."

"Trust me on this—in L.A. it'll run out. What do you plan to do then?"

"Be a mechanic. I'm already working on a deal where I can be an apprentice. I gotta go," Dylan said, looking at her watch.

"That's quite a timepiece," Kate said. It was polished steel, with a heavy band and numerous gauges on a face that took up much of her wrist.

Dylan looked fondly at the instrument. "Buying this—what a blast. I always wanted a watch like this." She touched the tattoo on her arm. "Getting this, getting my hair cut, buying these clothes, my shoes—God, it was . . . it was awesome. I belong in these clothes. I tell you, I'm happy. I just want everybody to leave me the hell alone. Including you."

"I'll make a deal with you. If you'll give me the phone number where you are—"

"Can't do that. I gave these people my word. I can't tell you where I am."

Kate knew she meant it, that this was where the line was drawn. She took out her notebook and pen. "Then I want you to check in with me at these times at these numbers—"

Dylan said proudly, "I've got a job, you know. It won't be that easy."

"Yes it will. The next time I see you, I'll give you a cell phone. Dylan, you're a minor—I shouldn't be giving you any rope at all. Either you do what I say or I'll have you picked up—case closed. Do we understand each other?"

"Yeah. Thanks for nothing." She got up, grabbed the paper from Kate, tossed five dollars on the table, and stalked off before Kate could say she'd pick up the tab.

Kate looked approvingly at the figure striding away. Tossing that money down—it was something she'd have loved to have done at age sixteen.

AT HOME, AFTER A FEW SIPS OF HER SECOND scotch of the day, Kate sighed in resignation and picked up the phone to call the station.

After she finished her recitation of Jerome Steinberg's testimony and the day's disaster in court, Cameron said, "I know I'm talking to a wall, but what the hell—hello, wall. Don't take this one on board, Kate. It's not your fault. It's one of those rare combinations of things that turn into a perfect storm. The Steinbergs didn't volunteer anything to us because they didn't know what they knew when you and the DA's office talked to them. You asked if they'd seen a strange car, and they said they hadn't, which was true. A car belonging to their son-in-law was not a strange car. You had to ask it that way and not identify the car so they'd volunteer what they knew, not agree with something you said, right?"

"Right," Kate said. It was indeed the correct questioning technique.

"Quantrill's guy didn't have to observe any niceties. He could just say, Did you see a new Mercedes-Benz, and they'd say, Sure, our son-in-law's. They probably didn't know what they knew till he talked to them. From what you say about Jerome, the Steinbergs also probably thought the defense investigator was a cop, and Quantrill's guy wouldn't bother to correct them—they never do, to get people to talk. So that's why they didn't call us."

"Right," she said. She had already considered the same scenario. It was still her fault.

"Right. I'm talking to a wall. Look, let me cover this with Walcott. Let me do this, Kate."

"She'll breathe fire all over you, Joe. It's my responsibility."

"This is your lucky day—I'm wearing my asbestos suit," he said, and she could hear the smile in his voice. "Kate, anything new with Aimee?"

"Nope. Miss Marple's pretty upset."

"I bet she is. Kate—you want to talk?"

After a moment she said, "I'm not very good at that, Joe."

"Yeah, so? Neither am I. It's something we've always respected in each other. But sometimes not talking is not so terrific an idea—you know that. We're good partners together, Kate. Better you should talk to me than drown your body and soul in booze. Or"—he chuckled self-consciously—"like we did when Janine walked out on me, we could maybe compromise and do both."

She was smiling as she answered, "Sounds like a plan. Let's see how things go."

"In the meantime, are you taking care of yourself?"

She looked at the drink in her hand. It would be her last of the night no matter what. "Yeah, Joe. Thanks. Thanks for everything."

THIRTEEN

Watching the courtroom fill up from where she sat in the fifth row, Kate was startled to see Lieutenant Carolina Walcott, well turned out in a beige pantsuit with a coral blouse, stride in. She seated herself next to Kate. "Thought I'd sit in on the closings," she said, and added with a dimpled smile, "Having nothing better to do."

"I'm sure," Kate said. "Glad to have you here." As busy as Walcott was, her appearance here was a significant show of support, and Kate was grateful.

As more people filed in, some sixth sense told Kate to glance over her shoulder. "The Talbots," Kate said, leaning toward Walcott. "Allan, Lisa—and Rikki. She's the one in the middle. First time she's been in court."

The three Talbots' faces matched the somberness of their dark suits. Kate had not seen Rikki Talbot in many months, and she studied the young woman as she made her way to the first row of seats behind the defense, walking slowly, precariously between brother and sister as if heavily medicated. Kate felt certain she was. The person Kate had first seen in a photograph in Lisa's living room had mutated into a shapeless mound of flesh, her eyes receded in a doughy face. As Rikki gingerly seated herself, she momentarily faced the courtroom, her eyes seeming dull, unfocused.

"She's a train wreck," murmured Walcott.

Kate nodded, remembering Lisa making the analogy with Cameron of her family as a car wreck. One fatality and three injuries, Lisa had said, one of them critical—meaning Rikki. Only the driver had escaped unscathed. Kate looked balefully at Douglas Talbot; he had turned and was watching his children.

Alicia Marquez was addressing the jury from the podium: "Ladies and gentlemen, look at the evidence. Use your God-given common sense. If you do those two things, you'll automatically accomplish the third, which is"—she pointed toward Douglas Talbot without looking at him—"to find this defendant guilty of the crime of first-degree murder."

A tactically sound opening, Kate thought, and Marquez was presenting herself well to the jury in her navy-blue suit and white blouse. She stood erect beside easels bearing an enlarged photo of Victoria Talbot, a poster holding a large schematic of the house and its grounds, plus several other photographs of rooms within the house. Only a single folder of notes lay open on the podium.

"The defense has taken you down the side alley of criticizing the police investigation of this case. But the evidence adds up—and it overwhelmingly points to this defendant.

"On the night of May twenty-eighth, Allan Talbot called his mother. She did not answer. Did not call him back. The fact that the Mercedes-Benz seen outside Victoria Talbot's house did not belong to the defendant gives even wider latitude for Douglas Talbot to have committed the murder of his ex-wife. It means the defendant could have arrived even earlier. It means he could have gone to the victim's house after he left the shooting range the night before. Those lights Alice Cathcart saw burning at two o'clock in the morning in the Talbot residence— they may be why the victim did not answer her son's call nor call him back: Douglas Talbot was in the house that a restraining order had expressly barred him from entering."

Kate watched approvingly. So this was the strategy for turning Jerome Steinberg's testimony around. Marquez's interpretation could indeed fit the circumstances . . .

"Only one person can account for the defendant's whereabouts during the previous night and at the time of Victoria Talbot's death the following morning: Marta Gonzalez."

As Marquez reminded the jury in detail of the reasons Marta Gonzalez had zero credibility as an alibi witness for Douglas Talbot, Kate studied the inner courtroom.

At the defense table, Gregory Quantrill never took his gaze from the jury except to make an occasional brief note on a legal pad. Talbot, wearing a gray suit and pale blue shirt, watched only Marquez, his face impassive, a pose he had successfully managed throughout the trial. The jury was listening intently but, save for juror number ten, was unreadable. Number ten's head was cocked to the side, his arms crossed over his paunch in a classic posture of resistance to Marquez's argument. The Talbot siblings were motionless, holding hands as they followed the proceedings.

Marquez continued, "Why did Victoria Talbot let this man

in? This man who had blighted her life, who had time and again physically attacked both her and her son? This man, who destroyed the childhood of her daughters with his drinking and abuse? This man, who put the mother of his children in the hospital with his escalating violence? This man, who would not accept the decree of the divorce court that she was now his ex-wife? This man, who made harassing phone calls and sent email messages to her every single day? This man, who drove obsessively past her house? This man, who refused up until the day she died to give her a moment's peace?"

Two of the women on the jury—the oldest two—had given almost imperceptible head shakes during this recitation; Kate's hope was that they would provide moral direction in the jury room.

"Perhaps Victoria Talbot had formulated the misguided hope that she could reestablish some kind of relationship after three years of separation enforced by a divorce decree. Perhaps she simply decided to confront or plead with her tormentor to cease his constant harassment. Or—consider this—perhaps Douglas Talbot somehow forced his way in."

Marquez consulted a note in her folder. "Why did Douglas Talbot visit a shooting range the night before the murder? Because it would explain his possession and firing of a gun. How convenient for him that his former wife still had the gun he had given her years before. Little did this defendant dream we would still be able to identify it as the murder weapon, thanks to the police work Mr. Quantrill so maligns—very good police work, exemplary police work.

"Whenever Douglas Talbot arrived at the house, however he got into the house, however he planned this crime, whatever Victoria Talbot did or did not do to let him in, this much is clear: It cost her her life."

Marquez stepped from the podium to indicate on the easel the photograph of Victoria Talbot. "Ladies and gentlemen, there was a particular cruelty to this crime, a callousness, a pure vindictiveness that has this defendant's signature all over it. It was particularly cruel because of where Victoria Talbot died. In the house that was her symbol of independence, in her favorite room, at her desk, looking out at the garden that was her passion. We may never know whether she sat there of her own choosing, realizing she would die, or whether this defendant forced her to sit there to be killed. What we do know is that this defendant"—she shook a finger at Douglas Talbot— "stood beside her and fired a bullet into her head. We do know that he splattered her blood and brains all over the window overlooking the garden she loved."

Movement caught Kate's eye: Rikki Talbot shuddering, and Douglas Talbot vigorously shaking his head, his shoulders rigid, the hand holding his pen clenched into a fist.

"Next came his callousness. You've heard the investigating detectives in this case testify to the almost surgical cleanliness in the house. And the fingerprint expert, Mr. Baker, who gave sworn testimony that in his twenty-three years of experience this was a crime scene as devoid of fingerprints as any he had ever seen. What does this tell us? It tells us that this defendant made certain no shred of any evidence of his presence would be traceable back to him.

"Next came the vindictiveness. From the manner of Victoria Talbot's death, we have a clear measure of the depth of this defendant's escalating rage at his ex-wife for daring to end the abusive dictatorship that was his family life. We know that after this defendant murdered his wife, he remained in the house with her dead body, putting the final touches on her murder.

He scooped up items of jewelry to make this crime look like a robbery. We know the bullet in Victoria Talbot's back was postmortem—fired into her body after her death. So filled with rage was this defendant that he walked back to where his wife lay murdered. So filled with rage was this defendant that he fired yet another shot into the body whose brains and blood he had already splattered all over the window."

The women and several of the men on the jury stared at Douglas Talbot, who continued to shake his head. Juror number ten's arms were no longer crossed, Kate saw. Like the rest, he sat hunched forward, motionless, held by Marquez's summation.

She moved over to the schematic of the house, and for the next few minutes laid out Douglas Talbot's probable movements through the house, then his escape into the backyard, leaving the back door ajar, then into the hedge, where he knew, from driving past the house many times, he could conceal himself until the coast was clear, then make his way out onto the street. "Leaving this bloody scene of horror for his own son to find," Marquez concluded, "leaving the body of his ex-wife and the mother of his children for his own son to find."

Marquez resumed her place at the podium. "These are the facts of this case. We have proved them to you. Thank you for your kind attention. Mr. Quantrill will soon address you with the defense's version of the events of this case. The rules of the state of California allow me to return with a closing statement. Then Judge Terrell will provide instructions about how the law applies in arriving at your verdict. I will ask again what I ask of you now: to bring in a just verdict. To hold Douglas Albert Talbot responsible for the reprehensible crime he has committed—the first-degree murder of his ex-wife, the mother of his three children. Thank you."

"LADIES AND GENTLEMEN," GREGORY QUAN-
trill said from the podium, "the prosecution has asked you to
look at the evidence and then use your common sense. On behalf of Mr. Talbot, I ask you to do no less. Contrary to Ms.
Marquez's histrionic contention that I've led you down some
byway, I've tried to keep our part of the case direct and simple
and to the point. Other than the diagram of the house, we have
no photos, no posters, no fancy exhibits to display. Because
this is indeed a very simple case."

Quantrill's voice was modulated, conversational, occasionally dropping in pitch so that the jurors had to lean forward to
hear him—a good tactic to keep them attentive, Kate knew.
He, too, was dressed in navy blue, apparently the universal
choice for closing arguments. Black was too funereal; gray too
bland and uninteresting. Like Marquez, his body language was
muted; he used few physical gestures in making his points, pre-
ferring the jurors to concentrate on his facial expressions and
his words.

"The prosecution's evidence is very easy to look at. They
have next to none. What little they have has proved to be, as I
promised you in my opening statement, tissue-thin. They've
brought in a truckload of conjecture. They've conducted a
wholesale trashing of Marta Gonzalez. Why? Because her testimony provides Mr. Talbot with a solid alibi. She has given her
sworn testimony—and we dispute their contention that Ms.
Gonzalez would come to this court and lie to you to protect a
murderer. You've seen this young woman and can judge her
character—her honesty and sincerity, her dignity under ruth-
less cross-examination.

"There is not a scintilla of evidence that Mr. Talbot was

anywhere near the house in Hancock Park either the night before or on the morning of the murder. So there is nothing left
for them to do but impugn the testimony and character of
Marta Gonzalez.

"The prosecution has its own very serious problems with
the truth. They called witness after witness—Marjorie Durant,
Gene Durant, Alice Cathcart, Paul Jankowski—to elicit testimony about a car purported to be Mr. Talbot's parked outside
Mrs. Talbot's house. You would have accepted this sworn and
sincere testimony in good faith and taken it into the jury room
with you except that we, the defense, found and interviewed
Mr. and Mrs. Steinberg and determined that the Mercedes-
Benz in question belongs to their daughter and son-in-law. The
prosecution has been forced to try and make lemonade out of
this lemon." Quantrill's voice had risen from its conversational
tone; a half-smile further conveyed his derision. "They smear
Marta Gonzalez, and characterize the investigation as exemplary police work when the question that should be asked is,
what else did they miss?"

Here it really comes, Kate thought, acutely aware of Walcott next to her, and knowing the jury was observing her. Her
heart rate accelerating, she concentrated on watching Gregory
Quantrill, and on holding a facial expression that conveyed
disagreement and incredulity.

"The police work in this case is nothing less than shoddy.
Nothing less than sloppy and short-sighted. The homicide detectives assigned to the investigation are hardly incompetent—
they have many years of experience between them. But you
heard their testimony. You saw and heard for yourselves how
they decided on the very morning of the murder that Mr. Talbot was their man, and went after him like heat-seeking mis-
siles. Their investigation of this case excluded all other

possibilities and led straight into this courtroom, to putting an innocent man on trial for murder. Only one obstacle stands between their botched investigation and this innocent man spending the rest of his days in prison: you, you, you, you . . ." Quantrill took time to point at each of the twelve jurors.

"What a ham," Walcott muttered from beside her.

Kate nodded, but she thought: It's working. As Quantrill singled out the jurors, each one seemed to sit a little straighter.

"The prosecution has concocted a scenario for this murder. We don't need to concoct a thing. We can tell you what happened. The evening before Mrs. Talbot's death, Douglas Talbot left work, went home for dinner, then made his way out to the Angeles Shooting Range. We have witnesses that confirm he did this. He is an American citizen with the constitutional right to own guns, and no matter how much the prosecution may attack him for it, he has used his guns for target practice on a regular basis.

"The next morning he drove directly to his company and arrived there at the usual time. He conducted business as usual, did everything as usual. Until he heard the shocking news about the murder of his ex-wife. And then the detectives showed up. And at that point, ladies and gentlemen, this grieving man became a murder suspect and his life became a living nightmare."

Like the jury, she too shifted her gaze to Douglas Talbot. He sat unmoving, his head bowed. His children were staring at him.

"Ms. Marquez says that we will never know why Mrs. Talbot let Douglas into her house. Indeed we never will—because it never happened and they cannot prove that it did. We do not deny Mr. Talbot's numerous, ill-advised, and misguided attempts to reestablish contact with his wife. We do not deny they were persistent, even obsessive. This man"—he gestured to Talbot, who continued to stare down at the table—"had been married for twenty-five years to the woman who was the love of his life. This man has no history of extramarital affairs. This man revered the sacrament of marriage. This man, at the same time, was a flawed man with serious and severe substance abuse issues. A flawed man who committed violence on his family. He is also a man who finally faced his demons and dragged himself out of his sewer and cleaned himself up. You heard the testimony from friends and associates, and members of his family who came here to testify on his behalf.

"Douglas Talbot is a man who never gave up hope that reconciliation was possible with the woman he loved. At the time of her death he was a man at midlife with many more years ahead of him, with hope that a reconciliation could still happen. Why would he give up on this hope and kill the only woman he has ever loved?

"The murder weapon has never been found, and the prosecution makes much of the two Talbot children's contention that only their parents knew the combination of the box in which that weapon was kept. One parent is no longer with us to support that contention. How do we know that she did not give the combination to one of these children, or to anyone else?

"The prosecution makes much of why Mr. Talbot would not have left his fingerprints on the steel box. None of Mr. Talbot's prints were found anywhere in that house. They ask you to use your common sense—yet they themselves indulge in the most fanciful and wild guesses to account for this crime scene. There is no trace of Mr. Talbot anywhere in that house. Despite the intensive labors of the best criminalists in the city of Los Angeles, there was no DNA, not a single hair, not a single fiber—nothing belonging to Mr. Talbot. Why? Surely not because Mr. Talbot cleaned up the house. It was because Mr. Talbot was never in the house.

"Ladies and gentlemen, let's look at this so-called cleaned-up house. Assume for the sake of argument that Mr. Talbot *was* there. Why would the entire place have to be cleaned up by him? Wouldn't Mr. Talbot know the exact places where he was and where he could possibly have left fingerprints?

"Let's also look at this interval between the shots that Marjorie Durant claims she heard. Dr. Green has testified that he cannot confirm the interval between the two shots. The prosecution says to you: Don't believe Marta Gonzalez's testimony. Then they tell you: But do believe Marjorie Durant—the only witness to testify that the two shots were fired anywhere from five to ten minutes apart. The actual murderer may have shot her in the head and then immediately afterward shot her in the back as well, to make sure she was dead because people can and do survive shots to the head.

"The prosecution's case is entirely circumstantial. Entirely. They have given you their scenario as to how and why Douglas Talbot killed his ex-wife. I submit to you that their scenario is preposterous.

"Let me give you another scenario, the one that is far more logical and therefore fits quite well into that realm of common sense Ms. Marquez urged you to exercise.

"On the morning of May twenty-ninth, Mrs. Talbot gets up and looks out her back bedroom window. Sees a stranger in her yard. Makes a crucial mistake. She runs upstairs, gets the gun out of the box she keeps it in, thinking she'll wave it around and frighten this person away. She opens the back door to her yard. Her intruder gets the gun away from her—something that happens all too easily to people who have never taken instruction as to how to use a gun. He forces her into her house, into her bedroom. Maybe he's looking to assault her, or rob her, or both. He's taken advantage of a sudden opportunity and he's nervous, knowing she can identify him. The gun at her head, he forces her to sit at her desk. Maybe he hears something. And panics. Pulls the trigger. He's not sure she's dead so he shoots her again.

"He's afraid someone's heard the shots. He grabs her visible jewelry, runs out through the back door and into the yard, then into the hedge—and is gone.

"Is this scenario possible? Of course it's possible. Did the police check out other alternatives? Yes, but we submit to you that they did not pursue those leads vigorously enough. You heard their testimony, all the testimony. Given the inadequate police investigation in this case, we may never know who actually committed this crime—the trail has gone cold. The transient who wandered into this neighborhood and into Mrs. Talbot's secluded yard, or the laborer who knew the neighborhood and knew Mrs. Talbot lived alone—that actual murderer is gone.

"Something else has come out in this case that should be important in your deliberations in the jury room. Mr. Talbot was not the only member of the family estranged from his ex-wife. We know from the testimony of Marjorie Durant that the two daughters rarely saw their mother, and blamed her as well as their father for the domestic violence in their childhood. Is this important? That's for you to decide. The bullet taken from the house where the Talbots originally lived in Hancock Park— we know that younger daughter Rikki fired that shot. Why was it fired? We don't know. Is that important? You decide.

"Gunshot residue tests were never performed on any of the Talbot children. Is that important? You decide."

Kate's eyes were drawn to Rikki Talbot, who was stumbling to her feet. Involuntarily, Kate clutched at Walcott. If Rikki did anything, said anything at this crucial juncture, it could result in a mistrial. Assisted by her grim-faced brother and sister, Rikki made her way down the aisle, her gait wobbly, tears streaming down her face.

Quantrill merely threw them a quick glance and continued imperturbably. "Ladies and gentlemen, the prosecution does not have an iota of solid, direct evidence that Douglas Talbot killed his wife. No one saw him arrive at the scene. No one saw him leave the scene. There is not a trace of evidence that he was ever in the residence of his ex-wife. Mr. Talbot has suffered enough in a case that, had it been investigated properly, would never have gone this far, never have come before you. Please do justice now for this grieving man. Please bring in your un-equivocal judgment that Douglas Talbot is not guilty. Thank you."

ALICIA MARQUEZ ROSE AND MARCHED TO THE podium, taking no notes with her.

"In all my years as a prosecutor," she said in a tone of ice, "I have never heard anything more outrageous than what has just been said in this courtroom. To even suggest that the Tal-bot children had anything to do with the horrifying murder of their mother is nothing less than a travesty."

Her voice rose. "Allan Talbot found the murdered body of his mother—an image he will carry with him for the rest of his life. The Talbot daughters are not only bereft of a mother, they're forever deprived of any opportunity to heal a rift that the passage of years and their own increasing maturity may have closed. To suggest that the Talbot children are implicated in this murder is unconscionable. It is no less than a final act of abuse on the children of this supremely abusive defendant.

"Everything points to this defendant as the perpetrator of this crime. Everything. He is a man of violence, of demonstrated violence, of escalating violence, and the testimony of the Talbot children and Victoria Talbot's visit to the hospital and the X rays of the broken bones in her dead body are the proof. This defendant's history shouts from the rooftops the kind of man he is. You heard Allan Talbot testify to what his father said when Allan confronted him and asked him to leave Victoria Talbot alone: 'What God has joined together,' Douglas Talbot told his son, 'let no man put asunder.' Douglas Talbot is a man who believed he owned his wife. Owned his children. That he could do anything he wanted with them and to them. This is a defendant"—she shook a finger at Douglas Talbot—"who spent a year going to a shooting range where he undoubtedly imagined his wife's face as the target he—"

"Objection!" shouted Gregory Quantrill, getting to his feet. "Your honor, this is—"

"Sit down, Mr. Quantrill," Judge Terrell said firmly. "Wrap it up, Ms. Marquez."

"Thank you, your honor. Ladies and gentlemen, the so-called scenario the defense raises is simply preposterous. If there was a stranger in her yard, why would this woman who kept a gun in a locked box even when there were no children in the house, this woman who showed nothing but aversion to guns—why would she put an instrument she loathed in her hand when she could pick up the phone on her desk and dial nine-one-one?

"The house was untouched, the jewelry taken was a small amount of minor value. Thousands of dollars in valuables were left untouched. Victoria Talbot was not sexually assaulted, her clothing not so much as disturbed. What did happen is that she was viciously and vengefully murdered by a man who could no longer abide her independence, who could not accept that she had left him, had left him forever.

"This defendant murdered his ex-wife as she sat looking out at the garden she loved. He murdered her because she was living the life she chose, a life that did not include him.

"That's what happened, ladies and gentlemen. Not the fanciful scenario foisted on you by the defense. Douglas Talbot shot and killed Victoria Talbot, and then left her body for his son to find. *That's* what happened.

"Don't let this man get away with yet another crime against his family. We have proven our case that Douglas Talbot is guilty of murder. I trust that you will bring in that verdict. Thank you."

"She's good," Walcott murmured to Kate amid the rustle of the courtroom as Marquez returned to the prosecution table. "If I ran this world, he'd get his balls fried." She glanced at her watch. "Gotta go." As Judge Terrell began his instructions to the jury, she rose and quietly left the courtroom.

At home, Miss Marple trotted to Kate, meowing piteously. "I miss her too," Kate commiserated, leaning down to pick her up. Fluffing the fur under her chin, she murmured, "I'm sorry you're stuck with just me."

The answering machine was blinking: three messages. Holding and stroking the cat, she pushed the play button. All from Maggie, all the same: "Kate, are you there? . . . I'll call back." Her voice conveyed urgency. Kate released Miss Marple and immediately called Maggie: no answer.

The phone rang as soon as she hung up. She looked at it for a moment, an ache in her throat. Yet another way she missed Aimee. This phone was an older model, without caller ID, which had never mattered because Aimee always answered the phone when she was home, and if she wasn't, Kate let it go to the answering machine to screen her calls. She picked up the phone and said huskily, "Kate Delafield."

"Thank God you're finally there," Maggie said, her voice tremulous. "Audie's dead."

Kate blinked in shock. She knew the breast cancer was fatal but not this soon—

"Killed herself. Sleeping pills. Took an overdose. She asked a bunch of us to come over—so all of us would find her, not just one."

"Maggie, I'm so sorry," Kate said, Audie's kind, motherly face vivid in her mind. "You're still there?"

"Yeah, all of us. A detective's doing a report, I need to give a statement."

"Rainey's there?"

"Sure. In a state of collapse."

That figured. Rainey was the ex-lover who had never stopped loving this partner of many years. Just as she herself had never stopped loving Anne. And would never ever stop loving Aimee. "Why don't I come over?"

"Don't do that. We've got way too many people here as it is. I just . . . I feel horrible, I need to talk, okay?"

"Okay," Kate said softly.

"So what's going on with you?"

"I thought you wanted to talk."

"Jesus Christ, Kate—"

"Okay, okay, I've gone through two terrible days in court—so bad the jury may come in with not guilty."

"This would be the child molester and wife beater and killer?"

"The very one."

"Jesus Christ, Kate."

"That's the bad news. The good news—I think it's the good news—I heard from my niece. Who claims to be my nephew."

There was silence. Then: "Transgender?"

"Yeah."

"That explains a whole hell of a lot. She looked peaceful as can be, Kate." Kate knew Maggie was referring to Audie but was unable to say her name again and was talking about her when she could, trying to maintain control. "She left a key in an envelope taped to the door and a note that said we should come in after we all got there. The house was filled with flowers, the windows all up, sun coming in . . . She was in bed, covers pulled up neat as can be, everything lovely . . . She looked beautiful, Kate . . ."

Something, there was something in what Maggie had just said . . . She needed to think about it. As soon as possible. "Maggie," she said, "Audie had a right to end her suffering—you know that."

"She had every right. I do know that. I feel okay about that part of it. I know she made it easy as she could. I just . . . What did Dylan tell you?"

"Pretty much that she's never going home—L.A.'s better for her."

"Yeah, with a transgender I can believe it. Audie left a note for each one of us on the bed, saying she wanted to be cremated and each of us should take some of her ashes and she asked me to put some of them"—Maggie's voice broke—"at the Nightwood Bar."

"God, I'm so sorry, Maggie," Kate said, tears welling.

"So what are you going to do about this nephew?"

"I told her she has to call me three times a day and I'll get her a cell phone. I've been thinking about her, though . . ."

"Him, Kate. Get used to it. Dylan is a him."

"I don't buy that, Maggie. She's only sixteen."

"For chrissake, don't you realize you sound like her fucking *father*? TGs come into the bar, Kate, so trust me on this: Dylan is a him, and you're never going to reach this kid unless you respect that. Why am I not surprised you know from nothing about this?"

The whole fucking world is on my ass these days, Kate fumed, but swallowed her ire: Maggie was at the suicide of a close friend and needed her support.

"Look, Kate. These folks know from the get-go about themselves, they don't choose how they feel about their gender any more than we chose our sexual identity. If you thought we had it tough, they have it *really* tough. The regulars at the bar don't want them, ridicule the hell out of them, resent the hell out of them. The few that do come in, it's at off-hours when they know the place will be pretty empty, and because they know I'm okay about them. So—"

"Maggie, give me a break. I'm willing to learn, okay? Aimee's still gone, so I'm thinking she—uh, he could stay here for a while."

"Are you hearing yourself?" Maggie's voice was stronger, assertive. "You listen to me, Kate. This kid is a minor. The parents have reported him missing. You're a police officer. You take him in, how many laws are you breaking?"

"Three that I can think of right away," Kate admitted.

"Where is he now?"

"Some flophouse in Hollywood with a dozen other people like, uh, him. He's got a sleeping bag. And some money."

"Jesus. Do this. Get Dylan to call me. He might agree to stay with me till we figure this out. If he does, you don't know one damned thing about it, you got that?"

"Got it." She loved Maggie Schaeffer.

"Marcie needs her cell phone back. Talk to you later," Maggie said.

"Wait! Marcie?"

But Maggie had switched off. *Marcie.* Aimee's friend. If Marcie was there, Aimee was too. That was why Maggie didn't want her to come over.

Kate groaned, her shoulders sagging. She pulled off her jacket, unfastened her shoulder holster, and removed the ammunition from the gun as she had every day of her police career. She sank into her armchair and sat unmoving, brooding over Audie, over Dylan, over Aimee, over the Talbot case. What do you know, she thought as she finally got up to change her clothes, I can think and not hold a drink at the same time.

Comfortable in jeans and a T-shirt, she picked up the phone, dialed Nancy Harrison's cell phone number.

"It's Kate," she said tersely. "Call when you can."

"I can talk now, Dale's out showing a house," Nancy Harrison said. "Please—do you have news?"

Dale Harrison was a real estate broker, Kate remembered. Like Jerome Steinberg's son-in-law. Coincidences. Her father was right, life was nothing but coincidences. But some were a lot more meaningful than others. "The news is that Dylan's been seen in Los Angeles and is okay so far."

"Did you get word—"

"There's a complication, Nan. No matter how you and I may feel about helping Dylan, I'm a police officer. She's a minor child who's been reported missing. If I approach her, I have strict obligations under the law."

"But you're also her aunt."

"By blood. Not under the law."

"I see. I see that you have to be careful. But as her parent I can surely give you permission."

"Yes you can. But an unwitnessed oral agreement isn't good enough."

"Okay, then it'll have to be a written one."

"I'd need a very clear statement authorizing me to act as her aunt on your behalf and as my judgment dictates. I'd need your signature notarized."

There was silence. Kate waited. She did not know if such a statement would give her true legal cover but it would be worth at least something. Nan Harrison finally said, "That sounds to me like a blank check."

"It's nothing less. You have the choice between my blank check or—Nan, maybe I should just wash my hands of this." It was a bluff she knew she would win.

"Wait. Wait. I'm sorry, it's just . . . I've never met you, and—"

"I understand."

"But I'll give you my trust. Whatever you decide, it has to be better than any of the alternatives. Please—do your best by her. I'll get the notarized permission off tomorrow."

"There's no time to lose. Not when it comes to a teenager on the streets."

"I'll FedEx it. Will you—I hear my husband, he's home. Thank you for this, Kate." She clicked off.

Kate replaced the phone in its cradle, then went to the kitchen to feed Miss Marple. Afterward she glanced at the kitchen clock: seven-thirty. Time enough for a quick trip into the station and then the next item on her list.

THE HOUSE IN HANCOCK PARK WAS DARK, the Coldwell Banker For Sale sign planted in grass that needed mowing. Bequeathed to the three Talbot children in the will

Victoria Talbot had signed the day her divorce from Douglas Talbot became final, the house had been put on the market many months ago. California real estate laws decreed that potential buyers must be advised if a violent death had occurred on the premises, and many buyers were deterred by such disclosures. Kate recalled that the two homes involved in the O. J. Simpson case had not been easy to sell.

She donned an LAPD raid jacket—its lettering would identify her as a cop if need be—and made her way down the flagstone path, let herself into the house with the key that remained in police possession. She had been here perhaps half a dozen times while the investigation was being completed, but not in the months since, and never at night, never with the house emptied of all furnishings. She flipped on the lights that remained connected for the benefit of Realtors, then paused in the entryway, remembering the French provincial table that had once been here, and the empty crystal flower vase on it. The living and dining rooms seemed cavernous, the glossy hardwood gleaming under recessed lighting, the one point of color the coral ceramic tile of the fireplace. The kitchen was virtually invisible in the gloom. She recalled the aroma of cleanser and furniture polish the first time she'd been here. Now there was only the dusty, indefinable smell of abandonment.

She made her way across the living room and down the hallway, flipping on wall switches as she went, her sneakers squeaking on the floor. As the lights came on and shadows vanished, it was as if ghosts were retreating ahead of her. Not much wonder home buyers were reluctant to live in a setting of violent death.

She paused at the threshold of the bedroom, her hand hovering over the light switch. The bay window gleamed faintly, and she stared at it through the darkness of the room, bringing from memory the two windowpanes to the left that had been dotted with bright red spots, the far left one sprayed more heavily with both blood and brain matter. She switched on the light.

A room once immaculately neat was now immaculately clean. Either Allan Talbot or the real estate agent had arranged for one of the crime scene cleanup companies to come in; the crew had restored the room to perfect condition.

She made her way over to the alcove where Victoria Talbot had met her death; then turned and walked out of the room, down the hallway, and into the kitchen. Beside the back door she flipped on the light switch; floodlights illuminated the backyard. For safety, Kate realized, and smiled ironically.

She returned to the bedroom, to the doorway. She pulled from her shoulder bag the four crime scene photos she had obtained from the station and looked from each one into the room. In the last one, a long shot, Victoria Talbot lay facedown beside her overturned desk chair, lying parallel to the windows, blood sprayed around her torso, her head angled to the left, her left arm under her, the right arm extended, the hand curled.

Finally, Kate replaced the photos in her shoulder bag, lowered the bag to the floor, and moved to the window. For a long time she stood gazing out at the brightly lit garden where the roses had been pruned back for winter, their once freshly tilled beds now dry and hard.

What were your last thoughts when you sat here looking out at your garden, knowing it was the final time? Did you ever dream any of this would happen? Your spirit is here in this place, I feel it, Victoria. Tell me what I should do now . . .

FIFTEEN

The jury foreperson—juror number nine as Kate had forecast—stood erect in the jury box, shoulders squared as if he were in line for a military inspection.

Peering sternly over his glasses, Judge Terrell said to him, "I understand the jury is unable to reach a verdict."

"Yes, your honor."

"You have exhausted every possibility?"

"We have, your honor."

"More time for deliberations would be of no further benefit?"

Kate knew the judge's questions were pro forma. The jury had already been ordered back into deliberations after previously reporting they could not agree on a verdict. The initial notification had come out of the jury room after only a single day of deliberations, a clear sign that the divide involved more than one or two dissident jurors and was unbridgeable.

"We're hopelessly deadlocked," the foreperson said stonily.

"Then I have no option than to declare a mistrial," Judge Terrell intoned.

Douglas Talbot did not immediately react, nor did Gregory Quantrill. A loud murmur rose from a courtroom packed with spectators—which did not include the Talbot children. The judge whipped a glance of such sharpness toward the audience that the reaction quickly died without need for further admonishment. Kate knew he was angered and frustrated by this verdict, as was anyone involved in a trial ending in a hung jury. Except, of course, for defense attorney Gregory Quantrill, who had earned his fee and would earn even more if he remained on the case.

As Terrell proceeded to thank the jury for performing its civic duty, informing them of their options as to whether they wished to respond to questions from the press, Kate watched the two deputy district attorneys at the prosecution table. Marquez stared morosely down at her legal pad; Martha Dicter sat expressionless, arms crossed. Kate knew Marquez had tuned out the proceedings and simply wanted this part of the trial to be over so that she and Dicter could begin their final step of interviewing anyone on the jury willing to talk about the issues that had divided it, to aid in the next prosecution of the case— if the District Attorney's Office elected to retry it. A new trial might or might not be reassigned to them. This, Marquez's first big case, was not an unmitigated failure—there had been no verdict, after all—but it was a failure nevertheless.

At the defense table, controlled jubilation reigned. Quantrill's hand was on the arm of Douglas Talbot, holding down his client, who squirmed on his chair as if in the grip of an electrical charge. Two female jurors looked balefully at him; the remainder were focused on the judge, and bore expressions ranging from sorrow to disgruntlement to anger. The eyes of juror number two glistened with tears.

Finally it was over, the case remanded back to the District Attorney's Office, the defendant free again on bail. Talbot leaped to his feet and shook hands with his defense attorney, then hugged him. Except for a few relatives and friends of Talbot, the courtroom rapidly emptied.

As Kate waited for Marquez, Douglas Talbot brushed by her in the push of the crowd. "Fuck you," he hissed.

"Same to you," she responded loudly to his back.

"I apologize on behalf of my client," Gregory Quantrill offered with a faint, bland smile.

"You were right," she told him. "We didn't do a good job investigating this case."

He was so astonished he stopped in his tracks. His smile widened. "Then you'll be dropping the charges."

"Nope. Not my decision."

"Detective, there is no way you or the DA's Office get to play games with this one."

Spotting Corey Lanier pushing her way against the flow of the crowd, coming toward them, Quantrill moved closer to her and lowered his voice. "For what it's worth," he said, "this guy's either innocent or delusional. My clients all say they're not guilty. This guy I actually believe."

"Try believing the truth," she said. "This guy is a monster. Who killed his wife."

Shaking his head, he moved on, pulling his sleeve out of Corey Lanier's grasp, saying to her, "Miss Lanier, I'll see you at the press conference."

"What did he say to you, Detective?" she asked Kate avidly.

"We exchanged mutual pleasantries and compliments," Kate said.

"Not from what I saw. So Gregory Quantrill wins again," she goaded.

"Did he? Not that I noticed, Corey."

"You see a guilty verdict next time?"

"No comment."

"You're so fucking consistent, Kate."

"So are you, Corey," Kate told her with a smile. "I'll see you around."

"You got that right, Detective." Yanking out her cell phone, Corey marched off.

As Alicia Marquez caught up to her, Kate said, "If it's any consolation at all, Alicia, you and Martha did a great job. The best you possibly could."

She gave Kate a wry grin. "It would be more consolation if you were our boss."

"As soon as you're done here, we need a meeting," Kate told her. "It's important. You, me, Joe Cameron, and my lieutenant. At the station."

Studying her face, Marquez said quietly, "I'll be there."

SOME FOUR HOURS LATER, JOE CAMERON, having picked up Allan Talbot at LAX, ushered him into an interview room at Wilshire Division. Cameron had expressed surprise that Talbot continued to do his job, especially one so stressful as being an air traffic controller, during the trial and jury deliberations; Allan had attended court proceedings only for his own testimony and the closing arguments. But Kate was not surprised; she sensed that he and Lisa had moved somewhere private in their grief, had washed their hands of their father, of directly and publicly following his fate, and had done only what was minimally expected of them.

"Allan," she greeted him from where she sat at the table, "how are you and your sisters doing?"

"Okay. We're all doing okay." He looked in puzzlement at the door closing behind the retreating Cameron, then scraped back one of the spindly metal chairs and sat down. Glancing at the acoustic tile, the mirror, the Formica table, he unbuttoned his suit jacket and leaned back, crossing an ankle over a knee. He asked with a slight smile, "Is this where you beat confessions out of your suspects?"

"The very place," she answered with her own smile.

The tight curls of his hair had grown into a dark brown nimbus around his thin face. He did not, she noted, look particularly distressed by the nonverdict in his father's case. "Lisa," she asked, "how's she doing?"

"As you might expect. Very pissed about what's just happened."

"How's she doing in general?"

"Not terrific. Once the shock wore off, Mother's death hit her like ten tons of brick. All that rage, all that fury just . . . melted away. She's in a really bad way knowing there'll never be any chance now to . . . heal things between her and Mother."

"I know," Kate said sympathetically. "Most of us would do more in the here and now if we could somehow know the way we'd feel if the person we're angry with vanished tomorrow." A lesson she herself had witnessed every day of her life in Homicide—how could she have been so blind to it at home with Aimee? "What about Rikki?"

"All she said was, 'He gets away with everything.'"

Kate nodded. "And how's she doing, otherwise?"

A smile illuminated his gaunt face. "She wanted to be in court for the closing arguments. We tanked her up on Valium to get her there. I was proud how she led us out when that god-damn lawyer—" He shook his head, then continued, "I think she's starting to get it that none of this was her fault, our family tearing apart. It's Douglas who put it all in motion. Nobody should ever have to go through the kind of hell she did to get to that better place."

"No they shouldn't. You really love Rikki," Kate said, pleased that he showed no eagerness to get to the reason for his presence here and that the interview was proceeding along the course she had planned for it. This preliminary conversation was necessary; in fact vital.

"Yeah. Lisa too," he said, drumming his fingers on the table. "Not a news item to you. Douglas is the reincarnation of a cockroach, and as for Mother—what can I say?"

"That you love her too," Kate suggested gently.

"Yeah." His expression soft, almost tender, he ceased his finger drumming and looked away from her. "We all do, you know. She wasn't an evil woman, Detective. She thought money and status and power—she thought being married to a man like Douglas was worth anything she had to put up with. She did it for our sake, too."

She nodded. "How do you feel about what's happened, Allan?"

He shrugged. "He killed my mother. That says it all." He settled his gaze on her. "What did you want to talk to me about? The retrial?"

"Yes. Exactly. We have a new theory of the case."

His gaze sharpened. "I heard on TV about that witness proving the Mercedes wasn't Douglas's car. Is that why the jury hung?"

"Evidence is always a mosaic, always more than one thing. A jury deadlocks if any of them finds reasonable doubt. The presence of the car was a key corroborating factor in our case—so it had to be a factor for them. It's a major factor in our new theory, too."

"Which is?"

"Some elements of this case never did add up, didn't have convincing explanations. As long as we could place your father at the scene, we could speculate about them and let it go at that. We didn't have definitive forensic evidence—in fact, as you know, we had no forensic evidence at all placing him there. But as long as we had the car—"

The vertical line between his hazel eyes deepened. "You have his history. His *history*. What are you telling me here?"

"More than anything we have his history," Kate said, nodding. "And evidence that his behavior was escalating. But once we had the true explanation about the car, a few things about the scene of your mother's death shifted into a new context. You told us something important when we interviewed you that morning. You said you noticed the house was unusually clean, considering your mother's housekeeping habits."

"Yes, I did tell you that," he said somberly, looking away.

"We'd have found it out anyway. Everybody could smell the cleaning products. No one has a kitchen that gleaming clean unless it's been freshly done. There was the quite striking absence of fingerprints. Your father's defense team knew our forensics people couldn't find a trace of your father there, a fact they were entitled to know. What we didn't have to tell them was that we could hardly find traces of anyone on any surface in that house—it had been that thoroughly cleaned."

"You said in court that Douglas—"

"Could have cleaned it up, yes. The question is—as the defense pointed out—why would he do anything more than wipe places where his fingerprints might be? Why would he throw away freshly cut roses? He didn't hate flowers—he had some flowering plants in his office when we talked to him."

"Then she cleaned the place herself for some reason we don't know," Allan said warily. "I don't see where you're going with this."

"When it comes to the circumstances around a death, anything that's uncharacteristic behavior is important. We talked to her housekeeper, Rosario. She said your mother never cleaned her own house in the nearly three years she worked for her, so that would be highly uncharacteristic behavior. Then there was the position of her body—"

He was staring at her in increasing agitation. She remembered his grief the morning of his mother's death, an agony that had lacerated its way through any balm of shock. "Are you okay?" she asked, leaning toward him. "Can I get you some coffee?"

"What you can do is tell me what's going on here."

"Okay." Crossing her arms on the table, she looked at him intently. "This is what I think happened the day your mother died. We found your message on her answering machine, the one you left the night before—she'd picked it up but hadn't deleted it. That morning you called again, and when she didn't answer, you came over. But you came over earlier than you told us you did. We think you got there at seven-thirty."

He did not reply; his fingers took up drumming again on the tabletop.

"You rang the doorbell. Waited. No answer. Then you heard a shot from inside. I can only imagine how you felt, Allan. As you rushed to open the door with your key. As you ran

through the house. When you found your mother and that horrible scene. Do I have this right so far?"

Allan Talbot's stare was frozen on her. "What *is* this?"

"You saw she was dead—checked her pulse to be sure.
There was nothing you could do to help her or save her. I think
what came immediately into your mind was your sisters. I
think your very first instinct was to protect them—something
you've tried to do all your life. Save them, if you could, from
what this would do to them. Especially Rikki, who's so dam-
aged. That's consistent with you . . ."

Her pause was deliberate. She did not take her eyes off him.
But he did not look at her, did not respond. His fingers continued to drum.

"I'm betting you immediately thought this would be the final straw to destroy Rikki entirely. You believed it would do so
much harm to Lisa that she'd never recover. Have I got this
right, Allan?"

He shook his head.

She sat back. "I believe I do have it right. You're a fast
thinker, Allan. Someone who works as an air traffic controller
at one of the world's busiest airports has to be. You stood back
from this scene and saw what needed to be done to protect
your family. There was a letter on the desk, maybe letters to all
three of you—only you would know. Her journal was open,
with her final thoughts about this last day of her life. You
picked up whatever she'd written to you and your sisters, tore
what she wrote out of her journal, closed it and wiped it clean
of prints, and put it in her desk drawer. All this time you were
listening for sirens—maybe someone heard the shot, called the
police. That would mean abandoning the whole plan. Then
came the hard part. And your mistakes."

His drumming fingers stilled.

"The gun had either fallen to the floor, or was in her hand, and I'm guessing it was in her hand—she's right-handed and in our photos of her that hand was curled. With a sudden and violent death rigor mortis sometimes is instantaneous in the hands."

A deep shudder ran through him. She said softly, "When I first saw you, Allan, I thought you were the most grief-stricken person I had ever seen in all my years at death scenes. Now I understand why. It was because of what you had to do. Which was to desecrate the body of your mother. You took the gun out of your mother's hand and it's my guess you then closed her eyes. Then you fired another shot into the body of your dead mother."

"Mistakes," he whispered.

Kate knew from the deadness in his eyes, the color draining from his face, that she had forced him into a chamber of acutely agonizing memory. "You knew you had to make it look like a murder. But you didn't know enough about the world of forensics. About blood spatter, its patterns, what it can tell us about the position of the body at death. Or that medical examiners can tell the sequence of shots fired into a body. Your presence of mind under the circumstances was remarkable, but you couldn't think of everything, and you didn't think about Marjorie Durant hearing both shots. Luckily for you, there was your father."

He jerked his gaze up to her. "Are you insinuating . . . you think this is some kind of frame-up of my father?"

"When we first talked to you, you knew it was his behavior that had led to this but you made no attempt to implicate him. You had no way of knowing his whereabouts—for all you knew he had an ironclad alibi. Do I have this right, Allan?" She needed an admission—and this was a man who was intelligent, perceptive, very quick thinking, and at this moment, exceedingly wary.

He shook his head. She continued, "You took the gun, the page from your mother's journal, and whatever else she'd written. You emptied a jewelry box. It wasn't much of a robbery, but you couldn't bear to take off her diamond ring or anything else on her body, you couldn't bear to take more of her things or to damage her house. You took what you'd collected outside and buried it in the rosebushes—a simple matter to conceal it under the very loose soil of any of those freshly hoed beds. Till the day came when the coast was clear and you could safely return and retrieve it all. After you hid everything, you came back inside the house, left the door ajar to further suggest a robbery, and called nine-one-one. This is what happened, Allan, isn't it."

When he did not reply, she said, "I read all your mother's journals. I'm guessing—"

"All of this is guessing," he muttered.

"—I'm guessing your mother could no longer bear her guilt over Rikki. Couldn't bear the pain of her estrangement from her daughters and grandchildren, couldn't bear the relentless stalking behavior of your father. She made up her mind to kill herself and that's why she didn't answer your calls—she didn't want the sound of your voice taking her out of her mind-set. She'd stayed up all night preparing for her death. Writing in her journal and composing her letters, cleaning up the house—it's why Alice Cathcart saw lights on so late. When your mother saw or heard you at the door, she knew she had to act on her preparations. She went into her bedroom, sat at her desk, looked out at that garden for the last time, and shot herself. That's what happened, Allan, isn't it."

He did not reply.

"When it turned out that your father had next to no alibi, when you found out about the new Mercedes seen on the street that morning—for all you knew, given his obsession with your mother, he'd actually been on the scene, and that made you even angrier. You allowed suspicion to fall on your father, allowed him to be arrested because in your mind he's guilty."

"It's more than in my mind. He's responsible for my mother's death, he's responsible for what he did to my sisters."

"I agree with you. I think he is too." This could be the breakthrough. "Allan, talk to me."

"Is this being recorded?"

"No," she said.

He looked up at the mirror of the interview room. "But we're being observed."

It was her turn not to reply. Alicia Marquez, Joe Cameron, Lieutenant Carolina Walcott, and Captain of Detectives Eric Delano were on the other side of the mirror, witnessing this interview.

"Assuming your theory is true," he said, "and I'm by no means saying it is, it seems to me there's no law against shooting a dead person."

"No," she said encouragingly. But there was: desecrating a corpse. There were also other laws—perjury, perverting the course of justice, not to mention what this trial had cost the city of Los Angeles. She was not required to admit any of this—and it was not in her best interest to do so.

"Bottom line," he said, "Douglas is guilty."

This man was no fool. She played her last card, her highest card. "We feel we should bring your sisters in, Allan. Tell them all about this and explain why we're not trying your father again."

He hunched forward over the table. "Listen to me. You,

and"—he gestured to the mirror—"whoever else is out there. You have no proof. There's no way in the world you can prove your so-called theory. Quantrill's theory of this case is just as good as yours. If you drag my sisters in here, if you give them even a hint of your wild-assed guessing, I'll take this to the papers, I'll sue the hell out of you."

"Relax, okay?" She held up her hands. "We have a problem with your sisters, Allan—can't you see that? If we don't try this case again . . . You know Lisa, she's no shrinking violet, she'll take this right to the papers and attack us tooth and nail."

He shook his head. "She won't. I can make Lisa understand what I understand: that it doesn't matter. He doesn't have to be in jail—he's already in jail. The whole world knows about him now. If you don't try him again, won't your announced explanation be that you have no additional evidence? And consequently you feel the trial outcome will be the same? Am I right?"

"Yes, that's substantially what we'd say."

"Which isn't saying—which doesn't mean he's not guilty. It'll be purgatory for him. He'll go crazy. Hiring Quantrill has cost him a bundle but it didn't buy him an acquittal. Rumor has it his partner wants him out of the business—people don't want to deal with a stalker and a murderer. I'm sure the drumbeat'll get a lot louder. Worst of all, he's lost his reason to exist—tormenting my mother. I'm fine not having him tried again and I can handle my sisters."

Allan Talbot scraped back his chair, got to his feet. "So we're done here, right?"

Kate shrugged. And again raised her hands. She'd done her best. And had realistically expected no other outcome than this one.

"I have one question." He leaned over, put his hands on the table, and peered into her face. He said carefully, "This very interesting theory of yours about how my mother died, how did you come by it?"

"It was the flowers," she told him, meeting his hazel eyes. "What bothered me most about this case was the flowers that had been thrown out."

"I didn't know about them," he said.

"No. How would you? It was the one element you had no way of knowing. For me it was the one element with no explanation at all. Then a friend of mine suffering from breast cancer took her own life. She was too ill to clean up her house as thoroughly as your mother did, but she tidied up, got ready to die," Kate said, remembering Maggie's account. "The day she died she filled her house with sun and with flowers. Your mother and my friend Audie were both suffering. The difference was, Audie welcomed her death. Your mother was in despair. Abandoning life. On the last day of her life, your mother couldn't bear the symbolism of those cut flowers. She threw them out, and died looking out on a garden of growing, living, sunlit beauty."

Tears glistened in Allan Talbot's eyes but he did not look away from her.

She said, "Once I considered the possibility of suicide, Allan, all the inexplicable details about that death scene made sense. Including something Gregory Quantrill should have brought up in his closing argument but didn't think of, apparently: There were no marks on your mother's body. Lisa told me your father broke things when he was on one of his rampages. There was nothing broken in that house." Except Victoria Talbot's soul, Kate thought. "If your father actually entered that house, I think he was very capable of killing her. But not before he smashed things and beat her the way he had before."

Allan Talbot straightened up. "There's another reason I'm not unhappy Douglas won't be in jail," he said, moving toward the door. "I intend to make his life . . . interesting." He walked out of the room.

A FEW MINUTES LATER, KATE, CAMERON, and Marquez were drinking coffee in the comfortable clutter of Lieutenant Walcott's office, seated in a semicircle in front of her desk.

As Marquez concluded a brief conversation on her cell phone and clicked off, Cameron offered, "Allan's carrying his own shitload of guilt over not doing enough to step on his father when his mother was alive."

"Yes, I may get another Talbot murder to prosecute," said Marquez with an attempt at a smile.

"I wouldn't bet on it," said Kate. "Judging by this case, smart as he is, it'll be a perfect crime."

"Not that this one was a crime," Walcott reminded them. Irritation spreading over her almond-colored features, she snapped, "We've wasted how many hours and police resources investigating the hell out of what's turned out to be a goddamn suicide? Alicia, can we get Allan Talbot on obstruction? On *anything*?"

Marquez considered her reply, then said, "Kate did a great job trying to get him to admit what he did, but he didn't come close—he's way too smart. If we'd only tested Victoria's hands for GSR during the autopsy—but that didn't occur to us, and now the body's been cremated. We have lots of circumstantial evidence of suicide, just like we had circumstantial evidence of murder. We have no solid evidence for what Allan did—none."

"What a screwup," grumbled Cameron. "If we can't prove suicide, it's still an open case."

"Not in my book," barked Walcott. "Case closed."

"It'll still go against our stats," Cameron muttered to Kate.

"I heard that, Detective," Walcott said. "You and your partner here can just work a little harder to bring up your numbers—clear your new and existing cases."

"Yes ma'am," Cameron said dolefully.

Cameron was right that this was a screwup, Kate thought, and she was culpable. From the moment she and Cameron had walked into the home of Victoria Talbot, the clues had been there—beginning with the empty flower vase and the smell of cleaning products. She had allowed Allan Talbot's extremity of grief to overcome the objective truth that he was at the scene of an apparent homicide and her job as a detective required her to suspect everyone. She should have ordered GSR tests on his hands and clothing to positively eliminate him. There were other more personal questions she needed to carefully consider. One was whether, after so many years on the job, she was relying too much on instinct in her investigations. The other was whether years of substantial alcohol intake had affected her judgment, however subtly.

Cameron, in his loathing for Douglas Talbot, had not been objective either; and as the more experienced lead detective, she had had the responsibility not to allow herself to become infected by his emotion. But she had. They were lucky, very lucky in the outcome of this case. Joe Cameron was a man she liked and trusted, but with his zeal for justice she needed to watch herself around him; she could not allow this to ever happen again.

"The call was from Martha Dicter," Marquez said. "The jury split was six-six. The acquittal voters wanted to convict but felt they couldn't do it without something definitive placing him at the scene. The ones to convict came from five of the women and one man. They told Martha they didn't care about the inconclusive evidence, they were convinced he was on a straight-line track to kill her. I think we might have got the guy the next time," she mourned, raking fingers through her hair. "With the Steinberg surprise package used up, Quantrill probably would've handed the case off."

"Earth to Alicia," Walcott said, "Talbot didn't do the crime."

"So what," Marquez said.

"My sentiments exactly," Cameron said. "I'd be very happy to see his worthless ass on permanent ice in the slammer."

"Kate," Walcott said, rubbing her chin, "this friend of yours whose death gave you your theory—when did she pass on?"

"Audie died the day of closing arguments."

Walcott's eyes narrowed. "So this new theory of suicide came to you while the jury was out?"

"I know what you're thinking, Lieutenant," Kate answered. "Why I sat with it, didn't come to you." *I asked Victoria Talbot what I should do when I was in her house. But I can't very well say that.* "The fact is, I came to realize this is one of those rare bird cases—whatever the jury came back with, it really didn't matter. Because—"

"Didn't *matter*?" Walcott held up a hand. "Wait, don't say anything, give me a minute here." She sat with her thoughts. "Okay, if they find him guilty, anybody could argue he deserves it on any number of counts—"

"Just for what the bastard did to Rikki," Marquez snarled.

"If they find him not guilty," Walcott continued, "anybody could argue he's technically not guilty. I see what you mean."

Again Walcott held up a hand for silence while she continued to ruminate aloud: "If Kate's theory leaves this room, it

gets back to Victoria Talbot's daughters—we all know that."
She sat back, allowing her words to sink in.

Kate, Marquez, and Walcott had already talked about this
while Cameron was picking up Allan Talbot. Their meeting
had been to plan strategy for the interview Kate would conduct
with Allan.

"If Allan admits he turned a suicide into murder," Marquez
had said to Walcott, "it'll mean a lot more to the family than
just prison time for Allan."

"Yes, I know," Walcott had replied. "I was in court for the
closings, I saw Rikki and the other two. Rikki's pretty fragile."

"She'll shatter to pieces if she finds out her mother committed suicide basically because of her," Marquez said. "The other
daughter won't be in such great shape either."

Walcott's gaze had traveled slowly from Marquez to Kate
before she said, finally, "We all have a job to do and we need to
do it."

And they had, Kate thought, as Walcott's gaze again moved
from her to Marquez, and then to Cameron. "In view of how
the interview went," Walcott said, "anyone who thinks we
have an obligation to convey Kate's theory of this death to
Douglas Talbot or his scummy lawyer—please raise your
hand."

"Aside from not wanting to do any favors for assholes,"
Cameron argued, "who can prove it? It's still just a theory."

Kate met Walcott's eyes, then looked at Marquez.

"Motion carried, case dismissed," Walcott said with a thin
smile.

"It's the right thing to do," Marquez said.

Maybe it was what they should do, Kate thought, but it's
the end justifying the means and it's not right. It can never be
right. "Marta Gonzalez," she said, voicing another concern.

"When Talbot finds out he doesn't need her testimony any-more . . ."

"Deportation," Cameron said. "This case has made her very visible."

Kate nodded. "Someone who's been here since she was five years old, she could be sent back to a country she doesn't even remember. I don't feel right about it."

"It won't happen," Alicia Marquez promised. "I'll look into it. I don't know why her parents wouldn't have applied for citizenship way back during the amnesty period."

"Thanks, Alicia," Kate said. "I owe you."

"No you don't," Marquez said. "Let's hope he elects to dump her instead of deciding she's his next candidate for the treatment he gave to Victoria."

Cameron began to say something, but after a glance at Walcott, he subsided. Kate was certain he would make it a point to have one of his allies keep an eye on Marta Gonzalez.

"Joe said something about Talbot's ass being iced in the slammer," Marquez said. "I'd love such a fate. The press is going to fry mine. Yours too."

Walcott waved a hand. "For a day," she said. "Then we get to rise from the dead and continue to do our jobs."

"I'll fill in my boss," Marquez said. "Under the circum-stances he may be okay with this, given what's happened."

"I'll talk to him too, Alicia," Walcott said. "As a prosecu-tor you've made our preferred list."

"Lieutenant—thank you," Marquez said. "God I'm tired. What a case."

Walcott was looking at Kate. "You look tired too, Detec-tive. You okay?"

Tired? She felt far worse than tired. After two more days without Aimee, those two days without a drink, she had been tempted numerous times to join Victoria Talbot in the hereafter. "You're right, I'm tired," she said.

"Why not take some time off," Cameron suggested.

The advice had been given casually but Walcott looked at him sharply before she said to Kate, "Taking time off is the one thing you've never been very good at. Maybe we should talk about it, Detective."

Kate nodded. "Maybe we should."

SIXTEEN

As soon as she unlocked the door, Kate could smell perfume—musk—and could hear muted sounds—a TV newscast. Her heart rate escalating, she moved quietly toward the living room.

Years of familiarity with Aimee's beauty had never lessened its impact, and once more Kate marveled at the lack of artifice—the dark hair, slightly graying now, but still in the same simple shoulder-length hairstyle; minimal makeup on classic features; a body with lovely curves and natural grace. How effortlessly beautiful she always was. Never more so than now. Still in her work clothes—a maroon silk blouse and black linen pants—she sat on the sofa, an arm along its back, her legs casually crossed, watching television.

Turning her violet gaze on Kate, Aimee somberly gestured toward the TV. "I heard the verdict on the car radio when I left work. I figured you could use a friend right now."

"I can always use a friend," Kate answered, smiling. "I'm so glad to see you. Where's Miss Marple? She's missed you . . . Nearly as much as I have."

"Took one look, turned her back, and went under the bed," Aimee replied, her expression still solemn. "You know cats. She won't deign to admit she cares one way or another that I'm here again."

Kate noted the choice of words. Not "I'm back" but "I'm here again." She wished she had, right now, an ounce of the prideful self-possession of a cat; it was all she could do not to throw herself on her knees in front of this woman she adored and beg her never to leave again, and she would do anything to make her stay. Maybe it was exactly what she should do. Or maybe Aimee would get up and flee in the face of such naked need. Kate stood awkwardly in the room, unsure of how to behave in her own house.

"Audie," she finally said. "I understand what she did, but still—"

"It was a real shock," Aimee said, nodding sadly. She reached for the remote control, clicked off the television. "Marcie was terribly upset when she told me, really shook up."

"Weren't you there?"

"No. I would've been but I've had to work a lot of late hours this week. She called me, said Maggie was with her and would be calling you. There's a memorial tonight—"

"Yes, I know."

"—I thought we might go together. But you look really tired, Kate."

Kate nodded. Along with tired she was also jittery, and getting more so by the moment, her nerves so raw-edged she clenched her fists and began to pace the living room to keep from trembling. She longed for even a sip of scotch to settle herself. "The week's been hell, it's taken a lot out of me," she conceded. "But there's no way I'd miss this. I owe Audie even more than you know. Of all things, her death gave me a new perspective on the Talbot case."

"Really? How are you feeling about the verdict?"

"I couldn't care less," Kate said.

Aimee's astonished expression was so comical that Kate chuckled. "It's a long story. I have a lot to tell you."

"We do have a few things to talk about," Aimee said.

She did not mean the trial. "I'm willing," Kate answered.

"Willing enough that we do our talking in front of a couples counselor?"

Jesus, she thought. Okay, all right, in front of anyone. An audience of millions if it meant getting Aimee back. "Sure," she said. "I think I've created a lot of problems and I need to look at why." She had survived the attacks of defense attorneys over the years; surely she could live through the personal onslaughts of a therapist. They couldn't come much tougher than Calla Dearborn, the department therapist who had counseled her when she'd taken the bullet in the shoulder.

"Aren't you going to sit down?" Aimee asked, puzzlement in her eyes.

She did not dare sit in her armchair. Always before when she came home, she'd get a drink and sit in that chair and savor the clean burn of that first scotch making its way down her throat. If she sat down now, the craving would overwhelm her. She moved to the sofa.

Aimee made room for her and, clearly unsettled by this unaccustomed behavior, said in a reassuring tone, "Don't worry, couples therapy isn't going to be an attack on you, Kate. The problems are my doing, too. Marcie arranged to have me see her therapist—I've been to her four times since . . . since I've been gone. It's why I had to work so much overtime to make up for the time out of the office."

"I see," Kate said. She was surprised. And deeply disturbed that Aimee was so troubled that she actually needed to see a professional.

"No you don't see, there's no way you could," Aimee said emphatically but without animosity. "She's been helping me with why we don't get anywhere when we talk, how everything goes into a knapsack of grievances that gets heavier all the time. I need some help getting my knapsack unpacked and I think you do too. I know you don't really want to do this, Kate, but we have to have someone ask us the right questions right now."

Kate understood that Aimee, without saying so, had framed this as an either-or proposition. She nodded. If she was to end up undergoing the ultimate surgery of separation from Aimee, at least she would be in the hands of a professional for the process, for whatever that was worth. "Is Marcie's therapist the one we'll be seeing?"

Aimee shook her head, with one additional shake to toss the hair off her face, a habit Kate loved so much she felt it now as a piercing pain. "She wouldn't do it if we asked her to," Aimee said. "I'd like you to choose the therapist. We can see more than one till we find somebody we're happy with."

Calla Dearborn, she thought. She'd phone Calla and get some names. "It's a deal," she said.

"In all our years together," Aimee said, sitting back to peer at her, "this is the first time you didn't come in the door and go right to the kitchen for a drink."

She felt embarrassed. So humiliated she wanted to crawl under the sofa. She longed so much to have a drink in her hand it was all she could do not to get up right now and go to the kitchen. Yet at some level she was inordinately pleased that Aimee had noticed. "I've stopped. It's been just two days, though," she said.

"Good for you. Kate, I'm really glad about that."

Kate got up, began to pace again; she had to. "I'll be honest, I have to be honest about this. I don't know how long I can go. A drink, it's . . . been like medicine. It really helps me with the worst of the job."

"I know that. I've always known that. I really do understand. But it takes you away from me. Beginning with that first drink, it leaves me with less and less of you."

"I'm not sure how long . . ."

"I know. I understand. Seeing it's a problem—that's what's really important. We'll go from there."

Kate nodded. At least Aimee hadn't called her a drunk, hadn't asked her to go to AA. She needed to get off this topic. "Have you talked to Maggie?"

"Maggie?" Aimee looked confused. "Not for ages. Why?"

"I just thought you might have. I found Dylan Harrison— Maggie helped me. He's on his way over here right now, I thought it would be good to bring him to the memorial with me. I can hardly wait for you to meet him."

Aimee was blinking in bewilderment. "Him? Dylan? You're calling Dylan a him?"

Kate grinned. "It turns out that my niece is actually my nephew."

"Your nephew," Aimee said, and ran her fingers through her hair.

"Yes. He's transgender—that's why he ran away. Instead of

behaving like my usual self, I decided to act like the detective I am and find out more about how he feels. There's a lot of information." She pointed to the bookcase. "I bought a half-dozen books, two of them are novels. I've been on the Internet a lot. Transgender people—they've been around a lot longer than any of us think. Like, forever. They're better at hiding themselves than you'd believe—"

Aimee was staring at her, and Kate broke off. "I'm babbling," she said.

"No you're not," Aimee said. "Let's see. In the week I've been gone, you stopped drinking, lost a court case and don't give a damn, you found a niece who's not your niece but your nephew."

"That's roughly the size of it," Kate said.

"Is . . . he staying here?"

"With Maggie, at the moment."

"You do have a lot to tell me. Everything you've been saying so far is really good to hear."

"How about we wait outside for Dylan?" If they left here, it would be easier not to want a drink. "Maggie will be at Audie's memorial—"

The doorbell rang. Kate rushed gratefully to answer it.

Dylan wore black jeans, a gray T-shirt under a black and gray vest, heavy lace-up boots, a watch cap. "Here as ordered, Aunt Detective," he said coolly, then his eyes widened and he stared past her as Aimee came up behind Kate.

"Dylan, I'm Aimee Grant," she said, extending a hand. "Kate's partner."

"Awesome," Dylan returned. He took her hand, so suddenly bashful and awkward that Kate would not have been surprised had he begun scuffing a boot toe into the floor. He darted a look at Kate that conveyed pure envy. "Awesome," he said again.

Kate grinned, thinking that Dylan might be a much different proposition than she herself had been at age sixteen, but she'd surely had a broader vocabulary.

"Kate, Dylan's the very image—he's like a clone of you," Aimee said, still holding Dylan's hand and frankly inspecting him; he was turning crimson under her gaze.

"Sure," Kate chuckled. "Forty years ago."

"Whatever." She said teasingly to Dylan, "I'd go for you if I hadn't already."

With Kate and Dylan both laughing, Aimee took Kate's hand as well. "Let's go be with our family, Kate."

"Yes," Kate said, and pulled Aimee to her and kissed her forehead. "Our family."

ACKNOWLEDGMENTS

To Jo Hercus, first and best critic and best everything else as well.

To Montserrat Fontes whose friendship and astute advice have spanned a suddenly amazing number of years, and virtually all my books. To my writer-brother Michael Nava, with many thanks, always with love and admiration. To Paula L. Woods, my sister-in-crime and L.A. maven, for her invaluable counsel, her talent, her friendship.

To Shannon Minter for his advice and pioneering transgender activism.

Very special thanks to Elaine Wolter, extraordinary mother of an extraordinary family, for sharing with me the story of her family and the emotional journey with Gus, her transgender son. I take this opportunity to share part of one of her letters to me: "The fact that a child is gay, straight or transgender doesn't change their soul. I love them all equally and only want them to be happy, healthy and fulfilled. Kids must live their own lives and parents should respect that. As I have said many times, love is not conditional but should be all encompassing." My wish for all transgender people is that they could be cherished by a parent like Elaine.

To Natalee Rosenstein for editing that has never failed to lift my work—and my spirit.